For my mum and dad

Bloody January

Alan Parks

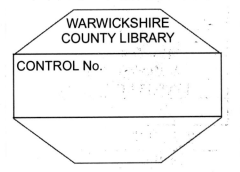

W F HOWES LTD

This large print edition published in 2018 by
W F Howes Ltd
Unit 5, St George's House, Rearsby Business Park,
Gaddesby Lane, Rearsby, Leicester LE7 4YH

1 3 5 7 9 10 8 6 4 2

First published in the United Kingdom in 2017
by Canongate Books Ltd

A CIP catalogue record for this book is available
from the British Library

ISBN 978 1 52880 131 7

Typeset by Palimpsest Book Production Limited,
Falkirk, Stirlingshire

Printed and bound by
T J International in the UK
Printforce Nederland b.v. in the Netherlands

MIX
Paper from
responsible sources
FSC
www.fsc.org   FSC® C013056

'For indeed any city, however small, is in fact divided into two, one city of the poor, the other of the rich; these are at war with one another.'

—Plato

'Every picture tells a story, don't it?'

—Rod Stewart

It became one of the cases cops mark their career by. Peter Manuel, Bible John and Bloody January. Nobody really knew where the name came from, probably some passing remark in Pitt Street or in a pub next to Central. The papers got a hold of it pretty quick. Banner headlines straight away. Most famous one still framed and hung up in stations across in the city.

BLOODY JANUARY: HOW MANY MORE TO DIE?

Years later the cops that worked Bloody January would tell the younger guys that they had no idea what it was really like back then. Six bodies in one week. They'd sit in pubs and reminisce, retired now, run to fat and drinking too much because they had nothing else to do. They'd tell their war stories, about how close they came to an arrest or finding one of the bodies. The younger ones would smile and nod, listen with one ear on the football results coming out the TV, thinking, 'It can't have been that bad.'

But it was.

1ST JANUARY 1973

CHAPTER 1

McCoy headed along the corridor towards the stairs, heels clicking on the metal walkway, breath clouding out in front of him. Never changed, Barlinnie. Freezing in the winter, boiling in the summer. The old Victorian building was on its last legs. Wasn't built for the number of prisoners they had stuffed into it now. Three, sometimes four of them locked up in a cell made for two. No wonder the whole prison stank. The smell of overflowing slop buckets and stale sweat was so thick it caught in the back of your throat soon as the big doors opened; stuck to your clothes when you left.

He'd been coming up here since his first weeks on the beat. Only good thing about Barlinnie was that it saved you going anywhere else. The whole spectrum of Glasgow's wrong-doers ended up in here. From rapists and murderers, nonces and kiddie fiddlers to bewildered old men caught coming out the Co-op with two tins of salmon stuffed up their jumpers and their wives not long in the ground. Barlinnie wasn't fussy, it took them all in.

He leant over the balcony rail, peered through the netting and the fug of tobacco smoke at the rec hall below. Usual crowd milling about in their denims and white plimsolls. Couple of boys whose names he couldn't remember playing ping-pong. Low-level troops from the gangs in the Milton gathered round the pool table, all long hair, moustaches and borstal tattoos. One of them pointed with his cue as Jack Thomson was wheeled in front of the TV, started sniggering. A year ago he would have been too scared to even look at someone like Thomson. Now the poor bastard had a dent in his head so deep it was visible from up here. That's what happens when someone takes a sledgehammer to each knee and then gives you a few whacks on the head for luck. Can't walk and your brain's so scrambled you don't even know where you are.

He buttoned up his trench coat, blew in his hands. Really was fucking freezing in here. A wee fat guy stood up from the card school, looked up, nodded. Steph Andrews. Still kidding himself that no one in here knew he was a tout. McCoy dug in his pocket, took out one of the packets of Regal he'd brought with him and dropped it over the side. Steph had caught it, pocketed it and was off before anyone even noticed. First rule of a visit to Barlinnie: bring fags. McCoy leant over a bit further, still couldn't see the reason he'd come up here.

'Feeding time at the zoo, eh?'

He turned and Tommy Mullen was leaning on the rail next to him. He took his cap off, scratched at his head. When McCoy had first started coming up to Barlinnie, Mullen's hair had been black. It was mostly grey now.

'How much longer you got now, Tommy?' he asked.

'Three more cunting weeks. Counting the days.'

'Not sad you're going then?'

'Joking, aren't you? Cannot fucking wait. Wife's brother's bought a wee caravan down in Girvan. Fresh air. Get the stink of this place out my nose.'

'What is it he wants anyway?' McCoy asked. 'All I got was a call at the station to get up here.'

Mullen shrugged. 'Think he's going to tell me?' He took a roll-up out his baccy tin and lit up. McCoy looked over the balcony again, tried to see him in the crowd.

'You'll no see him down there,' said Mullen. 'He's been moved. He's in the Special Unit now.'

McCoy let out a low whistle. The mysterious Special Unit. Nobody knew much about it or how it was supposed to work. Had been set up last year. Prison Services embracing the sixties far too late. McCoy remembered a news conference on the telly. A grim-faced warden sitting behind a desk flanked by two hippy professor types. The hippies blabbering on about Art Therapy, Positive Custody and Breaking Barriers.

Even though it was early days, any mention of

the Special Unit was enough to start the papers frothing at the mouth, most of the polis too. According to them the Special Unit was going to be Sodom and Gomorrah rebuilt on the banks of the Clyde. According to the hippies it was just a small section of the prison where top security prisoners would be treated like human beings. McCoy wasn't too bothered either way, wasn't like the usual stuff was working anyway. Bully squads beating the fuck out of troublesome prisoners, sticking them in cages in freezing wet basements. Far as he could see it just made those nutters worse; all the more determined to stab or batter any screw that looked at them the wrong way.

Mullen and McCoy left the main building and ran across the prison yard, coats over their heads, heading for a red door in the far wall. Weather was getting worse again, icy sleet, wind whipping leaves and rubbish across the yard. Mullen pulled the red door open and they were in.

McCoy just stood there looking, taking it in. Alice through the looking glass.

There were two greenhouses in front of them, full of flowers and tomato plants. Beds had been dug out the concrete, planted with neat rows of vegetables. A fenced-off area at the side was full of huge lumps of stone with half-finished faces or bodies carved into them, granite glistening in the wet. The door of a wee shed beside them opened and a thin bloke stepped out, long blond hair,

8

chisel in his hand, dusty leather apron. He lifted up his safety goggles.

'All right, Tommy?' he asked. 'No seen you for a while.'

Took a couple of seconds for McCoy to realise who he was. Bobby Munro. Couldn't help but smile. Bobby 'Razor' Munro standing in Barlinnie with a chisel in his hand? No wonder the papers were going mental. Must be the first time he'd used one for its real purpose; normally he'd have had it at someone's throat.

'Aye, all good,' said Mullen. 'Looking for Howie.'

'He'll be stuck in front of the TV as per.' He pointed to a door. 'Through there.'

'So you're Tommy now, are you?' asked McCoy, as they went in. 'All best pals. That how it works?'

'Don't fucking start me,' said Mullen, as they walked through the door. 'That took a lot of getting used to, I'll tell you. "The use of surnames is demeaning and depersonalising and must be phased out,"' he recited in a posh voice. 'Load of fucking pish.'

Last time McCoy had been in the washing block it was full of big industrial machines churning away, men standing behind big electric presses, half hidden in the clammy steam. Not now. Now it was almost empty, painted white, framed pictures and posters on the walls, huge iron sculpture in the middle of the floor. As far as McCoy could make out it seemed to be two dogs with human faces fighting each other, or maybe fucking each

9

other, couldn't quite tell. Mullen pointed at a door in the corner.

'Lounge is over there.'

McCoy stepped through. He didn't know what he was expecting, but whatever it was it wasn't this. It was like stepping into your auntie's cosy front room. Geometric wallpaper, two-bar fire going full blast and a three-piece suite with wooden arms positioned round a colour TV. Didn't even smell of slop buckets. Only one thing was spoiling the cheery atmosphere: Howie Nairn. He was sitting slumped on the couch. No denims and white sandshoes for the prisoners in the Special Unit. They got to wear their own clothes. In Nairn's case that wasn't much of an improvement. A dirty Che Guevara T-shirt, a tartan scarf round his neck, flared denims and long, wavy auburn hair tied back in a ponytail. Even had his slippers on. He was a bit thinner but looked much the same as last time McCoy had seen him. Was one thing hadn't changed: still had the raised criss-cross of scars running across his neck, disappearing down into the collar of his T-shirt.

'Get that screw to fuck,' Nairn said, eyes not leaving the TV. 'He's no allowed to be in here.'

'Suit yourself,' said Mullen. 'McCoy?'

He nodded an okay and Mullen backed out the door. 'I'll leave you boys to it, give us a shout when you're done.'

McCoy sat down on the arm of the couch, put a packet of Regal on the wee tile-covered coffee table. Waited. Was sure he could smell dope from somewhere. Wouldn't surprise him. Nothing about here could any more. Nairn didn't say anything, eyes stayed firmly fixed on the TV. Up to him then.

'I got the message. Supposed to be honoured, am I?'

Nairn grunted. 'Don't flatter yourself, McCoy. You were the only fucking polis whose name I could remember.'

McCoy looked at the posters taped up on the wall. Not the usual girls with their legs apart, not in here. A map of Middle Earth, picture of Chairman Mao. Books on the shelf were as bad. The autobiography of Malcolm X. *Stranger in a Strange Land. The Bhagavad Gita.*

'All this hippie stuff working, is it?' he asked. 'No feeling the need to open the warden's face any more?' No response. He sighed, tried again. 'So is this about Garvie, then?'

Nairn finally looked away from Zebedee and Dougal. 'Who?'

'Stan Garvie. Stuffed in a tea chest and chucked in the Clyde with some iron weights for company. Believe it was your doing. Staying in this holiday home made you want to confess all, that it?'

Nairn smiled, looked very pleased with himself. 'So that was the cunt's name, was it?' He shook his head. 'Naw, don't know nothing about that, *Detective* McCoy.'

McCoy raised his eyebrows. 'News travels fast.'

11

Nairn sat up, stuffed his hand down his jeans, scratched at his balls then sniffed his hand. 'Aye well, I've got some more news for you. Someone's gonnae get killed tomorrow.'

'What, you going to knife someone in the showers? Giving me a heads-up?'

Nairn smiled again, revealing a row of small yellow teeth. 'Always think you're the funny cunt, McCoy. About as funny as fucking cancer. Up the town, girl called Lorna.'

McCoy waited but nothing else was forthcoming. He realised he was going to have to play along. 'Who's going to kill this Lorna, then?'

Nairn looked disgusted. 'Fuck off. I'm no a grass.'

McCoy laughed. 'You're no a grass? Fuck am I doing sitting here, then?'

'You're sitting here because I'm stuck in this shitehole. I cannae do anything about it so you're gonnae have to.'

'How am I going to do that, then? Get on the radio and tell every girl called Lorna to stay in her bed all day? Away and shite, Nairn, you're wasting my time.'

He stood up. He'd been on since five this morning, was tired, wasn't in the mood. All he wanted was a pint and to be as far away from this prison and from Howie Nairn and his shite as possible. He leant forward to pick the cigarettes up off the table and Nairn's hand shot out, grabbed his arm. He pulled him close, face leaning into his.

'You start paying attention to what I'm telling you, McCoy, or you're going to make me awful fucking angry. Right?'

McCoy looked down at Nairn's tattooed fingers wrapped round his arm, knuckles white already. He was a prisoner and McCoy was a polis. There were lines and he'd just crossed them. Game was off.

'Get your fucking hand off me, Nairn,' he said quietly. 'Now. And don't you ever fucking touch me again. Got it?'

Nairn held on for another few seconds, then let McCoy's arm go, pushed it back towards him. McCoy sat back down. 'Either you start talking sense or I'm off. Last chance.' He waited. Nairn stared back at him, watery blue eyes fixed on his. If he was trying to intimidate him, it wasn't working. He'd been stared at by far worse than him. He shrugged and stood up. 'Time over.'

He walked over to the door, shouted on Mullen. He heard his boots coming down the corridor, segs clicking against the lino floor. Voice came from behind him.

'She's called Lorna, don't know her second name. Works in town. One of they posh restaurants. Malmaison or Whitehall's. Don't know who, but someone's gonnae do her tomorrow.'

McCoy turned. 'That it?'

Nairn was staring at the TV again. 'That's enough.'

'Just say I believe you and just say I stop it. You'll tell me what the fuck you're playing at?'

Nairn nodded. 'Now get to fuck. You're stinking up my living room.'

'What was all that about, then?' asked Mullen when they were back in the main building. Lock-up was starting. McCoy had to raise his voice to be heard over the catcalls and clanging cell doors.

'Fuck knows. Telling me someone's going to get murdered tomorrow.'

'No in here?'

McCoy shook his head. 'The town.'

Mullen looked relieved. 'Thank fuck for that. I'm on tomorrow. How come laughing boy knows about it anyway?'

'Christ knows. Think he's just pulling my string.'

They waited as a prisoner with a black eye and a bleeding lip was walked past them; hands cuffed behind his back, officer either side, still shouting the odds.

'That's the funny thing,' continued McCoy. 'I was there when he got done, but it was Brody's deal, no mine. Don't know why he wanted to speak to me.'

'Brody. Christ, nae cunt would want to speak to him. He fit him up?'

He shook his head. 'Nope, whole thing was straight for once. Nairn was as guilty as they come. Caught with a hold-all with three sawn-off shotguns in it.'

Mullen left him at reception, told him he'd let him know where his leaving do was. McCoy liked Mullen well enough but no way was he spending a night in the pub with a load of moaning-faced prison officers telling war stories.

A girl called Lorna. Maybe he would call the restaurants just in case. Couldn't be that many Lornas working there. Still couldn't think why Nairn had told him, he'd barely looked at him when he was arrested, too busy trying to kick out at Brody, calling him every filthy name in the book. His eyes drifted up to the calendar on the back wall of the turnkey's wee office, topless girl draped over a car trying to look like she was fulfilling her life's desire to hold a big spanner. Didn't realise it was Thursday. Maybe he wouldn't bother with Nairn's shite; maybe he'd go and see Janey instead. He was owed after all. The buzzer went and the lock shifted back with a loud clang. The turnkey opened the door, held on to it as the wind rattled it in its runners. McCoy peered out at the trees surrounding the car park whipping back and forth.

Turnkey grimaced. 'Rather you than me, pal. Rather you than me.'

He made a run for it, got in the unmarked Viva and slammed the door. He started the engine up and the radio came on. 'Chirpy Chirpy Cheep Cheep' suddenly filling the steamed-up car. He swore, turned the dial, Rod Stewart, 'Maggie May'.

Much better. He jammed the heater to full and pulled out onto Cumbernauld Road, heading for town. If he was going to see Janey, he needed to go and see Robbie first.

CHAPTER 2

'How long have we got?' he asked.

She grinned. 'All night. Stevie cleared it with Iris. She wasnae happy about it.'

He went to take a couple of the Tennent's screw tops off the set of drawers and she wagged a finger at him. 'Still have to pay for drink. You know that.'

He shook his head, took out a fifty pence, left it in the porcelain dish by the bottles.

The shebeen was big, one of those huge Victorian flats you got in Glasgow, every room converted to a bedroom apart from the kitchen. That was Iris's domain. She sat on an old kitchen chair in the doorway, crates of bottles and big Chas the bouncer looming behind her. She'd told him once that the shebeen made twice as much money out the drink as it did out the girls, whatever that said about Glasgow. She didn't mess about, Iris. Only sold whisky and beer. Take it or leave it. Tennent's and Red Hackle.

The real money was made after hours and on a Sunday. By midnight on a Friday or three o'clock on a Sunday afternoon, when the real drinkers started to get the shakes, she could pretty much

17

charge what she wanted for it. He'd passed enough shame-faced women and rheumy-eyed men on the stairs to know how well she did. Drinkers always found the money from somewhere. Even if it meant their weans didn't eat the next day.

Janey'd built a joint with the grass he'd brought, good stuff, according to Robbie, taken off some American band playing at Greene's Playhouse the night before. Half of it deposited into the lock-up at Central and half straight into Robbie's pocket. He'd only charged him a quid. By the expression on Janey's face should have been a lot more than that.

She put the thin joint in his mouth, closed her own over the burning end, lips forming a seal, and blew the smoke deep into his lungs. He held his breath as long as he could then let out a cloud of the sweet-smelling smoke. Didn't take long to kick in. He felt a bit woozy, good. Robbie was right. He took it back off her, had a couple more deep puffs and handed it back.

Janey'd put a scarf over the wee lamp on the bed-side table, lit a few joss sticks, stuck some pictures from magazines of beaches and expensive cars onto the peeling wallpaper. Anything to make the place a bit less like the back bedroom of a cold-water flat in Possilpark. 'Atmosphere' she called it. 'Punters like it, younger ones anyway.'

He sat down on the end of the bed, tried to untie the laces of his shoes. He giggled, was more difficult than he thought. He managed to get his tie and shirt off, tried and failed to unbuckle his belt, started giggling again. Janey'd put an album on the wee record player in the corner. *Their Satanic Majesties Request*. Had to keep it low, though. Iris didn't like her playing music, couldn't hear what was going on. Wasn't his favourite, but tonight it sounded good. Grass, drink and the music were starting to work together, perfect equilibrium.

Janey started dancing. Watching herself in the cracked mirror in the wardrobe. She was swaying to the music, singing along. She was a good-looking girl: long black hair, curvy body, funny wee button nose and a big smile. Too good-looking to be working here. Iris's shebeen wasn't exactly what you'd call high class. Punters were mostly labourers off the sites or men from the Iron Box factory with Friday night's wages burning a hole in their pocket. Every time he tried to ask her about it, tell her to find somewhere else, she laughed it off. Told him she liked it here, had worked in a lot worse places.

She caught sight of him in the mirror watching her, smiled and stuck her tongue out at him. He leant over and pulled her down onto the bed beside him. She laughed, pretended to struggle. He kissed her as she kicked off her platform sandals, wiggled out her hot pants. He kissed her neck, moved his hands down to her breasts, cock already hard against her thigh. Dope was really kicking in now; he felt heavy, slow, relaxed. He moved down her. She ran her fingers through his hair and he looked up at her, grinned.

'You and me, Janey. You and me,' he said.

The record stopped, arm lifted, went back and then the music started again. 'She's a Rainbow.' He was in her now, getting quicker, breathing heavy against her neck, getting there. She wrapped her legs around his back, moved in closer, whispered in his ear. 'Come on, my wee darling. Come on . . .'

He moved another few times, tried to hold back but couldn't. He moaned, collapsed on top of her, breathing heavily into her neck. He lay there for a minute, then raised himself up on his elbows, looked into her eyes.

'That was magic. How about you? You okay?'

She nodded, slapped him on the back. 'Let's do another, eh?'

He rolled off, sat up against the headboard and watched her. She was sitting cross-legged, bag of grass and fold of papers on the album cover nestling in her lap, long dark hair hanging down like a curtain over her face. She was a pro, could roll a joint in seconds flat, could even do it with one hand if she had to.

He looked at his watch. Ten past twelve. He wasn't going to any restaurants tonight, didn't care, too stoned to go anywhere. Nairn could fuck off. He wasn't his fucking errand boy. He wanted to be here, with her. She lit up another joint and took a deep drag.

'As of ten minutes ago it's my birthday,' he said. 'January second.'

'That right?' she asked. 'What age are you, then?'

'Thirty. Past it.'

She smiled hazily, eyes glassy. Leant over and kissed him, put the joint in his mouth. He took a drag, felt a rush to his head. He couldn't think of a better way to celebrate. He exhaled, lay back on the bed. Could hear Janey singing to herself as she built another joint. Could hear a closing door and the clatter of some punter's boots walking down the corridor, Iris answering the door and the clink of bottles as she handed them over.

Janey leant over him and gently blew a cloud of the grass smoke into his face. He breathed in, watched the headlights of the cars driving past making giant shadows that came and went. He listened to the rain battering against the window, remembered being in a caravan with his mum and dad when he was a wee boy. Janey switched the lamp off, snuggled up beside him. He watched the orange end of the joint glow and fade as she inhaled. He put his arm round her shoulders, pulled her in, let his eyes close and he drifted away.

2ND JANUARY 1973

CHAPTER 3

McCoy woke up freezing cold, all of the blankets wrapped round Janey, only a sheet between him and the ice starting to form on the inside of the windows. He tried to burrow under the sheets and fall back asleep, but it didn't work. Combination of a hangover and the cold meant he'd no chance. He tried to shake Janey awake, but she was having none of it, just grunted and turned away, burrowed back down under the blankets. He got dressed quickly, picking up his clothes from where he'd dropped them, pulled the front door of the shebeen closed behind him and walked down the stairs. Half five. Too late to go home, too early to go into work. Maybe he'd check the restaurants after all. He'd nothing else to do.

The city was starting to wake up, first buses rolling past, passengers leaning on the windows half asleep, bundled up against the cold. Despite the holiday New Year was over, back to normal, no matter how bad the hangovers were. Christmas lights hanging across the streets were still on, bells and holly weakly flashing on and off through the freezing mist and the snow that was starting to fall. A dog appeared round the corner of Sauchiehall Street, ran at the seagulls feeding on an overturned bin and they wheeled up and away, squawking into the sky.

McCoy was freezing, been standing in under the canopy of the Malmaison since half six, stamping his feet and blowing in his hands to try and keep warm. So far he'd watched a road sweeper trying to gather up all the soggy chip packets and empty beer bottles strewn round the street, bought a paper off a boy selling them from a pram, and stood out the way as two blokes pushed a cart full of old carpet and underlay up Hope Street. He conducted a thorough search of every one of his pockets, still couldn't find his other glove. He took the one he had off his left hand and stuck it on his right just as the restaurant manager turned up. Mr Agnotti, as he introduced himself. A right snotty wee bastard, as it turned out. Suppose you had to be to work in a place like that. McCoy'd only been in the restaurant once. Murray's fiftieth birthday dinner. Didn't think he'd be back, not unless he won the pools. It was a big room, wood panelled, hushed waiters going back and forwards with silver service trays and bottles of wine. Other clientele were all businessmen, stuffed with well-done steaks and prawn cocktails, after-dinner cigars plugging their fat faces.

Agnotti took McCoy into his office, asked to see

his badge before he would answer any questions. Wasn't happy about being interviewed. Turned out they did have one girl called Lorna working there, an under-waitress, whatever that was. He wrote out an address on a wee card and handed it over.

'May I enquire what this is about?' he asked.

McCoy smiled at him, couldn't help himself. 'No,' he said.

A kitchen porter was coming in as he was leaving, chaining up his bike outside. He pointed at a picture on the staff noticeboard in the corridor when he asked him if he knew Lorna Skirving. It had been taken at some staff night out. Four women sat round a table in a pub all dressed up, glasses held high, big smiles. Lorna Skirving was the one at the end. Nineteen, low-cut dress, dyed blonde hair, good-looking. He took it off the wall and pocketed it. Had to be who Nairn meant. He'd already been to Whitehall's and they didn't have anyone called Lorna working there: two Laura's but no Lorna.

According to the kitchen porter she'd no phone, so he called the shop, got them to send a panda up to her address to bring her in. He waited in the kitchen, was the warmest place, and watched them setting up the lunch service. Big pans of potatoes and carrots coming to the boil, trays of meat coming out the cold store. An Italian guy with no English appeared from the back and handed him a tiny wee cup of strong coffee. He said 'Gracias' thinking he was clever, was only when the guy walked away looking a bit puzzled he realised he wasn't. The shop called back fifteen minutes later. Uniforms had been on the radio, no answer at her door. Must have left for work already. He sighed, nothing else for it, and called Wattie from the payphone. This was going to be more than a one-man job.

The Golden Egg cafe was a right dump, like a Wimpy without the Wimpy name. Even had a menu with pictures on it – pictures that must have been taken somewhere else, if his bacon and eggs were anything to go by. But it had one virtue: it was right opposite the bus station. So close he could even hear the announcements from the station tannoy over the chat of the other customers and the orders being shouted through to the back kitchen. He rubbed at the condensation on the window and peered out. Eight o'clock and it wasn't even properly light yet, streetlights still on, snow getting worse, lying now. Cars and buses nose to tail as they queued at the big junction to Buchanan Street. Lorna Skirving's address was in Royston; all the buses from there came into the city via the bus station. She had to come in this way. Now all he had to do was spot her in the crowd before she got to work and some bloke who didn't like last night's lobster thermidor stabbed her to death.

'What time does she start?'

McCoy turned, had almost forgotten he was there. Wattie. Old mucker of Murray's at the Greenock shop had called him, said he had a bright boy, too bright for Greenock, should be up in Glasgow playing with the big boys. The bright boy was sitting in his chair ramrod straight, surveying the crowd outside like some sentry on guard duty. McCoy'd argued with Murray, tried to get out of it, tried to pass him on to Richards, Wilson, anyone but him, but Murray was adamant. He'd done three months in the shop answering the phones, making the tea. Was time for him to shadow someone for a few months. Murray got round him the usual way. Flattery. Bright boy needs watching, can't give him to some plodder like Richards. Didn't know why Murray was so keen, you'd think he'd have learnt his lesson by now. He'd had the complaints before, was sure he was going to get them again. Last secondment had gone back crying to Murray. 'He doesn't tell me what's going on, doesn't speak to me, blah blah blah.' But here the new one was, blond hair wetted down and neatly combed, big open face, dark suit and shined shoes. Twenty-six and he looked about fifteen. About as green as they come.

'Half eight, supposed to be,' said McCoy, yawning widely.

'Can I see the photo again?' asked Wattie.

He handed it over. Looking at Wattie was like looking at himself five years ago. Been a long time since he'd been as bright-eyed and enthusiastic. Been a long time since he'd come to work with his shoes shined and his shirt ironed too. He took a look at his reflection in the window, didn't look good. He needed a haircut and a suit that didn't look like he'd slept in it.

He stood up, looked outside. A layer of white settling on the tarmac. 'We'll head over there, see if we can catch her coming in.'

The bus station sat at the top of the town, hemmed in by the high flats at Dobbies Loan at one side and the new motorway that had destroyed the old Garscube Road on the other. It was a huge asphalt rectangle, must have been half an acre, lined with slanted bays for the buses to park. Shelters and benches ran round the outside, a cafe that made the Golden Egg look like Malmaison near the entrance. Buses came in from everywhere – housing estates on the edge of town, rich suburbs, even from the coast, Ardrossan and Largs. And the bus to London went from here, one every morning, always a big queue waiting for that one. The chance of a new life for a five-bob bus ticket.

A fat bloke with a hat and a whistle told them the Royston buses came in at bays 21 to 24 and pointed them up to the far corner. An old woman sitting on the bench by bay 22 gave McCoy a dirty look as he sat down, sniffed and moved herself and her plastic bags up a couple of feet. He watched Wattie pace up and down, stamping his feet to keep warm, flicking the top of his lighter open and shut, humming something under his breath. At least he was quiet; the last one had never bloody shut up. Some twat from Edinburgh with a science degree, in the accelerated promotion fast track, as he told you every five minutes. Went back to Edinburgh with his tail between his legs after he tried to arrest two women fighting outside the Barrowlands and got a broken nose and a black eye for his trouble.

A double-decker spun round the asphalt and pulled into the bay in front of them. McCoy stood up. The bus door hissed and folded back. A couple of old men muttering about the snow stepped down, followed by a bloke in a boiler suit with his piece in a loaf wrapper tucked under his arm, then a group of school kids all shouting and pushing each other. No Lorna Skirving.

She wasn't on the next one either. Wattie eventually got tired of pacing, sat down on the bench and pushed his heels out in front of him, stretched his legs, yawned loudly. McCoy sat, watched an old man throwing crumbs onto the wet ground, sparrows flying in from nowhere.

Another bus came and went, still no Lorna. He was beginning to think Nairn had been taking the piss after all when he saw the crowd across the other side of the station scattering. Shouts, a man falling backwards as he tried to run. A woman screamed.

McCoy started running. He was halfway across the forecourt when a reversing bus almost hit him. He jumped out the way, stumbled, looked up and saw what the crowd was backing away from. He was young, couldn't have been more than a teenager, anorak, jeans. His left arm was out in front of him, gun gripped tightly in his hand.

'Police!' shouted McCoy. 'Drop it!'

Clatter of heavy shoes and Wattie was beside him, breath coming out in clouds, eyes darting everywhere. McCoy grabbed his shoulder, pointed over at the crowd. 'Get them down and back. Now!'

Wattie nodded, ran off looking terrified. He didn't have time to worry about him, though. Had to get to the gun before the boy decided to fire it. He took a deep breath and started walking towards him. He tried to sound calm, wasn't easy, he could feel his heart going like a hammer in his chest.

'Just put it down, pal. No harm done, eh?'

His voice made him sound like he was trying too hard, being too nice, nothing he could do about that. The boy didn't even look at him, just kept moving his head from right to left, scanning the crowd, looking for someone. He could hear Wattie shouting behind him, trying to get the crowd out the firing line. A woman was crying, some wee kid screaming, more shouts. He tried to block the noise out. Just him and the boy with the gun, that's all that mattered. He kept walking towards him, going slow, hands held up, getting closer, keeping in between him and the crowd.

'C'mon, pal, gonnae have to stop this now. Just put it down, eh? It's not like—'

The boy's eyes suddenly focused, like he'd just seen McCoy for the first time. He spun his arm round towards him and lined up a shot, pistol aimed square at his head. McCoy froze as the boy adjusted his aim and squeezed the trigger. There was a sharp crack. A cloud of sparrows took off from the roof and the screaming started in earnest.

McCoy couldn't believe he hadn't been hit, would have sworn he felt a push of cold air just above his head. People behind him were running, falling, shoving each other out the road to get away. Wattie shouting at everyone to keep down. They started to drop and that's when McCoy saw her. She was lying half on, half off the pavement, body stretched across the kerb. Blonde hair, white coat, one shiny black shoe lying a few feet away from her. She tried to sit up, looked round bewildered. Blood was flowing down her legs, starting to turn the snow red. She looked down at it, her mouth opened to scream but no sound came. McCoy turned back towards the boy with the gun.

'Put it down, pal, come on, it's done now. Just put it down.'

The boy smiled at him, didn't look like he was all there. His eyes were blank, faraway. He held the gun up in front of him, looked at it. Snowflakes had settled in his hair, were melting, dripping down his face. He wiped his eyes and smiled again, and that's when McCoy realised what he was going to do.

He started running towards him, shoes trying to find purchase on the greasy ground. He was still a couple of yards away when the boy stuck the barrel up to his temple. He was screaming at him to stop, was almost at him when the boy closed his eyes and pulled the trigger.

The sound was muffled this time, no crack. A reddish mist appeared on the other side of the boy's head, bits of bone, then a thick jet of blood flew yards up into the sky. He wobbled, eyes rolled back in his head and he collapsed forward onto his knees, stayed like that for a second or so, then fell forward onto the ground.

McCoy ran over and kicked the gun out his hand, trying to avoid the blood still pouring out the side of his head. Up close he was even younger than he thought. A pair of dirty white plimsolls, quilted anorak with a tear at the pocket, sparse moustache barely covering his top lip. A froth of blood was bubbling out from the side of his mouth, big chunk of the back of his skull gone, bone and brain fragments all over the tarmac.

Wattie was kneeling down by the girl, fingers on her neck. He held them there for a minute then looked up and shook his head. McCoy wasn't surprised; amount of blood pouring out of her, she didn't have much of a chance. Tannoy was still going. The 14 bus from Auchinairn was going to be late. He looked up at the sky and let the snow fall on his face. He could hear sirens in the distance getting louder. He turned as a bus wheeled round into the bay in front of them, driver in the cab staring at the bodies open-mouthed. He stood on the brakes too late and his bus slid across the asphalt and into the station wall. There was a crunch and the driver fell forward and landed on the horn. It blared out, echoing round the walls of the station. McCoy looked back down at the boy, his left hand was spasming, fingers opening and closing, eyes going everywhere. He coughed up a huge gobbet of dark blood. Chest was only just going up and down, breathing shallow. McCoy squatted, took hold of his hand.

'You're going to be okay, just hang on, no long now.'

The boy coughed again, more blood came up and ran down the side of his face onto the fresh snow. McCoy sat there holding his hand, telling him it was all going to be okay, knowing it wasn't, wishing he was anywhere but there.

CHAPTER 4

He was sitting back on the bench by the Royston bay, smoking, when Murray turned up. Needed some time away from the blood and the uniforms bustling about and Wattie asking him questions every two seconds.

The ambulances had arrived first. The ambulance man had put his hand on his shoulder, told him they would take over. McCoy had tried to stand up but the boy's fingers kept squeezing his. He knew it was a spasm but couldn't let go, needed to feel he was some comfort for the boy. Ambulance man had eased his hand free. He stood there looking down at the boy until another one ushered him away.

Police cars had come next, then the vans with the uniforms in them, then the unmarked cars, then the lorries with the crash barriers. Now the place was bedlam, shouts, sirens, people crying and the tannoy still blaring out.

The line of uniforms that was blocking the entrance parted and a black Rover drove through the cordon and weaved its way through the maze of abandoned buses crowding the forecourt. Soon as it stopped a uniform scuttled over, opened the back door and Murray stepped out. Senior officers were around him in seconds, pointing over at the bodies, explaining what had happened. Murray listened for a while then held his hand up, silencing them. He pointed at the crowd gathered behind the rope cordon and sent one of them over there, barked orders at the others and they rushed off double-time towards the entrance.

McCoy watched as he strode over to where the bodies were, lifted the rope and went through. Uniforms and ambulance men stepped back, getting out his way. Wattie was standing there trying to look like he knew what he was doing. Even had his wee notebook out. Murray nodded a greeting at him, knelt down and carefully lifted the green sheet off the girl's body. Although the boy's body was surrounded by doctors and ambulance men, it didn't stop him pushing them aside to have a look at him too. He asked Wattie something and he looked around, eyes finding McCoy, and he pointed over. Murray gave out some more instructions, sent Wattie scurrying off, and made his way across the forecourt. Snow was still falling but Murray had no coat, just the usual tweed jacket stretched tight over his shoulders, trilby stuck on his head. He was a big man, Murray, six-foot odds, ginger hair fading to grey, moustache on a ruddy face. Looked like a prop forward gone to fat, which he was. McCoy wasn't sure why they got on; they had nothing in common as far

37

as he could see. Maybe everyone else was just too scared of him to have a normal conversation.

'You all right?' he asked, coming in under the shelter, taking his trilby off and shaking it.

McCoy nodded. 'I'm fine. Unlike those two.'

'Right fucking mess,' he said and sat down beside him. 'Wattie said you came up here looking for the girl before anything happened. Didn't tell him why. That right, is it?'

McCoy nodded.

'How come?' said Murray quietly, just the last remnants of his Borders accent remaining. He only had two speeds, Murray. Shouting, which meant he was annoyed, and talking quietly, which meant he was about to get annoyed.

McCoy sighed, knew he was in for it. 'It was Nairn, Howie Nairn. That's what the phone call was about, got me up to Barlinnie last night. Told me a girl was going to get killed today, wanted me to stop it.'

Murray was padding his jacket, looking for his pipe. Suddenly noticed two plain clothes had followed him over, were standing off to the side waiting. 'What the fuck are you two doing? Standing there like spare pricks at a wedding. Fuck off and get this site properly secured, now!'

The two of them looked terrified, hurried off. Murray'd finally found his pipe, stuck it in his mouth, sat back on the bench and pointed over.

'See that over there, McCoy? Those crashed buses, the blood, the bodies, the weans crying and

38

the crowds of fucking gawpers trying to get past the barriers. That's what's known as a right royal shite-show. A right royal shiteshow that I'm going to have to sort out. So why don't you just start again and tell me what the fuck went on here and what the fuck it's got to do with you.'

McCoy dropped his cigarette onto the ground, watched it fizzle out, started his story. 'Howie Nairn got me up to Barlinnie last night, he'd got the warden to call the shop. So I get there and he tells me there is a girl called Lorna who works at Malmaison or Whitehall's. No second name. Said she was going to get killed today. I thought he was playing games but I checked it and there is – was – a girl who worked at Malmaison, Lorna Skirving.' He nodded over at the body. 'Wasn't at home this morning so we came here to meet her, except she didn't come in on the Royston bus, so we missed her. Can't have stayed at home last night. First thing we know that bloke's standing there with a gun, and then she's on the ground.'

'And what's she got to do with Nairn?'

McCoy shrugged. 'He wouldn't say.'

'He wouldn't say? Well, fancy that. Maybe you should have fucking asked then!'

'I did . . .' He started to protest, but Murray was having none of it.

'Didn't ask him hard enough, then, did you? Might have stopped this fucking disaster happening. And, by the way, how come that cunt Nairn is suddenly telling you all his secrets?'

'Don't ask me. Call came in to the station last night, so I went, thought it would be something about Garvie. I hardly even know him. He was Brody's deal, no mine.'

Murray tapped the pipe stem off his top teeth, shook his head. 'Nope. You're not telling me something.'

'Eh?'

'Had to be a reason Nairn wanted to speak to you. What is it?'

McCoy looked at him, couldn't believe what he was hearing. 'What? You think I'm holding out on you, that it? That's shite, Murray. Why would I do that?'

'You tell me,' he said evenly.

'Fuck off, Murray, you're way out of order.'

Murray's face clouded over. 'So are you, son. You remember who you're talking to.'

'Aye well, you too. You really think I'd fuck you about?'

Murray rubbed at the stubble coming through on his chin, shook his head. 'No. But there's a reason it was you he wanted to speak to. You might not know it, but he does.'

McCoy stood up and watched two uniforms push a row of photographers back behind a rope line. Ambulances were backing up to the bodies, doors open.

'Where you going?' asked Murray.

'The boy still alive?'

'Barely. If you can call it alive. Half his fucking

40

head's gone. Who is he? Nairn let you in on that one?'

McCoy ignored him. 'He's nobody. According to Wattie, he's got nothing on him. No ID at all, no house keys, no wallet, no money, scars, tattoos. He's the invisible fucking man. Gold crucifix round his neck. That's it.'

Murray gave a half smile. 'Well, we know one thing then. He's one of your lot.'

McCoy ignored that too. 'So what happens now?'

'I walk back over there and try and get this mess sorted out. Try and get everything done and the place re-opened before the rush hour tonight. City centre's at a fucking standstill already. Buses backed up all the way from here to fucking Paisley.' He stood up. 'And you, away you go to Barlinnie and find out what the fuck Nairn's up to. And get some fucking answers this time. I mean it. He's an accessory at least. Lean on the cunt.'

'Here's done already. The bloke shot the girl then shot himself. What is there to find out?'

'What's to find out is what this has got to do with that cunt Nairn. This isn't bloody Chicago, we don't have shootings in the bloody bus station. Find out what Nairn knows and what it's got to do with him.'

McCoy sighed. Would have to try again later, no point when Murray was in this kind of mood.

'I'm sick of telling you. Get up to fucking Barlinnie now!'

McCoy held his hand up in surrender and

walked up towards the row of unmarked Vivas parked near the entrance.

'And McCoy . . .' He turned and Murray nodded over at Wattie, standing on the other side of the forecourt watching them. 'You've forgotten something.'

CHAPTER 5

Wattie hadn't said much since they'd got in the car. McCoy didn't blame him; he didn't feel like saying much either. Fuck of a first day on the job. Still, he hadn't done too badly with the crowd at the bus station, did what he was told, didn't panic. Rarer than you'd think.

'You all right?' he asked.

Wattie nodded; he didn't look it though. His face was pale, tiny spots of blood across his cheek that he'd missed when they went to clean themselves up back at the shop. He was fiddling with his lighter again, trying to keep his hands from shaking. Wasn't working.

'Look, it's not always like this. Fact it's never like this. Could be months before you see another body, never mind another shooting.'

Wattie nodded again, didn't say anything, just stared out the car window at the afternoon traffic on Riddrie Road. McCoy gave up. Maybe he was just a quiet bugger after all. They continued north through the city in relative silence. Suited him, only noise the rhythmic swish of the windscreen wipers fighting the sleet. The road to Barlinnie

43

took them through Royston, then Provanmill. Long rows of dirty black tenements lined the way interrupted by empty sites full of mud and piles of old tiles and bricks, any metal or lead from the roofs long gone. Driving through the north of Glasgow, a place he'd known since he was a boy, was like driving through a different city now. All the landmarks were gone, couldn't find his way any more. Garscube Road was gone, all that was left of Parliamentary Road was a few rows of tenements. Motorways and shitty high flats. The New Glasgow.

McCoy turned the steering wheel and his shirt cuff emerged from under his jacket. It was soaked in blood, cloth turned hard. Didn't know if it was the boy's or the girl's. Didn't matter much, he supposed. He was peering down into the footwell to see if he'd managed to get all the blood off his shoes when someone behind him sat on the horn. He sat up quickly, looked in the mirror. Ambulance. He held his hand up in apology, pulled over and it raced past them up the middle of the two lanes of traffic, lights and siren going full pelt.

Maybe he should have guessed then. Bad things did come in threes, after all. Then he wouldn't have been surprised when they pulled into the prison car park and the same ambulance was sitting there, lights slowly revolving, back doors open.

'What's that doing here?' asked Wattie.

McCoy shrugged, opened his door. 'Only one way to find out.'

They slammed the car doors shut behind them and made a run for the entrance, splashing through the puddles on the cracked tarmac. McCoy leant on the buzzer, trying to stand in under the awning out of the rain. He held his card up to the window and the big metal door rumbled back slowly. Tommy Mullen was standing there.

'What's going on?' asked McCoy, nodding at the ambulance.

Mullen looked surprised. 'That no why you're here? It's your pal, Nairn. He's been annoying somebody.'

They shook themselves off and followed Mullen along the corridor and up the stairs towards the wash block. Wattie wrinkled his nose, but McCoy was used to it. Barlinnie smelt the same as every other prison he'd ever been in. 'Sweat, shit and spunk', as Murray had memorably described it. Corridor got warmer the nearer they got to the showers, feel of moisture in the air. Mullen pushed the thick plastic door open.

'After you.'

The floor of the showers was swimming in water, covering the cracked and broken ceramic tiles. Steam was so thick it was hard to see what was going on; took a minute or so for their eyes to adjust. Mullen pointed over to the last shower in a row of ten or so. There was no sprinkler head on it, just an open pipe gushing boiling water in a big arc.

'Fucking thing's kaput,' said Mullen over the noise. 'Cannae get it turned off. Fact he's lying on the bloody drain's no helping either. Didnae want to move him.' McCoy nodded, still not sure what he was talking about. Mullen pointed into the mist. 'He's over there.'

Nothing for it, they splashed in. McCoy stupidly reminded of walking through the disinfectant footbath at the swimming baths, Wattie looking a bit peeved at the idea of getting his good suit wet. At least the water was warm. As they got closer two ambulance men emerged out the steam, dark stains seeping halfway up the legs of their grey flannel uniforms. They seemed to be standing over something. Stood aside to let them see. McCoy and Wattie sloshed their way towards them and had a look.

It never ceased to amaze McCoy how inventive men shut away with nothing to do could be. They became resourceful, turned their hands to making things out of nothing. Things like a murder weapon made out of a toothbrush, some insulation tape and a sharpened bit of glass. McCoy watched it spinning round in the water next to Nairn's outstretched hand. Whoever made it had done a good job; Nairn's throat was sliced right through, open sides of the wound moving in the current like a fish's gills. Gash must have been six inches long, neatly bisecting the old scars on his neck. A red string of blood was emerging from it, spinning and turning like ink dropped into a glass of water.

Nairn's head was back, mouth and chin just breaking the surface. His mouth was full of blood that was turning black, starting to congeal.

McCoy was doing his breathing. Ten, nine, eight . . . trying to stop the dizziness, missed what Mullen was saying to him. Another couple of breaths, in through the nose out through the mouth just like the doctor said. 'Think yourself calm. You are in control.' It was working. He started to feel a bit less like he couldn't get a breath, but he made sure he kept his eyes fixed a couple of feet above the body.

'What'd you say?' he asked.

'You deaf? I told you,' said Mullen, 'somebody wasnae happy wi' him.'

McCoy risked a look down. Wave of nausea, straight back up. 'Not wrong there. When did you find him?'

'Hour or so ago. B Wing landing came in for their shower and there he was.'

McCoy went to get his cigarettes out, realised he was never going to be able to light one in the damp atmosphere, stuffed them back in his pocket. Threes it was, right enough. A young girl shot dead, a boy just hanging on and Howie Nairn lying dead in a pool of water and blood.

One of the ambulance men was looking around. 'Probably be here somewhere.' He scanned the room, saw something floating by the far wall and waded over. 'There it is.' He fished in the water, picked something up, looked like a worn nub of soap. He held it up between his finger and his thumb, showed it to everyone.

'His tongue. They cut it off.'

McCoy heard a retch and the splatter of sick hitting the water behind him. He turned and Wattie was bent over, hand up, trying to say sorry. McCoy was just happy it wasn't him for a change. Wattie retched again, thin stream of vomit hitting the water. Ambulance man shook his head.

'Great. That's all I fucking need. Wandering around knee deep in water, blood and now fucking puke.'

McCoy felt a bit better, risked another look down at Nairn. He'd been one of those men Glasgow turns out all too often. Men in a permanent rage at the world and everyone in it. He'd been hitting out at everything since he was born and now, for once, for the first time maybe, he looked peaceful. He was naked, arms outstretched, red hair fanned out behind him. McCoy could just make out a tattoo through the water and the thick ginger fuzz covering his chest. A heart, blue scroll beneath it with a name in it.

'Who's Bobby?' he asked.

'His boyfriend,' said Mullen. 'Came to see him every fortnight, never missed.'

'His boyfriend?' said Wattie, wiping his mouth with a hanky. 'You're no telling me Howie Nairn was a poof?'

Mullen nodded. 'Queer as a three-bob bit and didnae care who knew. Man with a reputation like his, nobody was going to pull him up for it, were they?'

'What's he doing here anyway?' asked McCoy. 'Thought he was in the Special Unit?'

'He is. But they've nae showers over there. Complained to the governor, got allowed over here twice a week. Said he was being discriminated against.'

'That what this was about then?' asked Wattie. 'He try it on with someone on his weekly visit? Lovers tiff?'

Mullen shrugged. 'Could be.'

'Any witnesses we can talk to?' asked Wattie.

Mullen and McCoy looked at each other. 'He just started, has he?' asked Mullen.

McCoy nodded. 'Go easy. Rule number one, Mr Watson. Never any witnesses in prison, never are, never will be. We're on our own.' He loosened his tie, opened the top buttons of his shirt. 'Christ, it's like a fucking oven in here.'

'Plumber's on his way,' said Mullen.

'Aye, so's Christmas,' said McCoy. He stepped back from the body, tried to get nearer the door and the fresh air. Tried to think. 'I can't see some bloke Nairn's had a go at in the showers doing this, can you? Nairn was an animal. He asked you to touch your toes you'd do it, say thanks afterwards.'

'Speak for yourself,' said one of the ambulance men, looking disgusted.

'You'd have to be as much of a cunt as he was

to do this. So who does that leave us with then? Martin Walsh still in?'

Mullen nodded. 'Another couple of years to go. Martin Walsh definitely. Maybe Tommy MacLean? You know the suspects as well as I do. But if it's some jealous boyfriend, then fuck knows, bets are off. That sort play their cards close to their chests in here. Don't want it getting back to the wife or the boys in the pub who's tucking them in at night.'

One of the ambulance men moved forward, causing a wave in the water that broke against McCoy's trouser legs. 'You want him moved?' he asked.

McCoy shook his head. 'You're joking, aren't you? No way. Barlinnie's in Eastern's territory. They'll be here soon, they can sort it out. You okay now?'

Wattie was leaning against the tiled wall, still deathly white. He nodded, looked sheepish.

'I've got to get out of here, I'm fucking melting. All right if we use your office for a bit, Tommy? Think the High Heid Yin's on his way. I promise I'll no let Wattie here be sick in it.'

Tommy's office was right at the back of the prison, hidden away. He'd done it up over the years, tried to make it homely. It was a room not much bigger than a cupboard, strip of carpet on the floor, various pictures of him holding up fish, waders on, stuck on the wall. He'd a kettle on a tray, two

50

cracked mugs and a bag of sugar full of brown clumps sitting next to it. McCoy sat on the chair, started to undo his shoelaces. They were wet, couldn't get the knot to come loose. He stuck his half-bitten nails in and pulled, eventually came free. He nodded to the kettle.

'Penance for boaking your load. You can make the tea. Think you'll manage that?'

Wattie nodded, plugged it in and pressed the red switch. 'You ever seen anything like that before?' he asked.

'Like what? Somebody with their throat cut or with their tongue cut out?'

'Don't know. Whole thing, I suppose. All that blood in the water, him lying there.'

McCoy pushed the other shoe off with his foot, couldn't be arsed with the laces. 'Nope. But I've seen different and I've seen worse. Think yourself lucky you didn't want to be a fireman. That's the real gruesome stuff. Bodies mangled in car accidents, kids burned in their beds, all sorts of shite. No sugar for me.'

McCoy had just finished his tea and was lighting up a fag when he heard Murray shouting at somebody, as usual. He didn't care if they were a polis who worked for him or not, he was happy to shout at anyone. The door opened and he took in the scene. Face clouded over immediately.

'What the fuck's going on here then?' he said, looking at the two of them sitting there drinking tea in their shirts and skivvies.

51

McCoy nodded over at their socks and trousers steaming on the radiator. 'We got soaked, sir, just trying to dry off.'

Murray shook his head. 'Jesus Christ. Fucking pair of clowns. You see Nairn yet? What's he got to say for himself?'

'Not much,' said McCoy. 'You want a cup of tea?'

Wattie made him one while McCoy explained how they'd got so wet. Murray sighed, sat down on the edge of the desk and started padding his jacket. 'I don't even know why I'm asking this, but I will. Coincidence?' he said hopefully.

Wattie looked for something to say, to redeem himself from the shame of being sick at a crime scene. 'He was a poof, sir. Could be he fell out with one of his boyfriends? Or maybe he tried to get someone in the showers?'

Murray looked over at McCoy. He shook his head. 'Don't think so. Whoever did it cut out his tongue, didn't like what he'd been saying and wanted someone else to know. Howie Nairn was a big man in here, but there's others. Others that would have done it to him for the money. Somebody outside probably paid for it or called in a favour.'

'What? Because of what he told you?'

'Good a chance as any. According to Mullen, other than getting me up here for his wee story he's been a good boy. Quite happy doing nothing but parking his arse in front of *The Magic Roundabout*.'

'Christ, you telling me that fucking animal was

in the Special Unit? A murdering cunt like him gets a fucking colour TV and a vegetable patch after all he's done? What about the people he slashed and killed? What do they get?'

McCoy held up his hand, tried to stop the rant or they'd be here all day. 'It's Eastern's patch, maybe they can find out something about who did it.'

Murray grunted. 'Eastern? You're kidding yourself, aren't you? Even if they weren't worse than fucking useless they've no hope. Murder in a prison? About as much chance as winning the pools. You sure you've still no idea why he told you?'

'I'm sick of telling you, Murray. No, I haven't, and you know what? I wish he hadn't fucking bothered. Right?'

Murray held his hands up. 'Don't be so fucking touchy, McCoy, was only asking.' He'd found his pipe and was now tapping the bowl off the edge of Mullen's desk. 'Boy's dead, by the way. In the ambulance to the Royal.'

McCoy walked over to the radiator and felt his trousers. Dry enough. He shook them out, stepped into them. Remembered sitting there, boy's hand in his, eyes staring up into the sky. 'He say anything?'

'You saw him. He'd only half his fucking brain, what do you think?'

'Fair enough. What about the girl?'

'What about her? Dead as soon as the bullet hit.

Whoever he was he was a fucking good shot. Bullet went straight into her heart.'

McCoy was balancing on one leg, hopping about, trying to pull on a damp sock. 'Who was she, then? What's her story? Any connection with Nairn?'

Murray shook his head. 'Not so far. Came from Aberdeen. Only moved down six months ago and the parents haven't heard from her since. Worked at Malmaison, on the verge of getting the boot it seems. Turning up late, general uselessness. Theory is she spent the night at her pal's after a night at the dancing. We should get the pal in, see what she knows.'

McCoy shook his head. 'I'll go to her. Get more out of her that way.'

Murray nodded and stood up. 'Up to you. And what about laughing boy in the showers?'

McCoy finished tying his shoelaces. 'Eastern's problem now.' He brushed himself down, trousers looked a mess but that was no great change. 'Someone'll have to tell Bobby, by the way.'

'Bobby?'

McCoy tapped his chest where Nairn's tattoo had been. 'His faithful other half.'

Murray rolled his eyes. 'Fuck sake.'

'It's the seventies, Murray. Legal now and everything. Should send a woman, not some old copper who's going to sit there thinking he's a nonce. Be more sympathetic. Get more out of him.'

Murray started again on the Special Unit and

fucking nonces and sympathy for the bloody victims. McCoy let it wash over him. Couldn't help but think Murray was right. Had to be a reason Nairn had got him up here, had told him about Lorna Skirving. All he had to do was work out what it was.

CHAPTER 6

The last time McCoy had been in Bedlay Street it was still a proper street, rows of tenements, a few shops, even a pub. He'd run Janey up, sat in the car while she went up to buy hash from some guy who'd been to Amsterdam. Was only a year or so ago, but now Bedlay Street was just a strip of cobbles running through mud. Same all over. The Springburn he remembered, the big locomotive works, rows of tenements crammed full of people, was long gone. The works had all been shut down, people moved out to the new schemes on the outskirts of town. Schemes that were already riddled with damp, if you believed the people sent there.

Now Springburn was just motorways, half-demolished tenements with wallpapered rooms open to the sky and the odd pub left stranded in the middle of nowhere. Everything around it gone. Council may as well have firebombed the place, would have been quicker at least. He stood on the cobbles looking round, trying to get his bearings. Could see the big chimney at Pinkston, which meant he must be facing west, realised he must be standing across from where the baker's had been.

'What's up with you?' asked Wattie.

He shook his head. 'Nothing. Just trying to work out where I am. I used to get sent to the baker's up here. Saturday morning, get my dad's rolls.' He looked at the muddy patch of ground where Boland's should have been. The Black Lion next door was gone too. Number of hours he'd had to spend waiting outside for his dad he could have happily knocked it down himself. He turned away.

'What's the pal's name again?'

Wattie fished his new polis notebook out his inside pocket. 'Christine Nair,' he said, snapping it shut and looking up at the windows. 'Top floor.'

'Where you from, then?' McCoy asked as they walked into the close.

'Greenock. Down near Scotts.'

'Didnae fancy the shipbuilding, eh?'

'Didnae fancy me. Most of them are shut down. My da's been sitting at the kitchen table staring into space past couple of years.'

The close was dark, bulb gone, graffiti every-where. They trudged up, eventually got to the top landing. Stopped, caught their breath. Christine Nair's door was surrounded by plastic bags full of rubbish, half of them burst, eggshells and soup cans spilling down the stairs.

'What about you, then?' Wattie asked. 'Glasgow?'

McCoy nodded. 'Possil.'

'Where's that?'

He pointed behind him. 'About five minutes down there. What's left of it.'

Christine Nair answered the knock on the door in a shiny bomber jacket, big badge with 'The Sweet' pinned on it, yellow satin miniskirt, face all made up. Bored eyes stared out from under her feather cut. Didn't look very happy to see them.

'Off out?' McCoy asked pleasantly.

She looked the two of them up and down. 'Aye, and I'm late. What's it to you?'

McCoy held out his police card. 'We need to talk to you, hen, about Lorna.'

She sighed, held the door open and they walked in. The Marc Bolan posters and the tie-dyed bedspread weren't doing much to cheer up a single-end on its uppers. There were piles of dirty clothes on the floor, an overflowing bin in the corner, tap dripping on a pile of unwashed dishes in the sink. The room smelt of joss sticks just like the shebeen. Wasn't enough to cover the smell of damp, though. Big dark patch of it in the corner of the ceiling. She switched the radio off, the overhead light on and sat down on the bed. Didn't take her jacket off.

'What's she done, then?' she asked.

'She's no done anything, hen,' said McCoy. 'She's been killed.'

'She's been what?' She looked at them both, trying to work out if this was some kind of joke. 'She left here this morning . . .'

'Wattie, see if you can make a cup of tea, eh?' said McCoy. He nodded, went over to the cooker. Turned the gas on. Nothing doing. He sighed, reached in his pocket and stuck ten pence in the meter.

'I'm sorry, love. It must be a shock, eh? You all right?'

She nodded, tears starting in her eyes. McCoy searched his pockets for a hanky but couldn't find one. Wattie produced a neatly folded one from his coat pocket and handed it over.

'What happened?' she asked, looking bewildered.

McCoy sighed, wasn't really an easy way to do this. 'She was shot, she didn't feel anything, was very quick, it's—'

'She was what?' The girl was looking at him like he was mad. 'No! Lorna was shot?'

McCoy nodded. Wattie took the hanky out her shaking hands, handed her the tea. 'Drink this, loads of sugar in it, do you good.'

She managed to get the chipped Snoopy mug up to her mouth, took a sip. 'I cannae believe any of this, are you sure?'

McCoy nodded. 'She stay here last night, did she?'

She nodded. 'We went out last night, both on early shift at work. The Muscular Arms . . .' She faded away, tears started rolling down her cheeks. 'Who killed her?'

'We don't know that yet.'

'Why'd he do it?'

'We don't know that either.'

She shook her head. Took another sip of her tea. 'I cannae take this in, I cannae believe it.'

McCoy tried to find somewhere to sit, wasn't anywhere, leant back against the dressing table, caused a minor avalanche amongst the nail varnish bottles and wee pottery dogs covering it. 'Sorry about that, hen,' he said, righting them. 'What was Lorna like, then, Christine? She a good friend of yours?'

She nodded and then shook her head. 'Sort of. Met her at work. She could be a pain in the arse, but why would someone want to kill her?'

'Pain in the arse, how?' McCoy asked.

Christine shrugged. 'Borrowed money and never gave it back, was always late for her shifts, got me to cover up for her.'

'She have a boyfriend?'

She reached over to a wee yellow bag, rummaged in it, brought out a ten pack of Kensitas Club. Lit up. 'She didn't really have a proper boyfriend.'

'Good-looking girl like her? You sure?'

She chewed on her bottom lip, purple lipstick coming off onto her teeth, unsure whether to go on or not.

'Just tell us, love. Anything you know will help us find out who did it. Doesn't matter if he was married or something. Just need to know.' McCoy thought she was going to clam up; she took another drag of her cigarette and looked at him uncertainly.

'Come on, Christine, love. It's important.'

'The customers at the restaurant. She went with them sometimes. In their cars. Hotel rooms. Old men.' She screwed up her face. 'Pure disgusting, it was.'

'What? Lorna was on the game?' he asked.

She shook her head. 'No really, she didnae go up Blythswood or anything like that. She was good-looking, wanted a good time. Money. Clothes. "Sugar daddies", she called them. They gave her money, took her out to clubs, the dancing, maybe bought her a present. That cunt Agnotti pays us fuck all, you know.'

'What about you? You short of money, too?'

'Fuck off.' She held up her hand, showing half-moons of dirt beneath her nails and an engagement ring with a tiny chip of diamond. 'I'm getting married in the summer, saving up.'

There was a strip of pictures Sellotaped to the headboard behind her, kind you get from the photo booths in train stations. The two of them, Lorna and her, sticking their tongues out, then pulling model faces. They were both dressed up, looked a lot older than they were. McCoy leant over and peeled it off the wood, peered at it.

'Go out a lot together, did you?'

Christine shrugged, picked at a thread on the candlewick bedspread.

'That the problem, is it? Think your boyfriend'll find out what you've been up to?'

'Don't know what you're talking about,' she said, not looking at him.

McCoy waited, didn't say anything. Normally

61

worked. He wandered over to the window, rubbed some of the dirt off and looked out at the road heading up towards Bishopbriggs and its acres of new Wimpey houses. Spam Valley, they called it. People up there had spent so much of their money on their houses that was all they could afford to eat. The lights were starting to come on in the city below, already getting dark at four o'clock. January in Glasgow.

'You'll no tell him? He doesn't get to know?'

He turned round. 'Course not.'

'Promise?'

He ran his finger across his suit jacket. 'Cross my heart and hope to die.'

She seemed satisfied. 'I never even knew their names, honest. I only went with her a couple of times, she kept nagging me. Called themselves Ronnie or John, whatever came into their heads. Only did it when her bloke had a friend, wanted someone else to tag along.'

'No names. You're sure?'

She nodded. 'Might know a couple if I saw them, don't know . . . I've made her sound a right cow, haven't I?'

'Was she?' asked McCoy.

She shook her head. 'She was brilliant some-times, made you pee your pants laughing, but she was never gonnae stick to waitressing.' She smiled. 'Just as well. She's shite at it. She really wanted to be a hairdresser, work at the make-up counter in Fraser's. Something glamorous.'

She looked round the dingy room. She smiled again, wiped at her tears with the hanky.

'Cannae blame her really, can you?'

'Who was it arranged these dates, then? Someone at the restaurant?'

She shook her head. 'Lorna did it herself. Said she could tell as soon as they sat down, could pick them out. Changed her tables to serve them, got them talking . . .'

'These guys, all old were they?'

'Only ones with the money, she said.'

'She know a younger guy? Eighteen, nineteen, short hair, skinny? Wore a padded anorak?'

She shook her head. 'Don't think so. She wasnae what you'd call the romantic type. Unless he had money she wouldnae be interested. I still cannae believe she's dead.'

McCoy sat down on the bed and took her hand. The bed smelt sour, of unwashed sheets. How many rooms like this had he been in? More bad news for people whose lives were shitty enough as it was. 'Anyone we can phone for you, love? Want someone to come up and sit with you?'

'Who?' she asked, not really understanding.

'Another pal? Your maw maybe?'

She shook her head. 'I'll go into the work. Last thing I want to do is stay in here.'

'Fair enough.' McCoy stood up. 'Come on, we'll give you a lift.'

CHAPTER 7

'Funny smell in here,' said Wattie.

'Shut it,' said McCoy.

The waiter took their coats as Wattie looked round suspiciously. A big blown-up photo of an Indian market filled one wall. Windows overlooking the Kelvin making its slow and muddy way through the city the other. The restaurant was in Gibson Street near the university. Glasgow's very own bohemian neighbourhood, full of wee bedsits, bookshops, pubs full of hairy students and lecturers talking about Marxism and the struggle of the working classes. Might have talked more sense if they'd ever met a member of the working classes, but that wasn't going to happen up here. They couldn't afford the price of the drink.

They sat down. Wattie picked up the menu and scanned a list of things he'd never heard of.

'Have they got any normal food?'

McCoy just ignored him, ordered him a chicken dhansak when the waiter appeared. He eyed it suspiciously when it appeared, tasted a tiny bit on the edge of his fork then started wolfing the bloody

64

thing down. He settled back in his chair, empty plate in front of him, and burped loudly.

'Not half bad, this stuff. Don't think they have it in Greenock. Didn't think I'd like it but it's no bad at all.'

The couple of pints they had consumed in the pub next door beforehand seemed to have loosened Wattie up, he was happy to talk away now. His Greenock accent meant most of what he said was lost under the background sitar music. Suited McCoy fine. He had enough to worry about. He was going through everything in his mind, trying to make some sense of what had happened in the past twenty-four hours. Nairn, the shooting at the bus station. He wasn't getting anywhere. He was stuck, as always, on the things that didn't matter. Christine Nair and her hopes pinned on an engagement ring that looked like it had come out a lucky bag, the expression on the boy's face as he put the gun to the side of his head. He seemed happy, almost like he was looking forward to it. Could only have been eighteen or so – why would a young boy want to do that to himself? Two seconds away from blowing the side of his head off and he was smiling away like he'd won the pools. Didn't make any sense. He drifted back to Wattie's chatter. Was trying to recount the plot of some gangster film he'd been to see. He stopped, looked at him, must have asked a question.

'You listening to me?' he asked.

'Aye sure, shot him in the boat. Sounds great. What did they get from that cunt of a manager?'

'Nothing,' said Wattie. 'Was about to let her go. No idea about her extra-circular activities. Knew nothing full stop.'

'Curricular. They believe him?'

'Think so. He's a wee weirdo apparently. Managing the restaurant is all he cares about, wouldn't put that in jeopardy for the kickbacks of two girls on the game.' He looked at his watch. 'What time's he coming then?'

'Don't worry, he's always late.'

Apart from Murray, Alasdair Cowie was the only polis McCoy thought anything of. Not a good sign, seeing the Glasgow force was more than two thousand strong. Cowie was smart, smarter than him, would have been fast-track material but his wife got ill, MS, and he took his foot off the pedal. Liked to be home twenty minutes after his shift, no nights and no overtime. Bosses didn't know what to do with him, was obvious he'd be wasted as a journeyman polis, so he was shifted about different departments, kind of a troubleshooter. He was in vice now, trying to form a liaison group between the polis, some woman's group from the university and the girls who worked Blythswood and the Green. God help him.

'Who's it going to be, then?' asked Wattie, looking round the restaurant. A group of drunk businessmen in suits, young couple holding hands, two middle-aged women inspecting the menu.

'What?'

'Everywhere we've been today somebody's died. My money's on that couple getting poisoned by their curry.'

'Aye, very funny. Think I preferred it when you kept your mouth shut.'

The restaurant door opened and Alasdair Cowie appeared in a blast of wintry air. One of the waiters greeted him at the door, took his duffle coat off him, pointed at their table. Cowie looked over and waved, handed the waiter a long red scarf. He wasn't big, Cowie, but he was broad and getting broader as the years went on. Round face now sat above a couple of chins. He was ordering en route, waiter behind him scribbling in a notepad. McCoy could have told him the order himself, never changed in all the years they'd been coming to the Shish Mahal. Mushroom pakora, lamb rogan josh, saffron rice, two chapattis.

'All right, Harry?' Cowie asked, pulling a chair out.

McCoy pointed across the table. 'Wattie. Seconded. Stuck to me for two bloody months. And he's from fucking Greenock as well.'

Wattie nodded warily. Knew he was an unwelcome presence, but he was determined to stick it out whether McCoy liked it or not. Just like Murray'd told him to.

'That was a right fucking mess this morning,' said Cowie, sitting down and pulling his polo-neck jumper over his head. He put it on the chair next to him, tried to smooth out his hair and his wrinkled flannel shirt. Murray had called him a 'fucking unmade bed' more than once, wasn't far wrong. He leant across the table, scooped up the last of McCoy's curry with a bit of naan bread. 'And all your fault, I hear.'

He turned to Wattie. 'He been telling you his war stories, has he?' Wattie shook his head. 'What? Not even the one about the great bookies raid of 1969?'

'Fuck off, Cowie. How's Jackie?'

'Okay. The same. Not getting any worse. I would say she's been asking after you but she hasn't.' One waiter appeared with a tray of lagers, another with Cowie's pakora. McCoy watched him tuck in, pinched one of the little deep fried bhajis for himself. Cowie pointedly moved the plate back towards himself.

'No a great day for you. Blood everywhere. You okay?'

McCoy nodded. Tried not to notice Wattie looking at him with interest.

'You sure? You been back at the doctor lately?'

McCoy shook his head. Changed the subject quick. 'What do you know about girls working at Malmaison, Whitehall's, places like that?'

Cowie sat back, pretended to look pained. 'And here was me thinking you'd asked me out because you liked me. Amateurs, you mean?'

'Suppose so.'

He shrugged. 'Happens on and off in those kind of places, low level stuff. Businessmen in town for a night. Same as chambermaids. Nothing organised or official, mostly underpaid girls trying to make pin money.'

He dipped a mushroom pakora into the wee silver dish of pink sauce and grinned. 'I'm sure Lorna Skirving would have been able to tell you more about it.'

'Smart arse. How come you know about her?'

'Saw Gilroy at the station just before I came out. She was delivering the preliminary post-mortem report to Herr Führer Murray.'

'And?'

'And I earwigged on their conversation on your behalf, knowing full well that I'd have to sing for my supper. Cause of death was bullet in the aorta. It was the other stuff that was a bit more interesting. Funny I know more about your case than you do, isn't it? I'm quite enjoying it.' He waggled his empty pint glass. 'Finding it hard to talk, though, throat's awful dry.'

McCoy waved over at the waiter by the bar, got him to bring over another three pints.

'How kind,' said Cowie, taking a sip. 'Now I am replenished, I will continue.'

'Christ, I'd be quicker going and getting the bloody report off Gilroy myself.'

'Okay, here's the big news. Lorna Skirving had some unusual injuries apparently. Lot of bruises, faded whip marks on her back, ligature marks on her wrists and ankles. Bruising inside her anus and vagina, seem to have been caused by some sort of wooden stick or pole.'

Wattie let out a low whistle.

'I know,' said Cowie. 'Grim. And to top it off she had two razor cuts across her left breast. Forming an X.'

'Nasty,' said McCoy. 'How recent?'

'Week, maybe two.'

'Somebody beat her up?' suggested Wattie, eager to get in on the conversation.

'Maybe,' said Cowie. 'Bit too precise, though.' He sat back on his chair. 'More likely that's what she got paid for.'

'What do you mean?' said Wattie.

'Sorry, forgot you were from Ayrshire. You don't have sexual perversions down there, do you? Just sheep wandering around looking worried.'

'That likely?' asked McCoy, ignoring him.

'Not sure. Very specialised area, girls tend to be older. There's a small demand all right, but as far as I know it all goes through Madame Polo's up in Park Circus.'

'Christ, that place still going?' asked McCoy.

'Oh yes. She must be seventy odd now. You'd think the old bag would be sick of it, retired to a wee tearoom in Tillicoultry. But no, still up there, still paying the kickbacks, still open.'

'What?' said Wattie. 'What kickbacks?'

'Maybe she was moonlighting at Madame Polo's? As well as the punters from the restaurant?' suggested McCoy.

Cowie shook his head. 'If she was, she wouldn't have been working as a waitress and gobbling off some salesman from Newcastle in the back of his Cortina. Those girls earn a proper packet. Rich clients. Judges. Lawyers.' He leant forward conspiratorially. 'Even senior police officers, I hear.'

'What?' asked Wattie again, trying to keep up. 'That right? Who?'

Cowie tapped the side of his nose. 'Need to know, son, need to know.' He held up his empty glass, showed it to the waiter. 'My round, I think. Wife's at her mother's in Aberdeen. The night is young and I am free, but sadly not single, so we are going to get pished, my friend – royally pished.'

3RD JANUARY 1973

CHAPTER 8

McCoy stepped out his close, yawned, looked up at the sky. Rain had gone off but it was foggy, could barely make out the cranes and the big granary by the river at the bottom of the hill. He'd lived in Gardner Street for a few years now. Everyone knew Gardner Street, was the steepest street in Glasgow – looked like something from *The Streets of San Francisco* – big drop down to the Dumbarton Road below.

They'd eventually managed to get rid of Wattie around nine, and him and Cowie ended up in a lock-in at the Doublet until way past midnight. Was paying for it now. His stomach rumbled. Maybe he needed something fried, could go to the wee cafe by Partick Station. He was about to cross the road when a silver Zephyr pulled up beside him. The window slid down and a head leant out.

'Cooper wants to see you.'

He didn't recognise the particular bloke driving the car, but he looked the same as all Cooper's boys did. Bit too flash and a bit too thick. Feather cut, suit with big lapels, open beige shirt with pictures of Charlie Chaplin on it. The young hard man's look of choice.

'Now?' he asked.

The driver nodded. 'That's what he said.'

McCoy sighed, he didn't need this on top of a hangover and Murray doing his nut, expecting results in hours. Driver was chewing gum, waiting for him to get in. Cooper wasn't going to go away, though. Maybe he'd be better getting it over with before Murray noticed he was missing. He opened the door of the big silver Zephyr and got in the back. The cafe would have to wait.

McCoy hated sitting in the back of cars, always made him feel a bit sick, especially after what he'd drunk last night. Had vague memories of a hamburger from some van on the way home, no wonder he felt ropey. The driver didn't tell him where they were going but they ended up in Tollcross. It was in the East End, made Springburn look like a holiday resort. They stopped at the lights and McCoy watched the wrecking balls disappear in the clouds of dust as another big wall went down.

The driver muttered something about the dust ruining the finish of his motor and pulled the car in outside a pub called the Grapes. McCoy'd been in it once, when he'd first started, was still on the beat. Was a Friday night, packed full of punters, must have been fifty or sixty in there. Some bloke had got his face slashed twice while he was standing at the bar and nobody saw nothing. Not

76

one witness, just Duncan Stewart sitting in the corner with his cronies, grin on his face. No one would say anything, too scared. The bloke's girl-friend was screaming and crying while McCoy held a bar towel to the guy's wounds, trying to stop the blood while everybody kept their eyes down, supped at their pints.

'He in there, is he?' McCoy asked, looking out the window.

Driver shook his head, pointed. 'Next door.'

The Tropical Sauna consisted of a dingy-looking shopfront, cracked frosted glass windows with two palm trees etched into them. There was a hand-written sign taped to the window saying 'New Girls', just in case some passer-by was stupid enough to actually think it was a sauna.

'Starting a bit early, isn't he?'

Driver shrugged. 'Don't think he's been to bed yet.' He slumped down in his seat, closed his eyes. 'I'll be out here when you're done, just chap on the window.'

The woman behind the counter looked up from her copy of *Cosmopolitan* with a big smile until she realised who she was looking at. Smile disappeared immediately. She pressed a buzzer under the counter and the door behind her clicked open.

'He's in the premier suite,' she said, eyes back on her magazine. 'Blue door at the back.'

Cooper wasn't the only one starting early. Most of the cabin doors off the corridor were shut, moans and rhythmic squeaks coming from behind them. Tends to happen when you build cubicles out of plywood to save money, not exactly sound-proof. He knocked on the blue door at the end and a voice boomed out immediately.

'That you, McCoy?'

'Yep.'

'Well, get in here then, ya dozy prick!'

If this was the premier suite, he'd hate to see a normal one. The room was painted light blue, overheated, one of those paintings that Boots the Chemist sold by the bucketload of a naked girl on a beach hung above a wee table covered in bottles of lotion, faded towels and boxes of paper hankies. The window had a grille over it, only light coming from two fluorescent strips in the plaster-board ceiling. Cooper was sitting on the massage table in the middle of the room, legs dangling over the side, white towel round his waist not doing much to hide his obvious erection. He'd his arms wrapped round two girls, blonde on one side, brunette on the other. Both were topless, fancy knickers and high heels, Page Three come to life. Except Page Three girls didn't normally look scared, or like they needed a bath.

McCoy took in the scene. 'You want me to come back? Looks like you're busy.'

Cooper shook his head. 'Nothing that can't wait.'

Glasgow was a town of small men, wiry. Anyone over five foot eight tended to get called 'Big Man' but Cooper was the real deal. Well over six foot, built like a bear, as they say. Hair fashions had come and gone, but none of them had touched Cooper, blond hair cut into a short back and sides, side shed, just like he'd always had. Same as his clothes, unless it was a funeral or a wedding; he'd be wearing jeans, a short-sleeved shirt and a red Harrington jacket. James Dean had a lot to answer for. He pushed the blonde girl off the table and smacked her on the arse. She winced; he'd hit her hard.

'Away and warm each other up. I'll no be long. And you, ya prick, come here. C'mon, what's up? Gone all shy on me?'

McCoy shook his head. 'I'm no in the mood, Stevie.'

Cooper didn't say anything, just kept staring.

'I mean it, Stevie. I've got a hangover, give us a break.'

Nothing. Just Cooper staring at him with a stupid grin on his face. He sighed. Nothing much ever changed between him and Cooper; he always got his own way eventually. One day twenty-odd years ago Cooper had decided McCoy was going to be his pal and that was that. There didn't seem any real reason he'd picked him. He was just another one in the group of snotty, frightened boys in the playground, but for some reason Cooper had decided on him and McCoy's life had never been the same. Nobody hit him, he was safe. Mess with him and you had Cooper to answer to. And nobody wanted that. Protection came with a price, though. Cooper cared about one thing and one thing only:

loyalty. Jump over the gap between the roofs of two buildings, shoplift from Woolworths, wait outside Peter O'Hara's house for four hours keeping Cooper company so he could batter him when he came out. Anything Cooper wanted you to do, you did.

He walked over reluctantly, knew what was going to happen, thought he may as well get it over with. Soon as he got near enough Cooper grabbed him, got him in a stranglehold.

'Submit? Submit?' said Cooper, rubbing his knuckles hard on the top of McCoy's head.

McCoy tried to nod, head trapped under Cooper's arm, throat being crushed.

Cooper pulled him round again, squeezed his arm tighter into his neck. 'What? I cannae hear ye!'

'I submit!' McCoy managed to get out in a strangulated whisper. Cooper laughed, let him go and he stumbled, lost his balance, fell down hard on the lino floor.

The girls giggled. From down here on the floor he could see the bruises on their thighs, dirty feet squashed into stilettos. 'Beat it!' Cooper barked at them and they made for the door, tits wobbling. McCoy stayed down on the floor, rubbed at his neck.

'You're like a big bloody wean, Cooper. Give us a hand up.'

'Fuck off.' He yawned, stretched, scratched at the hair on his chest.

'Long night, was it?' asked McCoy, dusting himself off.

'Could say that.' Cooper seemed to have broken his nose again since the last time McCoy had seen him. Looked a right mess. 'I hear you're running with the big boys now.'

McCoy nodded. 'Detective Harry McCoy of the Glasgow Police Force.'

'Aye well, don't forget who put you there.'

Cooper eased off the table, re-tucked the towel round his waist and padded over to where his clothes were hanging from a peg on the wall. He fished out his fags; shook the packet and a little wrap fell into his hand. He opened it up and carefully raised it to his nose, making sure it stayed level. He inhaled deeply, grimaced, then held it out to McCoy.

He shook his head. 'Wee bit early for me. I've no even had my breakfast yet. So, what's up?'

Cooper wiped the powder from his nostrils, rubbed it on his gums. 'Need you to do me a favour.'

'Me?' asked McCoy.

'Aye, you. Why the fuck not? You're a polis, aren't you? Solve crimes, that no the sketch? You know the Ben Duncan?'

McCoy nodded. Was one of Cooper's pubs up in Lambhill. Funny-looking place. More like a big suburban bungalow plonked down by the road than a normal pub.

'Got turned over last night. Clowns broke open

81

the filing cabinet, took a couple of hundred quid in an envelope.'

'No exactly crime of the century.'

'That's no what's bothering me. They took something else as well.'

'What?'

'My book.'

McCoy whistled. Losing a tally book wasn't good. Had the record of who owed what, who was behind on their payments. For a loan shark like Cooper it was the equivalent of the Bible.

'It'll be amateurs, daft boys. No pro would do over one of my pubs, wouldnae be that stupid.' He dipped into the Agnew's bag sitting in the corner and pulled out a can of McEwan's. 'No questions asked. I just want the book back.'

'Why me? You've got loads of people—'

'Because I say so. That a problem?' Normally Cooper looked sleepy, even a wee bit dopey. Not now. His faced had changed instantly. McCoy knew not to argue when he was like that. Didn't take much figuring out. Cooper was chucking his weight about. *Even though you think you're a big boy now, you're still no as big as me.* He didn't mind really, seemed simple enough to ask around, and Cooper had helped him out a good few times.

'Okay, just asking, that's all.'

Cooper grinned at him, happy again. 'That's the boy.' He sat back up on the table and took a long slug of his lager.

McCoy turned to go.

'Heard you were in the shebeen the other night. Cashing in your chips, eh?'

'I'm owed, aren't I?'

Cooper took another slug of beer, swilled it round in his mouth. 'Christ, that speed's fucking strong.' He wiped at his mouth. 'You watch that wee Janey. She's mad for the drugs. Dope, acid, any shite she can get.'

'What does that mean?'

'Means she's no your girlfriend, McCoy. She sucks men off for a living. She's a whoor, a druggy wee whoor. I'd steer clear if I was you.'

'This friendly advice or an order?'

Cooper held his hands out. 'Up to you, pal, up to you.'

McCoy was just about to ask him what the fuck he meant when they heard banging and shouts coming from outside. The door swung open, blonde girl standing there, breathing heavy, looking panicked.

'The polis are here. They've stoved in the door!'

Cooper looked at him and McCoy shook his head. 'No way. Nothing to do with me.'

Couple of seconds later Raeburn appeared in the doorway, two other plainers behind him looking over his shoulder. Bernie Raeburn was a detective at Eastern, had been for years. First time they met, McCoy thought he was a prick and Raeburn thought he was a smart arse. Nothing much had changed since. Raeburn wandered into the room, looked the two of them up and down, Cooper in his towel, McCoy in his suit, and smirked.

'Hand job for your boss, is it, McCoy? Always thought you two were queer for each other.'

McCoy didn't say anything, seemed easier just to let Raeburn have his fun, and there was nothing a cunt like him could say would wind Cooper up. He was too fly for that, he'd just store it all up, bide his time. The two plainers were chuckling away like good yes-men should.

'So, if you've finished wanking him off, you can beat it before I call Murray. Some of us have got work to do.'

McCoy looked at Cooper and raised his eyebrows. Cooper nodded towards the door.

'Jesus Christ,' said Raeburn. 'You got to ask his permission before you can wipe your arse? Go! Vanish! Vamonos! Fuck off!'

McCoy pushed past the plainers, one of them blowing him a kiss, and left them to it. Didn't know why Raeburn bothered. Cooper's lawyer would have him out in a couple of hours. And Raeburn was even stupider than he thought if he thought he'd find anything that connected Cooper to the sauna. He'd be just another customer enjoying a medicinal massage for a slipped disc, doctor's note enclosed, once his lawyer was finished.

The corridor was full of girls in flimsy dressing gowns swearing at the uniforms, calling them everything under the sun. Two naked Indian men were standing in a cabin doorway looking terrified, hands cupped over their privates as a uniform tried to spell their names in his notebook. A uniform went to grab him and he held up his badge. A muttered, 'Sorry, sir', and the uniform backed away, looking sheepish. Usual shitshow from Eastern Division. If McCoy knew Cooper, the place would be open for business again by eight o'clock tonight.

Out in the street the receptionist and a couple of the girls were being hustled into the police van while a queue of old biddies waiting at the bus stop enjoyed the show. It wasn't that far from Tollcross into town and the rain was still off, so McCoy thought he'd walk. The driver and his silver Zephyr were long gone anyway. He'd be late into the shop, Murray'd be looking for him, but he may as well be hung for an inch as a mile and get this tally book stuff of Cooper's out the road.

Outside the Irn-Bru factory a man was selling the first edition of the *Evening Times* from an old pram. McCoy bought one, skimmed 'CITY CENTRE SHOOTING HORROR' on the front page and looked inside.

They'd managed to make the identikit of the boy look half decent. Actually looked like the person for once. Murray must be desperate, if he'd gone public this quick. Maybe rules get bent when you've no leads and you've got the Chief Super and the press breathing down your neck. There was a little picture of the crucifix the boy'd been wearing in the corner of the page. Looked the same as every other one he'd ever seen. Still, you never knew, might work. He tucked the paper under his arm and crossed the road to the City Bakeries. Stomach was still rumbling.

CHAPTER 9

A square battery, some wooden coat hangers, two well-thumbed copies of *Parade*, a naked Barbie and a shortbread tin with a picture of Ben Lomond on it. All of them arranged on a dirty blue blanket spread out on the wet cobbles.

'Anything you fancy, son?'

The old man standing on the other side of the blanket looked at him hopefully. McCoy shook his head.

'Not today, pal.'

The old man nodded, looked resigned, stuck his shaky hands back in his pockets. Another small defeat. One of many by the look of him.

McCoy relented. 'Tell you what, I'll take the magazines. How much?'

'Ten pence for the two. Good stuff in there, son.'

McCoy handed the money over, stuffed the magazines in the pocket of his coat and made his way down the alley. He kept to the centre of the path, avoiding standing on the blankets and sheets laid out either side, each blanket covered in a variety of clothes, old shoes, broken toys, cutlery. Anything the people standing behind them had found to sell.

Paddy's Market was under the railway arches down by the Clyde. It was the market for people whose kids didn't have shoes, who tea was bread and jam or a bag of chips if they were lucky. Glasgow was still full of them, no new high flats and colour TVs on the tick from DER for them. This is where they came every Friday to buy and sell broken biscuits in plastic bags, torn net curtains – anything. Paddy's was like some warped department store; there was nothing it didn't have, just nothing you'd want to buy.

McCoy squeezed between a bloke with blood all over his face shouting at nobody and a man with a pram full of stolen firelighters and walked into the railway arches at the back, out of the rain. Back here was where the upmarket stuff got sold; back here people had to pay to pitch their stalls. Stolen tobacco, dead men's suits reeking of sweat and mothballs, motorcycle parts, fur stoles stiff with age. Quality stuff. The divide was absolute. Under the arches and outside in the rain. Two different worlds.

He ducked in and headed for the cafe at the back. It was hard to see through the gloom. There were no windows back here, just strings of anaemic-looking light bulbs hanging over each of the stalls, shaking on their wires as the trains rumbled overhead. He smelt the cafe before he got there, bacon grease and stewed tea mixing with the general fug of damp and old clothes. He bought a tea, sat down on one of the orange plastic chairs and took out his wee red jotter with a laurel wreath on it. Started a new one for each case, got them out of Woolies specially. He'd stuck the picture from last night's *Evening Times* in it. Had drawn a question mark beside it. Next page was headed *CONNECTIONS – BOY GIRL*. List under it.

Work?
Punter?
Boyfriend?
Hired?

Then he'd written

Howie Nairn. How connected to the girl?

He sighed, shut it, sipped at his rotten tea and tried to think. Found himself listening to the couple at the next table arguing about where they were going to for Christmas dinner next year. Not his mother's again. Over her dead body seemed to be the gist of it.

'Mr McCoy.'

He looked up and Ally Jeffries was standing there. Bunnet and filthy car coat in place as usual. Dirty Ally by name and nature.

'Thought I'd catch you here, Ally. Have a seat.'

He looked pained. 'I've no opened up yet, Mr McCoy, stall's still sitting there.'

McCoy just pointed at the seat. Ally sighed and sat. McCoy pushed the two copies of *Parade* across the table to him. 'Got you a present.'

Ally put a pair of smeary milk-bottle glasses on and started flicking through them. A professional's eye. Dirty Ally's stall at the back of the arches sold second-hand porno mags, dirty books, photo sets of middle-aged women lying spreadeagled on flowery bedspreads. No one knew where it was, but he'd a photo lab as well. He'd develop anything. The kind of stuff that you couldn't give to Boots. Always printed off a few copies for himself as well, sold them on to special customers. That was the price you had to pay. He closed the magazines, took his glasses off.

'Think I've seen these ones before. After a while all gash looks the same to me.' Didn't stop him slipping them into his pocket.

'There's a fiver in one of them. A favour. Need you to put the word out. Some clown's broken into the Ben Duncan, stole something from Stevie Cooper. Something he wants back. Long as its back with him in the next couple of days he's willing to go easy, no questions asked.'

'That right?' Ally grinned, revealing a row of tobacco-stained teeth. 'You and the boy Cooper are getting awfy friendly these days. Thick as thieves, you two.'

McCoy stood up. 'Just get the word out, Ally.

Get the stuff back to me and that'll be another fiver in a wank mag for your collection. Money for old rope.' He pointed over to a man in a rain-coat and pulled-down trilby standing by Ally's stall. 'Better go, Ally. Think you've got a customer.'

'Where have you been?'

Wattie had a face on him like a girl who'd been stood up on a Saturday night. Half ashamed and half angry. McCoy ignored him, took off his coat and sat down at his desk, but Wattie wasn't giving up. 'You and me are supposed to be doing every-thing together, that's what you were told. Where were you this morning then? I've been sitting here like a right arse. Everyone looking at me asking where you are.'

'I miss anything?' he asked.

Before Wattie could reply the battered wooden doors of the office swung open and Thomson appeared. Face lighting up when he saw McCoy.

'Well, well, Harry Shagger McCoy, you're a quiet one, right enough,' he said, big grin splitting his face. He put his briefcase down on his desk and really got going. Started poking his finger into the hole he'd made with his other hand. 'You dirty bugger. And that early in the morning as well. Hats off to you.'

'Very good, Thomson. I was there seeing someone,' he said patiently.

'I bet you fucking were. Who was it? That wee blonde with the big—'

91

'McCoy! And you too, Watson. Now!'

Murray's bull-like head had appeared round his office door.

'What's all this about?' asked Wattie. 'Why do I never know what's bloody going on?'

They stepped into the office. Murray was holding out a piece of paper with an address on it. 'We got lucky for once. Someone's recognised the boy from the paper.'

CHAPTER 10

'Tommy Malone. That's his name. Thomas Gerard Malone.' The priest crossed himself. 'God rest his soul.'

'You sure?' asked Wattie.

He nodded. 'Oh, I'm sure all right. I recognised the poor lad straight away.'

'We'll need you to do a formal identification.'

'Least I can do, least I can do.'

And how did you know him, Mr . . .'

'I'm not a mister, son – I'm a father. Father McClure. I take it you're not of the Catholic faith?'

Wattie shook his head. 'Church of Scotland.'

McClure nodded, smiled. 'We can't all be lucky enough to enjoy the blessings of the one true faith.' Waited for some laughter that didn't come. He leant forward, picked his glasses off the desk and peered at a file. 'He was a resident here, Tommy was. With us for a while. Sixty-nine to seventy-two. Left us last year.'

'And why was he here? Did he have a record?'

'Nothing serious. Sure you lads won't take a drink?' He nodded over at the trolley by the book-case. Bottles and decanters, crystal glasses. McCoy wanted a drink, really wanted a drink, but he shook his head. Wattie followed suit.

'Not for me either, Father. Record? You were saying?'

Undeterred McClure got up from the desk and poured himself one. Half a crystal tumbler of Bell's. Took a gulp disguised as a sip. 'As I said, it was nothing serious, stole some cigarettes and a pint of milk from a shop when he was thirteen.'

'What age is he now?'

He thought for a minute. 'He'll be eighteen in a couple of months. Well, he would have been . . .' He trailed off.

McCoy couldn't take his eyes off him. Watched his fat fingers drum on the file, the tapping of the well-polished shoe, Brylcreem-slicked hair, a bead of sweat on his forehead as the whisky went down. Reminded him of every other priest he'd known. It was the smell in the building as well, floor polish and incense. Sacred Heart on the wall, Jesus gazing down on them, arms open, blood in each palm.

Soon as he'd found out where they were going it had started. Sick feeling in his stomach, clammy hands. Tried the counting down like he'd been told. Tried to imagine a peaceful scene in his mind. Didn't work. When Wattie stopped the car next to the chapel, McCoy thought he might just go, walk down onto Paisley Road West and find the nearest pub, leave him to it. Was sick of feeling like this. Didn't want to go back to the doctor, knew he should.

'He still at the home?' asked Wattie.

'No, no. He left almost a year ago.'

'Did he have a family?'

'None that I know of, part of the reason he was sent here. Mother died in childbirth, there was a father but . . .' He tapped the side of his head. 'Mental problems. Not been here since St Anne's took him in. It's a sad story, right enough.'

'And what was he like, Tommy Malone?'

Wattie had the bit between his teeth, notebook out, list of questions already written down in preparation. McCoy let him get on with it, glad he didn't have to do the talking. Didn't think he'd be able to, even if he wanted to. Kept looking at the priest's hands. The bead of sweat rolling down from his hair.

The priest sat back in his chair with a squeak of leather and rested the crystal glass on his belly. Was used to being listened to, took his time. 'He wasn't the brightest lad, but he was a trier. Could be easily led, talked into things by the other boys. Believe me, we have some right menaces in here, some right menaces. Thought if he did what they said, made them laugh or whatnot, they'd all be pals. Not a canny lad, if you know what I mean. That's why we were happy he got a placement at the estate. Assistant groundsman. Quiet there, no one to lead him astray. He had a room above the stables, was very thankful, happy as a sandboy he was.'

McCoy sat up in his chair. All this Bing Crosby shite had gone on long enough. Had to say something before he was too dizzy, while he could still think.

'He can't have been that happy. He shot a nineteen-year-old girl dead, then shot himself.'

The priest's face changed. 'I didn't catch your name,' he said.

'McCoy.'

'Irish name, isn't it? I trust you aren't one of these Church of Scotland heathens.' He smiled at Wattie. 'Present company excepted.'

'I gave up being a Catholic a long time ago, Mr McClure, so you can skip the "we're all in this together" shite. Tommy Malone shot a girl, then he shot himself. Why would he do that?'

His kindly manner disappeared. McClure leant forward, eyes narrowing. 'I don't know anything about that. Don't know why Tommy would do such a wicked thing, why he would want to bring shame on himself and the good people that looked after him. When I think of all the effort we put into that boy, the care he got from me, from all the nuns here, it makes me heartsick. To think he could have turned away from us, from his caring family here, from the teachings of the Lord.'

McCoy stood up. His time was up. He had to get out. Couldn't be in this hot wee office any more, couldn't listen to another angry priest talking about the care of the nuns. He put his hand out, steadied himself on the desk, stood for a minute. Wattie looked up at him, didn't know what was going on.

'You okay, sir?'

He nodded. 'You done?'

Wattie looked unsure, checked his notebook. 'Near enough, I think.'

'I'll get you outside.'

He walked to the door, could hear McClure starting up already, complaining as he shut the door behind him. Didn't want to listen to it. He headed up past the gym with its wall bars and yellow varnished floor and pushed open a door with 'Boys Toilet' painted on it. He ran the tap, stood there in front of the mirror, tried to calm himself down. He could walk out of here any time. No one was going to stop him, drag him back. He was thirty, a detective. He splashed his face with the cold water. Needed to a get a grip. Things were getting bad again. He took out his wallet. Wee card was still in there. The one the doctor had given him, the one he swore he wouldn't put on his record. Fine blue copperplate writing: 'Alison Horne MD MRCPsych'. In other words, the shrink.

He found a bench outside under some trees, sat down, tried to light a cigarette. Wind was up, trees rustling and swaying. Paisley Road West, with its pubs and cafes and people, was only on the other side of the wall, but it felt miles away. The chapel and the home were totally cut off. Gust of wind swung the wooden sign by the entrance on its chains. 'NAZARETH HOUSE'. McCoy heard Wattie say goodbye and thank you, saw the priest outlined in the light from the hall. The door shut and Wattie looked around the garden.

'What are you sitting here for?' he asked, sitting down and pulling his collar up.

'No car keys,' he said.

'What's up with you anyway? What was all that about?'

McCoy shrugged. 'Something I ate. He have anything else to say?'

'What? Apart from complaining about you? Took me ten minutes to get the bastard to agree not to phone Murray. What got into you?'

McCoy tried to light his cigarette again, didn't say anything.

Wattie sighed, knew he would get nowhere. 'Nothing really. Hasn't seen him since he went off to that job, doesn't know the girl. Never heard of her. Or Howie Nairn. He's going to do the formal at Crown Street tomorrow.'

'Big of him. Where'd he work then, this Tommy Malone? Next port of call, I suppose.'

'Somewhere out Drymen way.' He looked at his notebook. 'Place called Broughton House.'

McCoy stopped, looked up at him. 'Christ, you're joking, aren't you? The Dunlop place?'

Wattie nodded. 'That's it. You know it?'

'Oh aye, I know it all right.'

The Dunlops. That was all he needed. Perfect

end to a perfect day. He flicked his soaking cigarette away into the darkness.

'Come on, you can buy me a drink, see if it settles my stomach.'

CHAPTER 11

They started at Wypers. Used to be the hotspot years ago, dark bar with a great jukebox, Small Faces, Motown, Yardbirds. Always full of mods with their bum freezer suits on, lassies with big beehive hairdos and eyes like pandas. Not any more. Now it was just a dark bar full of drunken office workers and women who worked in the department stores in Sauchiehall Street. McCoy didn't care, all he was interested in was getting pissed. Wattie didn't seem too impressed though, moaned through a pint with his face tripping him, wanted to go somewhere with a bit more life. McCoy couldn't be bothered arguing, so they headed down to the Muscular Arms. Turned out Wattie didn't like that pub either. Took one look in and decided it was too full of posers. At that point McCoy gave up, started walking back up the hill, Wattie trailing behind him asking what was up. He pulled the brass door of Sammy Dow's open, letting out the smell of smoke, old beer and wet overcoats.

'This is where I'm going. Take it or leave it.'

Wattie muttered something under his breath

about 'bloody old man's pub' and followed him in. They squeezed in at the bar between two old boys nursing half pints and a couple of soldiers getting torn into it, Glengarries tucked under their epaulettes. McCoy ordered the pints, then another two, then two more. As Cowie always said, there weren't many problems that didn't look a bit better after a few pints. Nazareth House was retreating, being replaced by a fuzzy calm. He wasn't sure if Wattie was in the huff but he seemed happy to stand there, asking the occasional question or just drinking his pint. Or at least he was for a while, till the beer kicked in. They'd moved to one of the wee tables by then, round by the fireplace. Between the crowded bar and the coal fire the pub was boiling, both of them down to their shirtsleeves, jackets and coats over the backs of their seats.

'Can I ask you something?' said Wattie, face flushed, hair clinging to his damp forehead.

McCoy was expecting another question about shift times, or how to pass the sergeants' papers. He nodded, starting to feel a bit sleepy in the heat. 'Fire away.'

'Who's Stevie Cooper?'

He wasn't expecting that, wasn't expecting that at all. 'Stevie Cooper? What you asking that for?'

'Today, when you weren't there. When I was sitting all by myself like a right arse—'

McCoy held his hand up. 'Enough. Jesus Christ.'

Wattie grinned. 'So I had a sandwich in the canteen. Blokes at the next table were talking about him. He's a top boy? Runs Springburn? Up that way?'

McCoy nodded, not sure where this was going. 'Aye, what about him?'

Wattie was about to reply when an old man came up to the table, sweat ringing the armpits of his shirt, bunnet still clamped on his head. He stopped, leant in. 'Jesus, it's like a bloody Japanese prisoner of war camp in here. Any of you lads see us a smoke?'

Wattie handed him the packet, bloke took one, was about to start on another funny when he noticed the two of them staring at each other. He nodded a thanks and waddled off sharpish.

'Someone said he was your pal. Cooper is,' said Wattie.

'Oh aye, that what they said, was it? You sure?'

Wattie shifted in his seat a bit, steeled himself, shook his head. 'Not exactly. They said you were in his pocket.'

McCoy drained what was left of his pint and stood up. Wattie looked up at him, face all worried.

'I didn't mean to say anything out—'

McCoy leant over him to grab the wallet out his jacket and Wattie flinched, sat back in his seat. McCoy laughed. 'Christ, calm down. I'm only going to get another round in, not lamp you. Another pint?'

He was back in a couple of minutes, battled through the crowd, put the glasses down on the sticky wee table and lit up. 'So, who was it saying this then?'

Wattie shook his head. 'Don't know their names. One of them had reddish hair and . . .'

McCoy held up his hand. 'Don't worry, doesn't matter. All you need to know is I'm not in Cooper's pocket, never have been, never will be.'

Wattie nodded. 'I feel bad for saying it now. I never thought you were. Honest. No offence, eh?'

'Don't worry, takes a fuck of a lot more than that to offend me.'

Maybe it was the beer or the fact Wattie was so green it hurt, or maybe he just wanted to play the big man; whatever it was, McCoy was in the mood to give him some advice. 'This is no Greenock or wherever the fuck you come from. This is Glasgow. The big bad city, things work differently. They have to or we'd be at war twenty-four fucking hours a day. We use them, they use us.'

Wattie was trying to follow him but he was looking lost.

'We look the other way one day, or don't press charges or go easy, and they serve up some nonce cunt we can't get a hold of another. Get me? Some new boy from out of town starts causing trouble, trying to muscle in, we get a tip. We take him out the picture, send him back where he came from and life goes back to normal. Easier for everyone.'

Still looked lost.

'For that to happen there has to be some to and fro. You want to get ahead in this game you need an inside track, someone to talk to, connections on the other side of the fence.'

'And that's Stevie Cooper?'

McCoy nodded. 'And that's Stevie Cooper. Those cunts in the canteen just don't get it. Fifteen years in and still no hope of getting any higher than a duty sergeant. Make themselves feel better by saying things like that about me. I don't give a fuck and they feel better about their shitey lives. Everybody wins.'

Wattie nodded, looked serious. 'So how do I get to know someone like that? How did you get to know a Stevie Cooper?'

McCoy took a draft of his pint. 'That's my business. Now I'm fucked if I'm sitting here talking about work all night. Drink up, we're going.'

The billiard hall was upstairs from a bank at the corner of Ingram Street. Been there ever since McCoy could remember, had gone through a few names over the years, now it was Bob's Billiards. Not that anyone played billiards any more; all snooker now since it was on the telly. A nod from Johnny on the door and they went up the stairs. It was a huge place, almost thirty tables disappearing back into the gloom, quiet apart from the clacking of balls and the low hum of conversation. The hall had had a few different owners over the years but not one of them had got round to doing the place up. Still looked like the thirties inside, gas lamps poking out the wall thick with dust, patterned carpets worn through to the backing. It was a decent place though, good tables, well run.

That's how it kept its licence all these years; real players still came here to practise.

McCoy wasn't a great player but he liked the place, ended up here after the pubs shut a couple nights a week. Wattie'd started off okay, few good pots, matching him, only losing by a couple of balls. But by the time they were on to the third game he was all over the shop. Missed the ball completely a few times, wobbling on his feet.

Bobby, the Bob in Bob's Billiards, wandered over from behind the bar, stood by McCoy and watched Wattie trying to line up a shot.

'If that cunt rips my baize, you're paying for it,' he said amiably.

'Och, he's no that bad,' said McCoy as Wattie mis-hit the white ball and it skittered off the table and rolled under the one-armed bandit in the corner.

'Aye, so you were saying. Three hundred nicker to re-felt these things. You got that to spare?'

McCoy handed him his cue. 'Point taken.'

He sat Wattie down on the wee bench by the door, rang a taxi for him from the payphone. He was half asleep, lying slumped against the wall beneath the big picture of dogs playing poker. Couldn't really blame him, they'd been hammering it hard and he hadn't been working his way through a handful of Black Bombers like McCoy had. Present from Robbie when he got Janey's hash. Him and Johnny finally managed to get Wattie in a taxi, bunged the driver an extra quid to make sure he got home okay. He watched the cab drive off towards the West End, looked at his watch. Half twelve. He wasn't ready for going home yet, not by a long shot.

He walked back into town, wee guy in George Square was selling tomorrow's *Record*. He bought one. Front page was almost all type; they'd pushed the boat out, special red ink and everything.

BLOODY JANUARY: HOW MANY MORE TO DIE?

No wonder the guy was doing a roaring trade. Special edition. Pictures of Lorna Skirving in her school uniform looking innocent. Editorial lambasting Glasgow Police, the full ten yards. He stuffed it in a bin in Buchanan Street, kept going. Murray's job had just got about ten times harder.

He ended up in the basement of Maggie's up in Sauchiehall Street, watching the bikers play pool, too wired to go home. He got himself a pint and sat down in the corner out the way. The basement was like some sort of bikers' clubhouse. Walls were plastered with magazine pictures of big-titted girls on choppers, benches round the walls full of long-haired blokes and girls in denim waistcoats. Music was loud, only song he recognised was 'Silver Machine', rest just merged into each other.

He got his wee red jotter out, trying to use the speed concentration to think his way through what had happened. He wrote down

Dunlop?
Broughton House?
Connection there?
Malone?

But that was as far as he got, couldn't keep his mind on track, kept skittering off in every direction, so he put it away, supped at his pint and just watched the bikers. They all had big embroidered badges on their backs. Devil's Disciples. Some cut-price version of the Hells Angels, he supposed. He knew most of them were probably carpet fitters or joiners from Carntyne with wives and kids at home, but they looked the part. Oily denims and stringy hair. Probably just seen *Easy Rider* one too many times. He didn't blame them; he quite fancied a life on the open road. Drugs, drink, no responsibilities. Could be worse.

He liked the polis well enough, he was good at it and it had been good to him. Took him on at sixteen, no qualifications. Had been them or the army. Just that lately he'd the feeling he was about ten years too late for it. Detective ten years ago, that's what he should have been. Simpler times then. These days he was stuck halfway between Murray and the bikers round the pool table. Sitting in an after-hours club speeding out his mind with a police badge hidden in his suit pocket. Two didn't really fit together.

A bloke with a stinking Afghan coat, long dirty fingernails and yellow jaundiced eyes sat down and started talking to him. Just back from India, hippy trail to Kathmandu. Eventually got round to it and offered him a wee bottle of hash oil for a fiver. Took up his offer. Wasn't so much for him but for Janey. She loved hash oil, dipped the ends of her fags in it and smoked them when she was with the punters. They never suspected a thing, joss sticks working their magic.

He gave the Afghan coat bloke a bomber, took the last one himself, swallowing it over with a whisky. Glasses chinking. 'To Kathmandu!' Soon as he took it he realised he shouldn't have. He was getting too hyped up, too paranoid. Nazareth House had rattled him, put him off balance. Needed to talk to someone but Wattie had gone, bloke with the Afghan was gone, just him, the speed surging through his brain and the memory of Nazareth House rattling round.

Was the first time he'd been in a place like that for nearly twenty years. St Columba's Home for Wayward Boys in Dingwall was the last one. Dad came to get him at the end of three months. Got down off the bus, three days sober and shaking like a shitting dog. Took him home to Glasgow and started drinking soon as they got there. A week later his dad was back in the Royal and he was back in Dingwall getting the shit kicked out of him again.

He looked at himself in the cracked toilet mirror; he was starting to look like him now, grey hair at the temples and in his beard, same hands. His eyes were wide, light hurting them, jaw was grinding. He fingered the little bottle of hash oil in his pocket. He'd go and see Janey, that's what he'd do, smoke some of it and take the edge off. Lie in her bed in the light from the streetlamps outside, laugh with her at the noises coming from the other rooms and fall asleep. No more Nazareth House.

Iris sold him three screwtops before she told him Janey was on an all-nighter and he couldn't see her. She was in with some councillor that Stevie Cooper wanted taking care of. Needed a smooth passage through the planning committee for some row of shops he was putting the money up for. Strict orders that he was to get the full treatment, even free drink. McCoy listened to Iris, nodded, told her he understood, pushed her aside and started hammering on Janey's door. He needed to see her, needed to see her now, wanted to lie on the bed with her, fall asleep. Didn't give a fuck about the councillor or Stevie Cooper or his row of fucking shops.

'Janey, you in there?' he shouted. Tried the handle, door was locked, Iris screaming at him. The key turned and the door opened a crack. Janey peered out, dressing gown wrapped round her, middle-aged man sitting up in the bed looking terrified. The councillor's fat face was the last thing he saw before Big Chas grabbed him, wrenched him round off the door and punched him hard in the stomach.

He had to give Chas his due, he didn't really start hurting him until he'd asked for it, after he'd called him a cunt, punched him on the side of the head and tried to kick him in the balls. Only took two hard punches to his face from Chas to knock the fight out of him. He bundled him out, arm bent up his back. He'd a sense of doors opening, people peering out, then Chas ran him down the stairs, put a boot in his back and then he was lying sprawled on the pavement.

He lay there for a minute, trying to work out what hurt most, his arm or his face. He felt a shoe prod him in the side, opened his eyes. Chas was standing over him, big moon-face staring down at him, didn't look happy. Didn't look happy at all.

'I don't care if you are a polis, you do anything like that again and I swear I'll bust you, so I will. Got it?'

Another prod with the shoe, harder this time. McCoy nodded, cold wet pavement felt good on his cheek, just wanted to lie there and go to sleep, let it all be over. Chas sighed, pulled him up, sat him down on the steps of the close. He managed to squeeze his bulk in beside him and sat down with a grunt. He took out his fags, lit two and handed him one.

'You all right?'

McCoy nodded. Chas had been in Glasgow for years but he still had his broad Belfast accent, had worked on the shipyards before they got closed down. Rumour was him and Iris were an occasional item; she let him into her bed once a month or so, depending on how many gins she'd had. McCoy couldn't see it. She was a wee bird-like woman, Iris, and Chas was huge, feet like boats, always a sheen of sweat on his forehead. Still, you never knew.

'Fuck's up with you, McCoy?' Chas's eyes narrowed, saw something. 'Hang on.'

McCoy felt his head being grabbed and spun round, found himself staring into Chas's eyes. 'Fucking thought so. Here.' He reached into the inside pocket of his worn suit and produced a half bottle of Red Hackle, held it out.

'Drink some of this. It'll get you down from the fucking ceiling at least. Cunts on pills do my fucking nut in.'

McCoy took a big swig, coughed as his throat burned and it went down. Whatever it was, it wasn't Red Hackle.

'I hear you're a big polis now. That right?'

McCoy nodded, swallowed back some more of the whisky.

'Well, you shouldnae be in places like this then.'

'Didn't know you cared, Chas.'

The big man snorted. 'I don't. Just don't need you round here causing trouble.'

McCoy lay back, looked up at the cracked tiles on the close walls. 'Long you been working here then, Chas?'

'Christ, you're asking now.' He tried to work it out on his fingers. 'Three years here. Crownpoint Road for two years before that, shitehole that it was.'

'You like it here? Doing this job?'

He shrugged and his worn suit rode up, must have bought it a good few years and a good few stone ago. Could see the tattoos on his forearms. 'No Surrender, 1690, King Billy'. Looked like he'd done them himself with a pin and a ballpoint pen. Borstal tattoos. 'Money's no bad, you get a sore face once in a while but that's the script working in a place like this.' He grinned. 'Sure, where else is a fat cunt like me gonnae get his hole on a regular basis? Got some perks, this job.'

'Cooper ever come around?'

'Not really, not for a while. Think he prefers the saunas now, puts the better girls in there. Can charge more in those places.'

'Who does he put in here, then?'

'Old timers mostly, lassies that aren't the best looking. Most of the punters are so pissed they don't care.'

'What's Janey doing in here then?'

He stood up, brushed the dust off the seat of his shiny trousers. 'You know fine well. She's a druggy, isn't she.'

'That's no so unusual.'

'Maybe so, but there's druggy and druggy.'

They both stopped, looked up. A police siren up on the Garscube Road, another one behind it.

'Looks like your lads are busy the night.'

'What does that mean, Chas? Druggy and druggy?'

He sighed. 'Do you need me to draw you a bloody picture now? Heroin, that's what it means.'

McCoy sat up, looked at him. 'Fuck off. She's no intae that. Besides, you can't get the bloody stuff in Glasgow, you're talking shite, Chas.'

Chas looked down at him. 'You know, for a clever polis you can't half be a stupid bastard. Take a telling, this isnae a place for you any more. Find yourself a wee bird with big tits and settle down, or if you cannae manage that start going to the saunas. Just don't come here any more. Right?'

McCoy nodded, not really sure what was going on. Chas said goodnight, stepped over him and disappeared into the close.

'I mean it,' he said, walking up the stairs. 'No more, McCoy.'

4TH JANUARY 1973

CHAPTER 12

'What happened to you?' said Wattie, pointing at McCoy's black eye.

'Slipped on the bloody bathroom floor and banged it on the sink. I'll budge over, you can drive.'

Wattie revved the Rover, got it into gear and they set off down the Great Western Road, heading for out of town and Broughton House. The rain had finally stopped, clouds blown through. Morning was crisp and cold, bright blue sky, snow on the hills in the distance. The change in the weather hadn't done much to lift McCoy's spirits. He'd still been wired when he got home, couldn't sleep. Combination of the speed and trying to work out what Chas was really talking about kept his mind turning over. He'd eventually managed a few hours' kip on the couch, woke up with a banging hangover and an empty half bottle beside him.

'I'd some head on me this morning,' said Wattie. 'Last thing I remember is the snooker club, no idea how I got home. Landlady wasn't too happy this morning. Apparently I made a right arse of myself.'

McCoy nodded along as Wattie chattered on about being sick in his landlady's garden and waking up in his suit, but he wasn't really listening. He knew the silence had been too good to last. Amazing what a difference a night on the piss could make, was like they were big pals now. The Two Musketeers. Traditional Scottish way, he supposed, get pissed together and you were friends for life.

He fished the *Daily Record* out Wattie's coat pocket and looked at the front page, familiar red type. But it was a later edition than the one he'd seen last night, someone had been babbling meantime. He drew the air in between his teeth. Murray was going to be apoplectic by now. Double page spread.

SHOT GIRL WAS A PRO

The headline was followed by an exposé of the vice trade in Glasgow's leading hotels and restaurants on pages four, five, six and seven. No doubt some telephonist or secretary from Central had cashed in, got on the phone to the news desk with what they'd managed to pick up listening in. Usual story. Lorna Skirving's period of grace had ended and ended quick. Last night she was an innocent bystander tragically killed. Today she was a pro who probably got what she deserved.

'Which way?' asked Wattie.

McCoy looked up. 'Take the switchback, head for Drymen, it's out that way.'

Wattie nodded, turned off at the roundabout. Broughton House. So far McCoy'd managed not to think about it too much. Not for much longer. The home and now Broughton House. No wonder he'd got out his box last night. He lit a cigarette and watched the houses get bigger and more spaced out as they passed through the suburbs then into the country. This was where the rich people lived, as far from the slums and factories of Glasgow as you could decently get. The proper rich, that was, the factory owners, the building tycoons and the richest ones of them all: the Dunlops.

After another few miles and a wrong turning, Broughton House emerged from between the trees. It was a long, low building made of gleaming white stone, two curving wings and a round glass tower in the middle like some kind of lighthouse. It sat in a valley surrounded by thick woods and a high wall. Liked their privacy, the Dunlops. Wattie was craning out the window, trying to get a good look.

'I was expecting some kind of castle thing,' he said.

'Used to be one, knocked it down in the thirties and built that. Looks like the bloody bathing pavilion at Rothesay.'

They rolled up the drive between the rows of clipped trees, navigated round an ornamental pond and parked at the front of the house. The driveway was already littered with cars, all of them expensive. A Jensen Interceptor, a big Merc and what looked like a thirties Rolls-Royce. Wattie got out and looked up at the glass tower.

'People actually live here then?'

'Some of the time. They've got a big house in London, all sorts of places. That's what you get when you own a shipyard. Your dad probably paid for a few bricks.'

They crunched towards the door, feet sinking into the wet pebbles. McCoy pulled a brass handle and a chime sounded deep in the house. Wattie was pulling his tie straight, looking nervous. If he'd had a cap, he'd have been ready to doff it. The door was answered by a maid in a black dress, white pinny over it. She looked Filipino, Malaysian, something like that. Tiny. McCoy held out his card.

'Morning, Glasgow Police to see Lord Dunlop.'

She shook her head. 'Lord Gray not here.' She pointed past them to the hills. 'Hunting.'

'Okay, how about Jimmy Gibbs? He around?'

'Master Jimmy is here, yes. Please.' She bowed her head, held the door open and they stepped into the hallway. Was hard not to be impressed. The glass tower reached up above them, vast curved stairway swooping round it. The hallway was huge, light from the big windows bouncing off the white marble floor and walls. A lavishly decorated Christmas tree sat in the corner, must have been twelve feet high, boxes of wrapped presents scattered around it. Various vases full of white lilies dotted about the place.

'Who shall I say is here for him?' she asked, bowing again.

'Just tell him it's Harry McCoy, I'm an old pal of his.'

'Lovely flowers,' said Wattie.

'From the greenhouses. Lord Dunlop grows them,' said the maid. She bowed again, wandered off.

McCoy looked at Wattie.

'What?' he asked.

'Lovely flowers?'

'They are. My maw works in a florist. These are the good stuff.'

McCoy shook his head. Why him?

'Who's Jimmy Gibbs anyway?' asked Wattie, wandering over to look at an enormous tapestry of a stag being brought down by hounds.

'Jimmy? He runs the place for the Dunlops, takes care of problems. Knows where the bodies are buried.'

'How come you know him then?'

McCoy sat down on a long white leather couch by the fireplace. 'Was a girl working here, in the kitchens, killed herself. Turned out she was having an affair with the son and she was up the duff. All very convenient, so I started asking some questions. Got warned off.'

Wattie turned away from the picture. 'What? She was murdered?'

McCoy shook his head. 'No, was suicide all right but I'd rather find that out by myself than get told what to think.'

121

The maid reappeared. Smiled and bowed. 'Master Jimmy is in the sunroom; he'll see you now. Please.'

They followed her down a corridor lined with pictures, all modern, all abstract, all no doubt worth a fortune. An open door revealed a big ballroom off to the left, grand piano under a white sheet and stacks of red and gold chairs lining the wall. The corridor turned into a kind of glass tunnel coming out the back of the house and stretching across the garden towards a large greenhouse. The garden was full of artfully overgrown dark foliage with classical statues dotted amongst it. Wattie's head was swivelling from side to side trying to take it all in. The maid held the glasshouse door open.

'Through here, please.'

There was a swimming pool in front of them, slight steam rising up from it, tang of chlorine in the air. A man was ploughing up and down the middle of it at some speed. Head down in the water, arms scissoring. He reached the side, touched it like he was in a race, stood up, looked at his watch and smiled. McCoy coughed and Jimmy Gibbs turned to them, took his goggles off and wiped his hair back from his face.

'Thanks, Mary. That'll be all,' he said.

The maid nodded and retreated.

Gibbs pulled himself out the pool, stuck his hand down the front of his trunks and rearranged himself. He was wiry, looked fit. He padded over to one of the sun loungers, picked up a towel and hung it across his shoulders.

'Didn't think you'd have the balls to turn up here again, McCoy,' he said, rubbing at his reddish hair with the towel. 'Thought you'd have learnt your lesson.'

'Tommy Malone,' said McCoy, ignoring him. Knew he was going to rise to the bait at some point, was just trying to postpone it as long as possible.

Gibbs shrugged, reached down to the wee table by the lounger and picked up his drink, ice cubes clinking as he took a sip.

'The boy that shot himself, you mean? Funny business that.'

His manner was indifferent, seemed more interested in his drink than anything else. Acting like he knew something McCoy didn't, which he probably did. McCoy looked round at the swimming pool, the rattan chairs, the palm trees stretching up behind the wet bar.

'Long way from the Maryhill shop this, eh, Jimmy?'

Gibbs opened his arms, looked around. 'What can I say? Some of us managed to make something of ourselves.'

McCoy sat down on one of the loungers, took out his cigarettes.

'No smoking in here,' said Gibbs. 'Family don't like it.'

McCoy put them away, was still playing nice. 'Tommy Malone?'

'Hello, Harry.'

A voice he'd recognise anywhere. He turned and Angela was standing there. She looked a bit thinner, that was the only difference, still had the looks. Multicoloured robe over a swimsuit, dark hair piled up on top of her head, big round sunglasses on. She looked nervous, skittish, too thin.

He stood up. 'Angela,' he said. 'Looking good.'

She smiled, same smile she'd always had. The one that always made him do whatever she asked. Could smell her perfume as well. Worth. Cost a fortune. He should know, he'd bought it often enough.

'Wish I could say the same for you,' she said, looking at his black eye. 'You looking after yourself?'

'Like you're bothered,' he said. It was meant to sound funny, just came out sounding mean.

She sighed. 'I was only asking.'

'I'm okay, aye. How's you?'

Gibbs walked over, put his arm round her, kissed her cheek. 'You all right, love? Want anything?'

She shook her head. 'I'm fine, Jimmy.'

'Are you?' said McCoy.

'What?' said Gibbs.

She shook her head. 'You really can be a prick, Harry. A real fucking prick.'

'Only one reason you ever wore sunglasses. He getting that for you now, is he?'

Angela picked Gibbs' drink off the table and threw it in his face, wasn't much of it left but it was enough to make her point.

Wattie was looking back and forth at the three of them, no idea what was going on.

Angela kissed Gibbs on the cheek. 'I'll see you later, eh?'

The three of them watched her go, high-heeled sandals clicking on the floor of the glass tunnel. McCoy reached for a towel, started wiping his face down.

'Well done,' said Gibbs. 'Always were a charmer. Not surprised she fucking left you.'

Wattie stuck his fingers in his mouth and whistled. They stopped, turned to him.

'Fuck sake, pack it in, you two. I don't know what's going on here, don't even want to know, but we're here for a reason, not for a bloody rammy.' He pointed at the lounger. 'Mr Gibbs, if you could sit down?'

McCoy looked at him amazed, didn't think he had it in him. Gibbs looked as shocked as he did, but he sat down and Wattie took out his notebook. 'When you're ready, Mr Gibbs?' he said. 'Tommy Malone?'

Gibbs looked at them both, looked like he was about to start shouting again, then thought better of it. 'Been here for a year or so, kept himself to himself. Didn't see much of him.'

'How did he end up here?' asked Wattie.

He shrugged. 'Same way lots of lads do. Lord Dunlop is on the Board of Governors at Nazareth House, few places like that. He's a very charitable man, likes to give the less fortunate a leg up in

125

life. Poor boys whose parents have turned to drink and abandoned them. You know what I mean, don't you, McCoy?'

McCoy ignored that, was getting more difficult though.

'Anything else?' asked Wattie. 'Friends?'

Gibbs shook his head. 'Did his work, kept his nose clean. Nothing else I can tell you.'

'So who's the groundskeeper, the bloke he worked for?'

'Henry Mason. He's no here, though, gone off to visit his sister in South Africa.'

'Convenient,' said McCoy.

Gibbs shook his head. 'Watch it, McCoy, you're getting paranoid. Trip was booked last year, been saving up for years he has. You're seeing things that aren't there and you know what happened last time you did that.' He leant over, pressed a buzzer on the wall. 'Now if you and the boy wonder are done, I've got things to do.' He picked up the paperback lying on the table by the lounger, lay back and started reading.

'His bedroom, where he lived, we'll need to see that,' said McCoy.

Gibbs ignored them until the maid appeared. 'Mary, can you show these two the Malone lad's room? Gentlemen, let's hope we don't meet again.' He went back to his book.

'Didn't know you could even read, Jimmy. What is it? *Dick and Jane Frame a Punter*?'

Gibbs turned the book over, looked at the front.

'No, it's called *Harry McCoy Got Fucked Right Over*. Read it?'

That was it, he'd had enough. McCoy moved towards him, felt Wattie's hand on his arm. 'Leave it,' he said quietly.

'See these clowns out, Mary, before I lose my temper.'

McCoy followed Mary and Wattie back down the corridor towards the main house. Wattie was listening hard to what Mary was saying, trying to understand where she was telling them to go. McCoy fell behind, mind on other things.

Been a couple of years since he'd seen Angela. Couple of years since she'd told him she was going. Didn't believe her at first, Gibbs of all people, thought she was just saying it to wind him up. He stopped, let them walk on ahead and took his wallet out. Tried not to do this too often, didn't help him, but seeing her had made him want to look. He pulled the photograph out, corners were getting worn, he'd have to get it copied or something, was the only one he had. He looked at it and couldn't help but smile. He'd a blue jumper on one of the neighbours had knitted, wee fat legs in woolly tights. He was lying on his back on a tartan rug, teddy bear beside him. He rubbed his thumb over his face. He was smiling, about to start laughing, could tell from his expression.

'McCoy?'

He looked up. Mary and Wattie were standing at the end of the corridor waiting for him. 'Coming,' he said, putting the picture away. 'Coming. Hold your bloody horses.'

Mary walked them back across the vast hallway and opened the door. A bell rang somewhere and she looked up the stairs anxiously.

'You know him, Mary? The Malone boy?' McCoy asked.

She nodded. 'Very nice boy. Very sad.'

'Why would he do a thing like that, shoot someone? Any idea?'

She shook her head. 'He was a nice boy.'

'And he changed?'

The bell rang again. 'I have to go,' she said.

She looked back up the stairs, bell was going again, more insistent this time. She shook her head, began to close the door on them. 'Sorry, I don't understand. My English. I must go.'

CHAPTER 13

'She chucked a drink over you!'

'Wasn't the first time and, believe me, she's chucked a lot worse. We went out for a while, things got messy and she left me for Gibbs. End of. Happy?'

Wattie shook his head. 'Got to be more to it than that. And what was all that about the sunglasses?'

'Aye well, maybe there is but it's fuck all to do with you. Okay?'

McCoy sat down on the bed, rubbed his eyes. He shouldn't have looked at the picture, shouldn't even have come up here. Was basic stuff, just background, could have sent Thomson. Could even have sent Wattie by himself. But no, couldn't help himself, wanted to see Gibbs, wanted to see Angela, wanted to pick at it like a scab, make it hurt again, and he'd succeeded.

They were in Malone's bedroom, tiny place above the stables in the grounds of the big house. Place smelt stale, unaired. The single bed was unmade, still had the greasy imprint of his head on the pillow. Wattie was looking out the window, martyred.

'Come on,' said McCoy, opening the door of the wardrobe. 'Let's get this done and get the fuck out of here.' There wasn't much inside. A pair of jeans, few T-shirts, wash bag, jumper balled up on the bottom. He shut the door and looked round. Could tell this was a waste of time already. There was a calendar on the wall, 'Views of Bonnie Scotland', a crucifix hanging from a nail, picture of some sports day at Nazareth House. Malone holding a wee cup, Father McClure in the crowd behind. The dresser was old and scratched, looked like one of those utility ones from after the war. Couple of empty beer bottles on it, tub of Brylcreem, some Old Spice talc.

'Surprised he didn't do himself in earlier,' said McCoy. 'Living in this dump would be enough to send anyone over the edge.'

McCoy slid the bedside drawer open. Couple of scud mags. *Biker Orgy, Cavalcade.* Made him wonder how Dirty Ally was getting on. Cooper liked results fast. Maybe he'd go and check on him tonight. There was a book in there as well, old hardback, gold-edged pages like a Bible. He picked it up and looked at the spine.

'*The Confessions of Aleister Crowley.*'

'Who's he when he's at home?' asked Wattie.

'Not sure, heard the name I think.' He opened it and flicked through.

We had resumed Magical work, in a desultory way, on finding that Mathers was attacking us. He succeeded in killing most of the dogs. (At this time I kept a pack of bloodhounds and went man-hunting over the moors.) The servants too were constantly being made ill, one in one way and one in another.

'Bit advanced for young Tommy.'

He put the book back and closed the drawer, sat down on the bed again and looked round. Why would a boy living in a place like this, a place like anywhere else, suddenly kill some girl and then himself? Had to be a reason, but whatever it was he didn't think he was going to find it in this room.

'The gun,' McCoy said. 'Where did he get the gun?'

Wattie was flicking through *Biker Orgy*. 'Can't be that hard to get hold of a gun round here, all that hunting, shooting and fishing.'

McCoy shook his head. 'It was a .45 pistol. He didn't get that kind of a gun here. Looked like an old war thing, filed-off serial number. A hot job. Where would an ordinary lad like Tommy Malone get a gun like that?'

Wattie stopped at a page, turned the magazine vertical and peered at it. 'Maybe he wasn't so ordinary after all.' He looked up to find McCoy staring at him.

'What did you say?' asked McCoy.

Wattie looked puzzled. 'Nothing. Just that maybe he wasn't so ordinary.'

'That might be the first useful thing you've said.

Still doesn't make up for following me around like a bad smell, but it's a start. Anyway, he could only get a gun like that in town.'

'Who would he ask?'

'Davey Waters.'

'Who?'

'Been at it for years, smart enough to never get done. Never touches the guns himself, gets wee lads to deliver them. Sits in the Vale all day.'

Wattie was staring at the page of the magazine, not listening to him.

'What's up with you, Wattie? They no have scud mags in Greenock? Take it with you if you're that interested. Tommy Malone doesn't need it any more.'

Wattie didn't say anything, just held out the open magazine. A newspaper picture of a young woman's face, good-looking, blonde, had been stuck onto the centrefold. It had been pasted onto the body of a woman lying on a couch with her legs open.

'Who is that?' asked Wattie.

McCoy took it, had a closer look. 'Sharon Tate, I think.'

'She the one that got murdered by those loonies in America?'

McCoy nodded, flicked through the magazine and found another picture. This time a picture of Sharon Tate's face was stuck on a woman tied to a motorbike, nude, rope looking like it hurt, some bloke with a Hells Angels jacket and a big cock looming over her. 'Not what you'd call your average wank material.' He shut the magazine, gave it back to Wattie.

'Tommy Malone's still waters are starting to look pretty bloody deep. C'mon, let's get out of here.'

They heard them before they saw them. Barks and whelps ringing round the yard outside the stables. They stopped and watched as six or seven gun dogs of various sizes appeared round the corner. They were panting heavily, tongues lolling out their mouths, steam coming off them in the cold, crisp air. A brown one at the front saw them and barked, others' heads up in an instant, and they ran towards them. McCoy stepped back, then noticed with relief that their tails were wagging. Couple of seconds later they were surrounded by them, all jumping up, all wanting patting or scratching.

'Thank God they're friendly,' said McCoy, trying to avoid being pushed over by a big Great Dane-looking thing with its paws on his chest. A sharp whistle sounded and the dogs froze, turned and moved as one, running back down the gravel path leading towards the house.

'Shite,' said McCoy under his breath.

Two men were coming towards them. Black swept-back hair, waxed jackets, broken rifles hanging over their arms. Both walking with the air of self-confidence that only generations of money, privilege and public school can bring. Lord Dunlop was in his mid-fifties, looked ten years younger, neat moustache, military posture, still had the good looks that had made him a society pin-up when he was younger. The son was broader, coarser, not as good-looking. As far as McCoy remembered his mother had been a model, some American heiress that ended up taking an overdose in a shitty hotel in Venice. Strange how two good-looking people can make one that isn't. The two of them stopped, dogs milling around their legs.

'Mr Gibbs let us in,' said Wattie, sounding apologetic. 'Police.' He started digging in his pocket for his card. Lord Dunlop ignored him, was staring straight at McCoy.

'McCoy. That was your name, wasn't it? What in god's name are you doing roaming round my property? I thought you'd been dismissed.' His voice was cut-glass English, Scottish upbringing hadn't made a dent.

''Fraid not,' said McCoy. 'Still gainfully employed.' He looked back at the stable block. 'Tommy Malone.'

'What of him?' asked Dunlop.

'What of him? He's dead. Shot a girl in broad daylight then blew the back of his own head off.'

No response from either of them.

'We're just up here doing some background, having a look at his room. You have much to do with him?'

Dunlop Junior laughed. 'Hardly.' Same accent as his father. 'He was a junior groundskeeper, I believe. Went missing about a week ago, didn't turn up for work. I only met him once and I'm

134

quite sure my father never did. There're almost thirty staff on this estate, you know.'

'That right?' said McCoy conversationally. 'Well, that's not that many. Remember him, do you, Lord Dunlop?'

He shook his head. 'I'm afraid not. Dreadful business, by all accounts, but not something I can help you with. Now if you'll excuse me.' He held up seven or eight dead birds tied together, heads lolling. Grouse? Partridge? McCoy had no idea.

'How about Lorna Skirving – ever meet her?'

Lord Dunlop shook his head. 'Sorry. No idea who that may be.'

'Sure?'

Dunlop Junior looked up, spaniel still nuzzling in at his hand. 'Who is she?'

'Doesn't matter,' said McCoy. 'If you don't know her, you don't know her.'

Lord Dunlop started walking, dogs crowded round him. 'You've had your fun, McCoy. Now get going before I have to call one of your superiors. Again.'

McCoy tugged at an imaginary forelock as he passed. 'Sorry to have disturbed you, sir. Good day.'

'He's a bit of a prick, isn't he?' said Wattie, opening the car door. 'Who does he think he is?'

'Who he thinks he is, is Lord Dunlop of Broughton, Chief of Clan Dunlop, Right Honourable Member for West Stirlingshire. It goes on and on. That's who he thinks he is.'

'What's the son's name? Looks just like him.'

'Teddy, I think.' McCoy settled into the passenger seat, found a tube of Polos someone had left in the glove compartment. He got one out, rubbed the dust off it. 'If our Tommy Malone wasn't such an ordinary boy after all—'

'That was my line,' said Wattie proudly.

'Then maybe Lorna Skirving wasn't so ordinary either. Maybe she wasn't just a waitress giving hand jobs for spending money. Maybe she was something more, maybe both of them were.'

'No sure what you mean . . .'

'No, me neither.'

Wattie turned the engine over. 'Where we off to?'

'Back to the shop, then off to the Vale.'

'Davey Waters?'

McCoy nodded. 'And the hair of the dog that bit my arse last night.'

CHAPTER 14

Soon as they walked in the shop they could tell something was up. The main office floor was normally frantic, people joking, arguing, shouting into phones. Not today, though. Even Thomson was quiet. Head bent over a new electric typewriter, tongue stuck out in concentration.

'What's up?' asked McCoy, sitting down at his desk. 'Somebody die?'

Thomson looked up. 'Not yet, but you better start saying your prayers. Murray's looking for you and he's fucking beeling, been shouting the odds all afternoon.'

Wattie had sat down at his desk in the corner; he'd been shoved over in the space below the noticeboard, lowest of the low. He held up a sheet torn out of a yellow telephone message pad.

Wattie plonked the note down in front of him. 'Alasdair Cowie wants you to go and see him. Maybe he wants to go for another curry.'

McCoy took it and stuffed it in his pocket, straightened his tie, whatever good that was going to do. Was aware everyone on the floor was watching him. 'Better get this over then, eh?'

Murray was on the phone, gestured for him to come in and sit down. McCoy listened for a minute or two then tuned out, some rubbish about quota rearrangements. Nothing to do but wait. Murray was leaning back, talking away. He was wearing a thick tweed suit for some reason, shoulders and arms protesting against the seams. Even the chair he was sitting in looked too small for him. His office was neat, same as always, everything in its place, picture of two smiling kids in a frame on the desk. Framed back page of the *Scotsman* on the wall. 'HAWICK TAKE TITLE!' A much younger Murray in rugby kit, covered in mud, holding up a trophy, big grin on his face. Must be nice to have a life that ordered, everything in its right place, kids, wife, job. Click of the receiver being put down brought him back.

'Well?' he asked.

McCoy shrugged. 'You wanted to see me?'

Murray shook his head, looked more disappointed than angry. 'Just couldn't help yourself, could you? You're supposed to be a senior officer, McCoy. Responsible. What the fuck were you thinking?'

The penny dropped. 'Christ, that didn't take them long, did it, we just left the bloody place.'

'That it? That all you've got to say? Think being your usual smart arse is going to get you out of this one, do you? Not a fucking chance, son, not this time.'

McCoy suddenly realised he'd called this one

wrong. He'd only seen Murray really angry a couple of times, didn't want to see it again, especially if he was at the receiving end. His neck was already starting to go red, big fingers crushed into fists. He leant across the desk, voice quiet, another danger sign.

'Do you think I like having the Chief Super speak to me like I'm some sort of cunt? Do you think I like the fact I didn't know you were up there so I looked like an incompetent cunt as well? Think that's all a big laugh? Another chance to shrug your fucking shoulders, is it?'

McCoy held his hands up, started to apologise. 'Sir, I'm really sorry, I didn't know that—'

'You shut your fucking mouth!' Murray was standing now, leaning over the desk. 'Don't you ever do anything that fucking stupid again. You're a senior officer, not a bloody cadet. I fought for you last time, McCoy, not this time. You hear me? Stay away from the Dunlops, from Broughton House, from anywhere within five fucking miles of them.'

McCoy nodded, tried to ride out the storm. 'I only asked him some routine questions, sir, the boy worked there—'

Murray was up out of his chair and round. McCoy jumped back, thought he was going to hit him. Murray grabbed his lapels, red face pushed into his, veins in his neck sticking out.

'A few questions? Last time you went up there to ask him a few questions you were drunk, accused his son of killing someone—'

'It was just after wee Bobby died, I wasn't right, I—'

'Do you know what I had to do to get you out of that? Even when you had some sort of excuse? Dunlop, the Super, Personnel. Every one of them wanted you canned. I wish I'd fucking listened to them now.'

He pushed him away and McCoy's chair tipped, dumped him on the floor. He stood up, was starting to get annoyed, something he didn't often do. Tried to keep calm, remember where he was and who he was talking to.

'Sir, with all due respect you put me on this fucking case. What was I supposed to do? Not investigate it?'

'And that's your excuse, is it? Nothing's ever your fault, is it, McCoy? No fucking flies on you. Too smart for the likes of us.'

He opened his mouth to protest, but Murray had already turned away.

'Just get out my sight, McCoy, go on. Fuck off before I do something I shouldn't.'

McCoy came out the office just in time to see everyone look back down at their desks. Was so quiet he could hear the big clock on the far wall ticking. He sat down, tried to slap some of the dust off his trousers. Lit a cigarette; let the general hubbub start up again. Could see Wattie looking over at him anxiously, wondering what was going on. No question, he felt like a total arse. He hadn't

140

expected Dunlop to do anything, thought he'd be on the back foot with a murderer working for them, so he went up there chucking his weight about, looking for Angela, looking for a scrap with Gibbs. All the time forgetting how fucking bulletproof the rich really were. All it took was one phone call from Lord Dunlop and he was fucked.

'You okay?' asked Wattie.

McCoy nodded, picked up a report from the desk and pretended to read it, realised his hand was shaking. Murray's door opened again and he headed for the big blackboard at the back of the office, pile of papers in his hand. Told everyone to gather round. A scraping of chairs and bums settling onto the edge of desks then a silence. Nobody whispering or making jokes during the briefing today.

He sat on the edge of the desk, put his papers down; room was silent, everyone waiting for him to go on. 'Forty-seven hours, gents,' he said. 'Forty-seven hours since Lorna Skirving was shot dead in the middle of town. We know who did it: Tommy Malone. Up until then a quiet boy working as a gardener, keeping himself to himself. What we don't know is why. Why he got on a bus to town and shot the Skirving girl. Why he shot himself. Where he was between the time he left Broughton House and got to the bus station. We don't know what his relationship to Skirving was and we don't know why he killed her.'

He looked round the room at them all. McCoy

141

tried to look concerned, everyone else just looked scared. This wasn't an ordinary Murray briefing. None of his usual terrible jokes, no reading out of scores from the Police Rugby League that nobody cared about. This was serious.

'I want to know why this happened – why a young girl is dead and why a young man shot himself. We've got about three days' grace before the Super decides to shut us down. Three days for us to find some answers.' He stood up again, pointed. 'McCoy, you work from the girl towards him and for fuck sake stop before you get anywhere near the Dunlops, clear?'

McCoy nodded.

Thomson put his hand up. 'Sir?' Murray nodded at him. 'This might be a stupid thing to say, but maybe he didn't kill her.' A general sniggering, relief of tension. Thomson reddened.

'Shut it,' barked Murray. 'On you go.'

'What I mean is maybe he was just killing someone. Someone who turned out to be Lorna Skirving. Just a girl. Maybe there's no connection after all?'

Silence, everyone looking at Thomson. Murray ran his hands through what was left of his hair. 'Christ,' he said. 'I hadn't thought of that.'

Wattie put his hand up and Murray nodded at him.

'He was looking in the crowd, sir, could just have been looking for any girl, but I don't think so, seemed to know her when he saw her.'

'That right, McCoy?'

McCoy nodded. 'Think he was looking for Lorna Skirving. Don't know for sure.'

Murray didn't look happy. 'No way a boy's just going to go to the bus station and kill someone he doesn't know. Why would he do that? Has to be a connection.' He rubbed at the bristle coming through on his chin. 'Christ, if there's not then god help us. Wilson? You here?'

Man at the back of the room stood up. Marcus Wilson, old hand, only a couple of years from retirement. 'You, and only you, deal with the boy's background and his time at the Dunlops. I don't have to tell you this, but tread bloody lightly. Whether we like it or not, the Dunlops have some very important friends. Someone here has already fucked them off, make sure it doesn't happen again.'

Wilson nodded. 'Sir.'

'And you.' He nodded at McKee. 'Touts, grasses, someone must know something about this.' He stood up to go. Stopped. 'The boyfriend. What was his name?' He was looking at McCoy.

'Nairn's boyfriend, you mean? Bobby.'

Murray nodded. 'What did he have to say for himself?'

He was about to say he thought Murray was sending a woman to interview him but he didn't. 'Haven't spoken to him, sir.'

'You haven't spoken to him?' McCoy shook his head. 'Playing a blinder today, McCoy, playing a blinder right enough.' He pointed at Wattie. 'You speak to this Bobby as well. Let's just hope Mr McCoy hasn't forgotten to interview any other important witnesses, eh?'

A few smiles, teacher's pet getting a doing. Murray stood up. 'What are you all still doing here? Move!'

CHAPTER 15

Che Guevara with his beret. Angela Davis with her Afro. 'Bringing the Boys Home' written over a picture of a coffin draped in the American flag. Cowie's office had certainly changed since the last time McCoy had been here. Posters covered one half of the office now. Still had that stupid goldfish swimming round in its murky water though. Been there for years, had to be the world's oldest goldfish by now. Cowie'd bagsied the old horse tackle room at the back of the station, moved in a couple of years ago and refused to leave. Place was becoming more and more like a junkshop every day. He'd bought an old desk, faded rug. Every so often Murray'd come in and scream at him to get rid of all the junk. He'd nod and say 'Yes, sir' and never shift a thing.

McCoy didn't sit down, kept by the door, held up the yellow page from the message pad. 'What d'you need me for, Cowie? I've just had a kicking from Murray, need to get going.' He took another look round, empty space on the wall. He nodded over. 'What happened to your Pirelli calendar, by the way?'

Cowie smiled. Girl sitting at the other desk didn't. Combat jacket peppered in wee badges, long blonde hair, nice figure. Desk in front of her was covered in books and folders, overspill on the floor beside her.

'Contrary to appearances, McCoy isn't quite the arsehole he seems,' said Cowie. 'That comes with the job. Much as it pains me to say it, he's quite a nice guy underneath it all.' He wagged his finger between them. 'Susan Thomas, meet Harry McCoy.'

'Like looking at girly calendars, do you, Mr McCoy?' She was English, sounded faintly London.

He went to nod, then shook his head.

She smiled. 'Oh well, at least you tried.'

'Susan's doing a PhD up at the university,' said Cowie, picking a pile of papers off an old chair and nodding for McCoy to sit down. 'Researching deviant sexual behaviour and its commercial exploitation. Under the counter Super 8s, fetish magazines, specialised prostitution, things like that. Helping me out with this liaison group for a few months. What's your thesis title again, Susan?'

'Deviant Sexuality as New Commodity – Exploitation, Capitalism, Fetishisation and the Rise of the Disembodied Self.'

'Kinky,' said McCoy. 'I'll have to read that when you've finished. Funny subject for a woman, mind you.'

Susan held her hands out. 'What can I tell you? Needlework class was full up.'

146

'You walked into that one,' said Cowie.

'The case you're working on . . . Lorna Skirving?' Susan asked. 'Alasdair explained that her body bore traces of S&M activity – activity she may have been paid to perform?'

McCoy nodded again. Wasn't sure what S&M stood for exactly, but he wasn't going to tell her that. 'Might have been, but was all amateur stuff, according to her flatmate. Blowjobs for out-of-town businessmen, that sort of thing. You said all that whipping stuff went through Madame Polo's up in Park Circus.'

'Susan's got another theory, think you should hear it,' said Cowie.

'It used to,' she said. 'One of the subjects I've been interviewing for my dissertation is a lawyer who lives in Edinburgh, comes through here every couple of weeks on business. While he's here he likes to "indulge" himself, as he calls it.' She took a slightly battered roll-up out a metal tobacco tin and lit up. 'Have you heard of a woman called or calling herself Baby Strange?'

'Baby Strange? You having me on?'

'It's not her birth name obviously, that's the name she goes by. I've heard her mentioned a few times in my interviews but nobody seems to know much about her. Very hard to track down, I've been trying for a month or so.'

'Who is she, then?'

'Difficult to say, seems to be formulating a new mode of practice . . .'

147

'Eh?' said McCoy.

'Go slowly,' said Cowie. 'He's not as bright as he likes to think. That right, Einstein?'

'Shut it, Cowie. Mode of . . .'

'Basically she seems to be reordering the notion of pimp or madam. No fixed premises, no fixed stable of girls working for her. She operates in the margins, outside of the usual commercial structures surrounding prostitution. She's more of a fixer or a connector. Specialises in the more extreme stuff – younger people, drugs, made-to-order pornography, that sort of thing. Seems the sexual revolution, for all the good it's done, had a downside too. It's left people jaded, looking for something different, and that is what she is able to supply.'

'A sort of new Madame Polo?' asked Cowie.

She shook her head, tucked some strands of hair behind her ear. 'No, completely different, to be honest. I've interviewed Madame Polo. She looks like Margaret Calvert, talks like a schoolteacher. She's there for the rich businessmen and judges wanting their arses caned by nanny and a small sherry in the drawing room afterwards. That's why she's in Park Circus, makes them feel at home. Baby Strange is different.'

'How different?'

'I'm only working on gossip and what I can pick up here and there. Seems she can arrange just about anything. Girls, boys, orgies, voyeurism. You name it.'

'You think Lorna Skirving was working for her?'

She shrugged. 'No idea. But it might explain her injuries.'

'You got an address?'

'Sorry, no. I wish I had. I'd love to interview her. If she's doing what I hear she's doing, then it's an economic reinvention of the conventional model, very valuable for my thesis.'

'But . . .' said Cowie.

She smiled, took his cue. 'But I'm meeting another interview subject tomorrow . . . if she turns up, that is. Be the third time of trying. She may well know her, or at least know someone who does.'

Cowie clapped his hands, rubbed them together, interview clearly over. 'Sorry, McCoy, need to get on, you can thank Susan for helping solve your case later, we've got a lot to get through this afternoon.' He stood up, held the door open. 'Jackie and I are taking Susan for a curry tomorrow; she has still to experience the wonder that is the Shish Mahal. Fancy joining us? Got to promise not to talk shop though or Jackie will empty a dish of pakora sauce over me. No kidding.'

'What time?'

'Eight o'clock?'

McCoy stood up, smiled at Susan. 'Thanks for that. I'll see you tomorrow then?'

'Looking forward to it,' she said, pushing her hair back again. She smiled. 'Maybe you can bring the nice guy underneath this time.'

149

CHAPTER 16

Wattie was struggling to keep up, half walking, half running, following McCoy up Buchanan Street. It had just been turned into a pedestrian precinct, as the signs everywhere were proud to tell you. What that meant was they'd paved over a decent, busy street, sat some benches on it and scattered round a few tubs of dying shrubs.

'You know what?' he said. 'He'll kill you. He'll find out and he'll kill you.'

McCoy kept walking, trying to get there before he was completely frozen by the snow that had started up again. Wattie caught up with him, grabbed his arm, pulled him round.

'Murray tells you to stick with the girl, to leave everything else alone, and first thing you're going to do is march into the Vale and ask Davey Waters if he sold Tommy Malone a gun. He'll go nuts.'

The two of them stood there in the gently falling snow, staring at each other. McCoy pushed his wet hair back from his eyes. 'He's not going to find out because I'm not going to tell him and neither are you. So either you stop moaning or you can fuck off. Up to you.'

The Vale was opposite Queen Street Station, that's why Davey Waters liked it. Not too many nosey regulars. Most of the clientele were either about to catch a train or had just come off one. Crowd changed all the time. The big illuminated sign above the double glass doors of the pub promised a lot more than it delivered. Inside was long room with toilets at the back, couple of one-armed bandits blinking mournfully and a TV above the bar with an out of order sign taped onto the screen. McCoy took his coat off, shook the snow off it and looked round. The usual. Couple of old jakeys nursing half pints, group of pinstriped businessmen waiting for the train back to Edinburgh, and Davey Waters sitting on the padded bench at the back.

'That him?' asked Wattie.

McCoy nodded. 'Get us a pint, eh?' He wandered over to Waters, pulled out a wee stool with a ripped vinyl cushion and sat down. 'Evening, Davey.'

Davey grunted a hello, sipped his pint and kept his eyes firmly fixed on the broken TV. He was fifty odd, in a non-descript suit. Heavily oiled quiff was all that was left from his days as a Teddy boy. McCoy got out his wee red jotter and opened it up at the picture of Tommy Malone he'd cut out the paper, held it up in Davey's line of vision.

'Sorry to interrupt your viewing pleasure, Davey, but I need you to take a look at this.'

Davey grunted again, took the jotter and peered at the picture. 'Nope,' he said, handing it back.

'Nope, I'm not telling you or nope, I've never seen him before?'

Wattie appeared with two pints and sat down.

'Who's this?' said Waters, looking him up and down.

'This is Wattie. May look like he's just left school but he's a right hard cunt, Davey, station's new heavy. No qualms, this one, bust you as soon as he'd look at you. Wattie, this is Davey Waters. If you need a hot job in our fair city, he's your man.' The door banged open and three red-faced men in tweeds came in; Inverness train must have arrived. 'Been selling many jobs lately, Davey? Sell any to the lad in the picture?'

He shook his head.

'Well, that's great, Davey. You've put my mind at rest because if you had you would be in a whole world of shite. This lad shot a girl a couple of hundred yards up the road, sure you heard about it, and Big Boss Murray isn't happy about it, not happy at all. Wants it wrapped up quick. So he's got everyone out trying to find who sold him the gun and when he finds out . . .' McCoy shook his head. 'Not going to be pretty. First of all he's going to get Wattie here to knock seven shades of shite out of him and then he's going to make sure he goes to Barlinnie for a very long time. Getting the picture, Davey? It all becoming clear? Selling him that gun was a big mistake, a very big mistake.'

Davey was starting to look worried. 'I didnae sell that boy any gun. That's the truth. End of story.'

McCoy sat back, took a swig of his pint, didn't think he was lying. Unfortunately. Another fucking dead end.

Davey stood up. 'That it?'

McCoy couldn't think of any reason why not. 'Tell you what, Davey. I'll tell Murray I don't think you got him the gun and you tell me where else he could have got it from.'

Davey shook his head. Professional pride showing. 'Nowhere in Glasgow. I can tell you that for nothing.' He nodded over at the pinstriped suits. 'There's your problem. No seen those adverts with Jimmy Savile? "This is the age of the train". Plenty guns in Edinburgh, Newcastle, Manchester. Take your pick. All yours for the price of a cheap day return. Now if you'll excuse me, I've got a business to run.' He walked out, letting the door swing behind him.

McCoy watched him go. 'That's us told then.'

'Right hard cunt?' said Wattie.

'What?'

'Don't know whether I'm flattered or insulted.'

'Aye well, just think yourself lucky you didn't have to prove it. Waters would have knocked your teeth out in seconds flat.'

'What now?' asked Wattie.

'You go back to the shop. Need to find some connection with Tommy Malone and Lorna

153

Skirving. Check his records with the social. Maybe she was in care at some point and they met up. See if he was in any mixed homes. Think there's one in Dundee, couple in Edinburgh and a big one just outside Dyce. See if the two of them ever overlapped. They have to have known each other somehow. Then after that—'

'You're kidding, aren't you?'

'Nope. Go and have a look at Lorna Skirving's flat. Have a poke about, see if you can find anything.'

'Thomson's already done it, there's nothing there.'

'Thomson's a good guy to have a drink with, but he's not the sharpest knife in the drawer.'

'And I am?' grinned Wattie. 'Is that what you're saying?'

'Aye right.'

'Where you off to?'

'Going to go and have a chat with Madame Polo. Not sure Cowie was right. If this girl did do kinky stuff, there's a chance they ran into each other.'

'So you're going to some high-class brothel while I give a single-end in Royston the once-over?'

'Them's the perks. Now get going.'

Park Circus was part of a series of grand Edwardian terraces built on a hill overlooking Kelvingrove Park. They were unusual for Glasgow, looked more like something that should be in Edinburgh. It was a posh area, townhouses for rich people, some lawyers' and bankers' offices and a couple of hotels.

The door had a buzzer and an intercom, no name. McCoy pressed it and said he was here to see Jean Baird. Waited a minute or two and then it clicked open. A girl was standing there dressed in a maid's outfit. She opened the door wide and he stepped in.

He wasn't sure what he expected. Red flock wallpaper? Chandeliers? It wasn't anything like that. Dark wood panelling, the tick of a grandfather clock, fresh flowers on a marble stand and some paintings of hills and glens dotted up the stairwell.

The maid beckoned to follow her. There was a door sunk in the panelling; you'd miss it if you didn't know it was there. She knocked twice, there was a muffled 'Come in' and she pushed the door open and stood aside.

It was a small office, mostly taken up by a large Victorian desk. There was a woman sitting behind it. She was old but well preserved, hair swept up, face perfectly made up. She gestured to the chair in front of the desk.

'Well, Mr . . .?'

'McCoy,' he said.

'Well, Mr McCoy, you certainly managed to get my attention. Not many people call me by that name, not any more. What can I do for you?'

McCoy reached into his pocket and held out his police card. She glanced at it, nodded, and he put it back into his pocket.

She smiled confidentially. 'I assume you are aware of certain, how shall we say . . . arrangements I have with some of your colleagues in the higher echelons of the force.'

McCoy nodded. 'I'm not here about kickbacks, Mrs Baird.'

She held up her hand. 'Helene, please. I haven't answered to that other name for many years.'

He took out the little picture of Lorna Skirving and pushed it across the polished desk. She picked it up, looked at it and pushed it back.

'I need to know if she worked here.'

She looked at McCoy as if he was mad. 'Mr McCoy, I assume you are aware of the kind of establishment I run. For me and my clients, discretion is paramount.'

The door opened, the maid again.

'I thought I told you to always knock,' Helene snapped at her.

The maid looked terrified. 'It's Mr Cameron, he's . . .'

She held up her hand. 'Enough,' she hissed. She stood up, edging round the desk. 'If that's all, Mr McCoy? Something needs my immediate attention.'

He smiled and stayed put. 'It's okay, I'll wait,' he said. 'There were a few more things I wanted to ask you, if that's all right?'

She wavered, torn between leaving McCoy in the office and dealing with Mr Cameron, whoever he was. There was a thump like furniture going over and a muffled scream, seemed to be coming from directly above. It made her mind up for her. She hurried out, telling him she'd be back in a couple of minutes.

A couple of minutes was more than enough time. McCoy walked round the desk and started going through the drawers. Nothing much in the top one, mostly bills and office stuff. Nothing much in any of the other ones either. A half bottle of vodka tucked at the back of the bottom drawer. That was about it. There was a large cardboard box tucked into the leg space of the desk. It was all taped up, printer's bill stuck to the top, addressed to 12 Park Circus. Nothing ventured, nothing gained. McCoy got the letter opener from the top of the desk, sliced through the tape and pulled up the cardboard flaps. It was full of magazines. Full of copies of one magazine, to be exact. *Jezebel.*

McCoy took one out and started flicking through it. What you'd imagine really, reasonably high-quality dirty pictures, mostly of naked girls tied up and blokes standing over them with whips and, in one instance, a cricket bat. He should pocket one for Dirty Ally. Was just about to put it back in the box when he saw her. In the picture she was tied to a chair, nothing on but a pair of high-heeled boots, bloke with a whip, a mask and a big cock standing over her. Seemed the rummage was worth it after all. He put the magazine in his pocket, closed the box up again, slipped it back under the desk, sat back in the seat and waited.

A couple of minutes later Helene reappeared, looking slightly less put together than she had before. She sat back down, tucked some errant strands of hair back into her bun and opened the bottom drawer.

'Drink?' She was holding up the vodka. McCoy nodded. She filled two glasses and handed one over.

'Trouble?' he asked.

She shook her head. 'Nothing we can't handle.' She took a sip of the vodka.

'What else was it you wanted to ask me, Mr McCoy?'

He took the magazine from his pocket, opened it at the page with the girl and put it down on the desk in front of her.

'Someone shot her the other day in the bus station. We know who it was, but we have no idea why.'

Helene looked at him, not a flicker. 'What exactly has this got to do with me, Mr McCoy?'

'Did she work here?'

Nothing.

He sighed. Things were never easy.

'You're not a stupid woman, Helene. What you've got here takes building up, years of work. Do you really want me to tear it all down?'

Not a flicker. 'As I said, Mr McCoy, there are arrangements in place with certain ranking

158

members of your force. Ranks undoubtedly far higher than the one you hold. You had best think about what you are saying.'

He tapped the photo of Lorna. 'Did she work here?'

She sipped her vodka and stared at him.

'I'm giving you a smart way to do this, Helene. Tell me what I need to know and I'll be out of here in ten minutes, you'll never see me again; your establishment won't get mentioned anywhere, I swear.' He put the photo of Lorna back in his wallet. Still nothing. One last go.

'My boss is called Chief Inspector Murray,' he said. 'I doubt you've heard of him, doesn't mingle with the great and good at Central and the High Court. All he is interested in is finding who killed the girl. He does not give a fuck who or what he brings down to do it. If it means raiding this place in broad daylight with the papers outside, he will do it. Believe me, he will do it. This is a murder case. Help me.'

That was it, the grand pitch. It was up to her now. McCoy wasn't lying, Murray would take the place apart, but it would take time and warrants, time he didn't have. He stared at her, she stared back. He could hear the clock in the hall ticking and the rhythmic squeaking of a bed somewhere upstairs.

'Lorna Skirving,' she said eventually, 'worked here for a month or so around November. She was never, how shall I say, up to the standard of our usual girls, but she had an interest in more specialised areas, areas we have a demand for. Became more trouble than she was worth, one of the clients thought he'd money missing from his wallet. I had to let her go.'

McCoy nodded. All understood.

'Private visits with the clientele are banned. Lorna never managed to stick to that rule. She became friendly with one of them. He was a younger man, an exception. Most of our clients tend towards the middle-aged or the elderly. Very proud of him, you know, talked about him to the other girls. Spoke about him a little too freely, in fact.'

'What do you mean?' I asked.

'Told them she had started doing visits off premises, strictly not allowed. Not safe for the girls or the clients, but it happens. The girls get greedy, do jobs where they don't have to pay the house. Told one of the other girls this boyfriend had paid for her for a whole weekend.'

'Where was this?' he asked.

'Funnily enough it was just a couple of doors down. A townhouse in Park Circus. The townhouse is usually empty. The man rarely uses it apparently, has other homes.'

'Do you know what number?'

She shook her head. 'No, but it was next to the Bon Accord Hotel, overlooking the park.'

'And this boyfriend was?' McCoy asked.

Helene shook her head. 'I don't actually know,

but even if I did I wouldn't tell you. That's how it works here, Mr McCoy. Anonymity as soon as you walk through the door.'

'What did she tell the others about him?' he asked.

'Just said he was a cut above the kind of man she'd met before. Lorna wasn't a bad girl. Not too bright, but she didn't deserve a fate like that.'

He stood up to go and she walked him through the hall to the front door. 'Just find out what happened to her, Mr McCoy.' She looked older in the light from the hall, tired. 'People look down on the girls here, think they're worthless. But they are just girls, no better and no worse than anyone else.'

He told her he would do everything he could and stepped out into the quiet of Park Circus, waited. Rang the bell again. The maid answered the door and McCoy put his finger to his lips. *Shush*. Held out his cigarettes. She looked behind her, up and down the street, then stepped out onto the stair and he lit it for her.

'You know Lorna Skirving?' he asked.

She nodded.

'You know who the boyfriend was?'

Nodded again. McCoy got the message, took a couple of quid out his wallet. She tucked it under her wee black skirt.

'Don't know his name. She never told anyone, said he wanted to be discreet.'

'Christ, well what do you know? I'm a few quid in remember.'

161

'He liked, you know, the stuff she did professionally.'

'Pain?'

She nodded. 'All that stuff. Wasn't short of a bob or two. Lived out in the country somewhere. Aberfoyle? Somewhere like that.'

'Drymen? Broughton House?'

She shrugged. 'She didn't say.'

McCoy went to walk away.

'She said he was her ticket out. Whatever it took, she wasn't going to lose him.'

CHAPTER 17

McCoy didn't know why he was sitting back at his desk. He could never think in the shop, couldn't get any peace. Still, he supposed he'd better show Murray he was at his desk working, even if he was spending most of the afternoon staring into space. Wattie put a mug of tea on the desk. McCoy sipped it, grimaced.

Wattie shook his head. 'Never bloody happy, are you?'

He watched Wattie sit back down, take out his notebook and square himself up in front of his typewriter. For want of anything better to do, McCoy got his wee red jotter out. Opened it. Sighed. No inspiration there. He swallowed over some of the rotten tea. If Lorna Skirving's boyfriend was from Drymen or somewhere round Broughton House that would connect her to Tommy Malone. And who did he know in Drymen that was sleazy enough to be fucking a nineteen-year-old girl behind his girlfriend's back? Jimmy Gibbs. The more he thought about it, the better a fit he was. He had the run of Dunlop's properties; if they owned a townhouse in Park Circus, he would have access to it. He suddenly realised Murray was standing over him.

'Busy?' Murray asked.

'Was just having a think abou—'

'Aye, bollocks. Wattie! Get over here.' Wattie scrambled over. 'Where would he go?' asked Murray.

'Who?' asked McCoy.

'Malone was missing for four days, must have gone somewhere. Where?'

'He'd have gone home,' said McCoy. 'Except he hasn't got a bloody home.'

'Everyone's got a home, somewhere they go to,' said Wattie.

'That's very bloody lyrical, Wattie. Some song, is it? Fat lot of fucking good that's goin—' Murray stopped and looked at McCoy, who was starting to realise what was coming. 'You know people who don't live anywhere, don't you, McCoy?'

'Give us a break. It was one fucking case, sir, that's all.'

'Tramps, alkies, nutters – I thought you were the great saviour?'

'What?' said Wattie.

'You no hear? McCoy here solved the great murder case of 1970. One tramp murders another. Nobody cares but our golden boy here.'

'That's not fair, sir.'

'Seems some bastard living rough was running the jakies down by the Clyde. Taking their benefit books off them, taxing their fucking two bob begging money. One of them couldn't take it any more, stabbed him. Thanks to McCoy's heartfelt speech from the dock the murder charge got reduced to culpable homicide, only got eighteen months. Since then McCoy cannae walk down the street without some jakey shaking his hand, telling him he's a fucking hero.'

Wattie started to laugh. 'King of the Jakies, eh?'

'McCoy, away down and see your pals, see if he'd been there, or if they know anything at least.'

'Sir—'

'Just get down there – doesn't look like you're doing anything else. Ask around, you never know. And Christ knows we could do with a fucking break.'

CHAPTER 18

As far as McCoy could tell, the fall down through the cracks happened in stages. Living at home. Chucked out of home. Living in a flat with other jakies. Living in a hostel. Living in the Salvation Army shelter. Living in any shelter that would still take you. Living in an abandoned building. Living on the street, usually the hot air grates behind St Enoch Station.

After that, it got really hopeless. Down at that level no one's too fussy. Meths, water with gas from the pipes bubbled through it, hairspray filtered through milk, anything. Aftershave, boiled-up boot polish.

So they started at the Grates, as low as you could go while still expecting coherent answers. The people they talked to were friendly, most of them anyway. They looked at the picture, tried to think. Said they'd maybe seen him, weren't sure. Mostly just trying to help McCoy out. Wattie stood off at the side for most of it, trying not to wrinkle his nose up or look too disgusted. Wasn't really managing it. They were just about to leave, head for the soup kitchen at the Broomielaw, when they heard someone singing 'Danny Boy' and two figures bundled up in coats and old blankets emerged from the walkway under the station. The walkway was like a cloister, huge stone pillars holding up the arches. The woman had her head thrown back, singing for all she was worth. Her voice, what was left of it, echoing round the cloister. Her voice must have been great in its day, hoarse now, top notes missed, but the emotion was still there. Everyone stopped talking as they grew closer and listened. She finished, 'Oh Danny Boy, I love you so!', bowed with a flourish and fell over. The man helped her back up on her feet, stuck his half bottle of red biddy into her hand.

She bowed again, managed to stay upright this time. Her companion was peering at McCoy. He looked like a docker or a builder, woollen hat shoved down on his head, bright blue eyes in a ruddy, bearded face.

'Jesus Christ, it is you. Mr McCoy. How's the boy?'

'I'm good, Eamonn, good. How's you?'

'You know he passed away in the jail?'

McCoy nodded. 'I heard.'

Eamonn crossed himself. 'God rest his soul. You did a good thing there, son, a good thing, won't be forgotten.' He shifted his weight, deposited the woman on the grate beside a wee man with no teeth. 'Bit much of the biddy, eh? Who's this?' he asked, looking at Wattie.

'Wattie, new at the shop, helping me out.'

Eamonn held out an extremely dirty hand, one finger missing. Wattie shook it, nodded.

'Not from Glasgow, are you, son?'

'How'd you know?' he asked.

Eamonn shrugged. 'What you down here for, Mr McCoy?'

McCoy held out the photo. Pointed at Malone. 'Seen him anywhere? Think he might have been living rough.'

Eamonn shook his head. 'Looks like a lot of the young lads you see on the street. What's he done?'

'Nothing. He's dead, just trying to find out what he was up to before he died. You doing anything for the next hour or so?'

Eamonn grinned. 'No. Want me to hold your hand?'

McCoy drove, Eamonn in the front, Wattie in the back. It was snowing, coming down hard now. Heater was on full but Wattie rolled down his window, tried to do it without them noticing. Didn't escape Eamonn.

''Fraid I don't smell as fresh as where you're from, son. Used to work on the tattie fields down Ayrshire way. Me and every other poor Irish bugger. Beautiful place. That where you're from?'

'Greenock,' he said. 'Further up.' He hadn't really spoken since they'd got to the Grates. Was still looking shell-shocked.

'Lovely part of the world, working the fields, two weeks then a dance in the camp. Everyone drunk. Girl from Gweedore let me pull her—'

168

'Left?' asked McCoy, not sure where he was, somewhere round the back of Dalmarnock power station at a guess.

Eamonn looked out the misty windscreen. 'Aye, stop at the next building.'

They pulled up outside the gates of a half-demolished factory. Side of it had collapsed, avalanche of brick and masonry pouring into a muddy puddle the size of a swimming pool. A bent iron sign stuck out the water, surrounded by a thin layer of ice: THOMSONS 'BEST IN THE WEST OF SCO . . .'

'What is this place?' asked Wattie.

'Fuck knows. Eamonn?' said McCoy.

Eamonn took the bottle of biddy out his pocket and had a swig, handed it to McCoy, who did the same. He tapped on the windscreen with his knuckle. 'This? This, son, is where you don't want to end up.'

They were walking round the back of the factory, picking their way through the frozen puddles, when Wattie pulled McCoy aside. 'You sure about this? I don't have a fucking clue what's going on.' He sounded scared, was shifting his weight from foot to foot, looking off into the distance. 'What is this place anyway?'

McCoy looked over at the abandoned factory. 'This? This, Wattie, is the end of the road. Where the Legion of the Damned are. Polis never come here. Fuck, even the Salvation Army doesn't come in here. Too dangerous. That's why we need

Eamonn. If Malone really had nowhere to go, he might have ended up here.'

Wattie looked away, rubbed at his mouth with the back of his hand.

'Tell you what,' said McCoy. 'You stay out here. If we're not out in an hour, call for two pandas, eh?' Was only his third day on the job, after all, and it had been a hellish few days.

Wattie nodded gratefully. 'That okay?'

It wasn't really, but he'd rather have Wattie out here than in there making it dangerous for all of them. 'Off you go.'

Eamonn was waiting for him outside a boarded-up window on the ground floor. Handed him the last of the bottle of red biddy. 'You fit?'

McCoy swigged it down. 'As I'll ever be.' He moved forward and Eamonn stuck his hand out, stopped him. 'We're just asking about your man in the picture, aye? Nothing else for you to worry about. Deal?'

McCoy nodded. 'Deal.'

Eamonn pulled a couple of the loose boards back and they scrambled in. Was dark inside so they stood there for a minute, let their eyes get used to it. Eamonn pointed to a dim light coming from the back of the building, staircase just visible. They walked towards it, going slow, watching where they stood. Floor was covered in bits of old machinery, broken bottles, fair few dead pigeons. A man was sitting at the bottom of the stairs, middle-aged, thick specs, raincoat, notepad in his hand. He was

170

writing in it, tiny letters covering each page. He didn't look up as they went past, just kept writing, muttering under his breath.

McCoy could hear noises as they climbed the stairs. A radio turned down low, someone crying. They got to the first floor and McCoy looked round amazed. The internal walls of the factory had been knocked down, making a room the size of a couple of tennis courts. There were wee fires burning, groups of people round them, couple of dogs wandering about. He heard laughing behind him, turned as a woman emerged from the darkness. She was nude, fat body pale in the flickering light. She was wiping a towel between her legs with one hand, swigging cider from a bottle with the other. She approached the line of elderly men ranged along the back wall, nodded at one and he got up and followed her back into the darkness.

McCoy was about to say something, but Eamonn shook his head. The bargain had been made. Nothing to do with them. He pointed over to a small fire in the corner, people sitting round it, passing a bottle.

'You sit over there. I'll no be long. You got the photo?'

McCoy gave it to him, and Eamonn headed off towards the furthest corner. McCoy walked over to the fire and nodded a hello. The people sitting there didn't seem to pay him much mind; they'd seen him with Eamonn, that was enough. He took a seat on a big burst couch next to a heavily pregnant

171

girl holding hands with a boy whose face was almost all an angry red birthmark. McCoy held out his cigarettes, everyone took one, some mumbled thanks. Always the easiest way to make friends. An old woman with a shaved head and a row of stitches crossing it handed him the bottle, fingers with long tobacco-stained nails wrapped round it. He took it and swigged back before he could think about it too much. Hit him like a rock, he spluttered, was like battery acid. The woman smiled at him, no teeth.

'Good stuff, eh?'

He nodded, tried to hand it back but she pointed to the pregnant girl. He handed it to her and she swallowed a big glug back without flinching, handed it to the boy with the birthmark.

McCoy sank back in the couch, tried to take in what was going on. A teenage boy, face made up like the bands on Top of the Pops, glittery shirt, baggy trousers and yellow platforms appeared at the top of the stairs. He was giggling, leading a well-dressed middle-aged man by the hand. Suit, overcoat, good black shoes shined by his wife no doubt. The boy moved over to the window, man still being dragged behind him, and stood in front of a tiny wee woman with a row of cans and bottles arranged on a plank in front of her. He turned, kissed the man on the mouth and pointed at a bottle of vodka. The man took out his wallet, handed over a fiver without flinching and they moved away into the darkness. Boy singing now, about a long-haired lover from Liverpool, not a care in the world.

McCoy watched him go, remembered what him and Eamonn had agreed. He was here for Malone. End of. He had had another couple of slugs of whatever was in the bottle as it went round again, handed out his cigarettes again in return. He looked at his watch. Half an hour Eamonn had been away. An elderly man dressed in what looked like homemade priest robes appeared out the darkness reciting the books of the Old Testament over and over. McCoy found himself joining in, residual memory kicking in. 'Genesis, Exodus, Leviticus, Numbers . . .' he was repeating under his breath when he realised Eamonn was standing there shaking his head.

'Didn't take long for you to go native, eh? Come on. Found someone that saw him.'

McCoy followed him up the rubbish-strewn steps to the next floor. Soon realised it made the one below look cosy. No fires up here, few candles, that was it. He could hear groaning, someone crying. There was a smell of piss everywhere. Eamonn walked towards the back, McCoy keeping up, didn't want to get separated. A girl was sitting cross-legged on a filthy mattress in the corner, boy passed out beside her. Candle illuminated a pretty face, mid-teens, illuminated the scars and cuts up her skinny arms too. She had a wee puppy in her cardigan, head poking out between the buttons.

'This is Beezy,' said Eamonn. 'Recognised your man.'

'That right?' said McCoy, sitting down on his hunkers. 'Where'd you see him?'

She looked at him, didn't say anything, companion grunted and rolled over. He reached in his pocket, found a couple of quid.

'You know the Hamilton?' she asked, putting the money under the mattress. 'Up by Parkhead?'

McCoy nodded. Old fever hospital that had been shut for years, half derelict now.

'In there. There's people living there, security clear them out every couple of weeks but they cannae find everyone, place is massive. Me and Ivan were staying there one night and this guy – Tommy?'

'Aye, Tommy.'

'He was dossing there. Hadnae any money, nothing, so we gave him half a loaf we had. Asked us if we wanted some acid.'

'What did you say?'

She gestured behind her. 'Ivan took some, I didnae fancy it. That guy Tommy said he'd been on it for days. Didnae surprise me – his brain was pure scrambled.'

'How?' asked McCoy.

'Kept talking about his "mission" and how he had been chosen to do it. Wasn't making any sense. Said some guy called Alistair was guiding him, that he was communicating with him on a different plane. Usual acid shite.'

'Did he say what this mission was?'

Ivan sat up, leant over. 'Said he had to free someone and then he could free himself. That the time was coming for him to leave.'

'Leave?' asked McCoy. 'Leave where? The Hamilton?'

Ivan shook his head. 'Here. The Earth.'

They must have been waiting outside his flat. Biding their time, choosing their spot well. They'd had a lucky break too. The streetlights had failed on Gardner Street, road was pitch black. McCoy'd dropped Eamonn off back at the Grates, then Wattie off with his landlady. Was closing the car door, yawning, looking forward to his bed, and before he knew what was happening someone had bent his arm up his back and was pushing him up the street and into the wee alleyway that ran between the tenements. He tried to turn to see who it was, but the guy was good: every time he turned, he pushed his arm up higher, increased the pain. He could hear more than one person behind him, had to be two or three of them. They ran him into a wall, hard; he knocked his head, felt the blood burst from his nose and went down. And then the kicking started. He tried to get his hands up but a good few went into his head before he managed it. The kicks kept coming. He felt a tooth break, a boot slam into his kidneys, sound of grunts and heavy breathing. He pulled himself into the wall, tried to make himself as small as possible, but one of them grabbed his foot and pulled him out into the lane so they could get into him easier. He looked up, thought he saw someone he recognized, and then a boot hit him square in the side of the head and that was that. His hearing went, everything sounded like it was happening far away, could still hear the grunting as they kicked in at him but it was getting fainter and fainter. He could feel the blood pooling in his mouth and the steady thump of the kicks. Then nothing.

CHAPTER 19

8th July 1951

He started to cry when he saw her coming out the kitchen door. She'd the plate held out in front of her, white linen tea towel covering it. He looked round at Stevie, but he had his head down, he couldn't do anything about this, nobody could. She took the tea towel off. The smell hit him and his stomach rolled, couldn't breathe properly. Her voice was soft, reasonable.

'Now, are you going to eat this, young McCoy?'

He was sobbing now, shaking his head, tears and snot running down his face.

'There are children in Africa that are starving and you won't eat the good meal God has provided.' She set the plate down in front of him, pushed the spoon into his unwilling hand. 'Your behaviour is an insult to me, to those starving children and to the Good Lord himself. This plate will keep reappearing until you have finished what is on it. Now eat.'

He looked down at it through a blur of tears.

Cold lamb stew, lumps of fat and gristle in watery gravy, all of it mixed in with the vomit he'd thrown up into it yesterday when she tried to force a spoonful down his throat. He wanted his mum, his dad, wanted anyone, anyone that could make it stop. The dining room windows were open, summer sunlight coming through the trees, dappling the walls. Everyone was silent, almost two hundred boys with their heads down, thinking themselves lucky it wasn't happening to them, at least not today. He picked up the spoon, hand shaking, and pushed it into the horrible mess on the plate, Sister Agnes looking down at him, an encouraging smile on her lovely young face. He got the spoon halfway up to his mouth, then dropped it, dry retching spasming his body. She hit him on the back of the head. Hard.

'Stop that crying. You're putting it on, there's nothing wrong with you. Just get on and eat it. Sooner the better, we'll both be here as long as it takes.'

'Fuck off, you fucking cow, just leave him alone.'

A collective gasp, forks stopping halfway to mouths. Stevie Cooper was standing up, an eleven-year-old knot of anger and hurt, fists balled at his sides. He leant over and pushed the plate of stew off the table. It smashed on the stone floor, stew and sick splattering Sister Agnes's legs.

'You're a fucking cow, a fucking cow!'

Stevie was screaming at her now, calling her

everything, trying to get across the table to her. Father Kelly already running towards them from the back of the hall. Stevie started running, made a break for the open doors, thought he'd made it until one of the Christian Brothers stepped out from behind a table and tripped him. He went flying, crashed into a row of chairs and the brother was on him in a second, pinning him down.

McCoy tried to run towards him, but Sister Agnes was too fast, grabbed him, nails digging into his left arm. He was struggling, but her grip was too tight, he couldn't get away. Father Kelly was striding towards Stevie now, pulling his thick leather belt through the loops of his trousers. He raised it above his head and swung it down as hard as he could across Stevie's face. He shrieked in pain, noise echoing round the big hall. All around McCoy, children sat bent over their meals, refusing to look, some of them crying, shoving the food into their mouths as fast as they could as Father Kelly dragged Stevie along the floor and out through the double doors.

He must have escaped somehow. Everyone knew where Father Kelly had taken him, down to the lock box in the cellars. He'd get three days at least. Nobody got out the lock box, had a padlock on it, key on Father Kelly's belt. He'd done it, though. He woke up and Stevie was standing at the end of the bed. He started to cry as soon as he saw him. He was covered in blood; it was everywhere, in his hair, all down his body, staining his white underpants red. One of his eyes was red too, white filled with blood.

'Shove up,' Stevie said. He crawled onto the bed and got under the sheets. 'Don't know what you're crying for,' he said. 'I'm the one that got the doing.'

They lay there all night, neither one of them sleeping much. Stevie in too much pain and McCoy too scared. The blood was gradually soaking the sheets. He was getting covered in it. He tried to roll to the other side of the bed, but it kept coming, he couldn't get away. He could feel it on his arm, a cold stickiness, could smell it too. Knew if he turned round he would see Stevie covered in it, in his hair, his face, everywhere.

Worse than that, he was ashamed. Ashamed that he wanted Stevie to still be in the lock box, to not have covered him in his blood, to not be here in the morning when Father Kelly discovered he'd gone and that McCoy might have something to do with it.

He must have fallen asleep somehow. He woke up, it was light, morning, and Father Kelly was at the side of the bed. The priest held Stevie in an iron grip, Stevie looking terrified.

'You too, lad,' Father Kelly said. 'Thick as bloody thieves.' He grabbed his upper arm, long nails pressing into his flesh. 'Come on now.' Nails pressing into his arm, pressing and pressing . . .

★   ★   ★

180

McCoy opened his eyes. Bright light. Nurse standing over him holding a syringe, wiping at his arm with a swab.

'That's it over now, go back to sleep, Mr McCoy, back to sleep.'

5TH JANUARY 1973

CHAPTER 20

He could smell stale pipe smoke. Ralgex. Had to be Murray. McCoy opened his eyes and sure enough he was there, sitting on an orange plastic chair by the end of the bed, folded *Glasgow Herald* in his lap.

'Still alive then,' he said.

McCoy tried to sit up, arms and legs felt heavy, he felt heavy. Tried to speak but his throat was too dry. Murray pulled the yellow cellophane off a bottle of Lucozade by the bed and poured a glass, held it up to his lips. He drank it down, fizzy and incredibly sweet.

'Where are we?' he managed, looking around.

'The Western. You not remember coming in?'

He shook his head. Took in the white curtains round the bed, distant noise of chatting, clattering pans. 'I remember getting kicked to fuck, don't remember coming here.' His left hand felt funny, he held it up; two fingers bandaged together with a splint in between them.

'You wouldn't. Did you over well and good. You were out cold for a while. Your neighbour called it in, found you lying outside the close.' He sat back

185

on his chair. 'You've been moaning away in your sleep, talking nonsense. Telling someone to run, and blood, and something about some woman called Agnes. What's all that about then?'

He shook his head. 'No idea. Any more of that?'

He drank the whole bottle, started to feel more human. He lifted up his bedclothes. They'd put pyjamas on him. Stripy ones. He pulled the jacket up, saw all the bruises and cuts and pushed it back down again. He lifted the waistband of the trousers up and peered down, balls were twice the normal size, nice shade of browny blue. Must have got a good few kicks in there.

'A total of twelve stitches, two broken fingers and bruising similar to what you would find in a car crash victim, so the doctor says. He wants you to stay in for a few days.'

McCoy shook his head and Murray sighed. 'How'd I know you were going to do that?' He stood up, looked at his watch. Ten to eleven. 'Stay here the day, I'll come back for you at six. Deal?' McCoy nodded. 'You know who did it?'

'I thought I recognised one of them. Only saw him for a couple of seconds before he booted me in the head.'

'Now who'd want to beat you up, McCoy? The usual queue?'

He shook his head. It hurt. 'I've been a good boy lately.'

'That'll be right. They took your money and your watch. Maybe it was just a robbery after all.'

McCoy's face fell. 'My wallet?'

Murray held up an empty wallet. 'Uniform found it down the lane. Picture's still in it, don't worry.' He put it down on the bedside cabinet. He looked at McCoy, at the stitches and the broken fingers. Left him it.

They made him sign himself out. Young doctor looking at him like he was mad. Sent him home with six codeine tablets and a strict warning. If he got a sudden headache or became sensitive to light, he was to come straight back. If he started pissing blood again, he was to come straight back. If either of the two taped-up fingers started to go black, he was to come straight back. He stood nodding as they told him, not really listening, just waiting for them to finish. Murray was beside him, car keys in one hand, his plastic bag of clothes in the other, like some dad come to fetch his kid home. Took a good twenty minutes to get up the stairs to his flat even with Murray helping. By the time they got to his door the sweat was pouring off him, never felt so sore and tired in his life.

He must have looked bad. Murray even called him at home that night to make sure he was okay. Phone was only on the sideboard on the other side of the room, still took him twenty rings before he got there. Told Murray everything was fine even though it wasn't. Everything hurt and the edges of his vision were blurry, but there was no way he was spending another night in hospital.

He managed to get himself settled onto the couch, bucket beside him to piss or be sick in, half a bar of chocolate he'd found to eat, bottle of Lucozade Murray had left to drink. He pulled the bedspread over himself and took three of the tablets washed down with a good whack of Bell's, hoped he'd sleep soon, hoped the dream wouldn't come back.

Hadn't had one for a while, the dream about being back in the home. Sometimes it was about Sister Agnes and sometimes about the time Father Kelly broke Stevie's arm after he got them downstairs to the cellar. Always the blood though, that was always there. In the dreams he was covered in it, he tried to wipe it off and it wouldn't go, couldn't get it off himself. Still woke crying sometimes, not sure where he was or what was going on. Must be talking to that bloody priest, bringing memories back.

He felt the pills kick in, mind starting to drift. Wondered if this was what heroin was like. If it was, he couldn't blame Janey. The pain slowly dissolved. Still couldn't remember who the guy was he'd glimpsed as he'd been kicked. Almost had it, just out of reach. He lifted up the bedspread and looked down at his balls again, tried to tell himself they were getting back to normal. He took another slug of the whisky and stared at the TV. Some film with John Wayne. He'd no idea what was going on and he didn't care, happy to just look at the colours, listen to the voices, feel the cotton of the pillow under his cheek. The whisky tumbler slipped out his hand as he drifted off and rolled along the carpet. John Wayne shot someone, the clock on the mantelpiece ticked on. McCoy slept.

6TH JANUARY 1973

CHAPTER 21

He woke up with the TV running static, neck stiff from sleeping against the arm of the couch. Felt better, though. Still in pain but a lot better. Took him an hour to give himself a bath, trying to avoid getting the dressings and bandages wet. He dried himself off and stood in front of the wardrobe mirror. His whole body was blotched with black and yellow bruises; one around his kidneys was as big as a dinner plate. No wonder he'd been pissing blood. Balls looked better, though. He moved in and peered at his face. Not a pretty sight. Swollen nose and the last of the black eye he'd got from Chas.

He'd just managed to get his skivvies on, after ten minutes of moaning and groaning, when there was a knocking at the door. Murray come to check up on him no doubt. He wrapped a blanket around himself and slowly made his way down the hall, leaning on the wall for support. Knocking came again.

'I'm coming, I'm coming, give us a break,' he said, flicking the lock and opening the door. Angela was standing there.

She took her sunglasses off, looked him up and down. 'Christ. You going to ask me in?'

He held the door open and she walked past him, familiar smell of perfume and cigarettes. He followed her into the living room and sat down on the couch; just getting up and answering the door had half killed him. She was looking round, at the couch with the balled-up blankets, empty whisky bottle beside it, bucket, newspapers and an overflowing ashtray on the coffee table.

'If I'd known you were coming, I would have tidied up a bit,' he said.

She took off her black maxi coat, knelt down and looked at him. 'What the fuck happened to you, Harry?' She held his chin, moved the side of his face into the light. 'Look like you've been hit by a lorry.'

'It's no that bad.'

She touched the big bruise over his kidneys. He winced. 'You should be in the hospital.'

'I was. You here checking up on the boyfriend's dirty work?'

She stood back up, walked over to the window. 'It's the sixth,' she said. 'I just wondered why you weren't there.'

Suddenly her black coat and dress made sense. 'Shite. These bloody pills have knocked me sideways.'

'Flowers there again,' she said. 'Big bunch.'

'Your mum?'

She shook her head. 'God knows.'

194

'Definitely no mine, that's for sure. Might be Stevie.'

'Always had a big smile for his uncle Stevie, didn't he?' she said.

'Had a big smile for anyone, you know what he was like.'

'The two of us miserable gits managed to make the happiest baby in the world.'

She moved a pile of ironing he'd never quite got around to off a chair and sat down at the table. Started smoothing out the newspaper opened in front of her.

'That's three years,' she said.

'Doesn't seem like it.'

She opened her handbag, took out a hanky and dabbed at her eyes, trying not to ruin her make-up. Didn't work, too many tears. Black mascara started running down her cheeks.

'Come on, don't do this, Angela. It wasn't our fault. Not yours, not mine. It happens. You know it does.'

She shrugged.

'Cot death is cot death, you know that. The doctors told us. You're just twisting the knife in yourself. Wouldn't have made any difference what state we were in.'

She smiled at him. 'I don't believe you, Harry. Wish I could, but I can't. Maybe if we hadn't been so out of it we would have noticed something, heard him crying, I don't know . . .' Tears started again. She dug into her bag, took out a folding mirror and opened it, tutted, dabbed at her eyes. 'Christ, I look a right state.'

McCoy sat and watched her repairing her make-up like he'd done so many times before. She'd sat in 'her' seat, the one nearest the kitchen. Habits die hard. He remembered them sitting at that table when she told him she was pregnant. Didn't know who was more scared, him or her. She put everything back in her bag, snapped it shut and stood up. A wobble. Put her hand out and steadied herself.

'Hasn't stopped you, though,' he said.

She nodded at the empty bottle of Bell's by the couch. 'Nor you either. Bad as each other, always were. That was the trouble.' She smiled at him. 'Still, whatever gets you through the night, eh?'

It had become a habit. They dropped the wee man off at her mother's on a Friday night. Picked him up on Sunday afternoon. A weekend free to do what they wanted and what they wanted was always the same. Whatever he could get off the vice squad, whatever she could nick from her mother's medicine cabinet, whatever they could get they took. Didn't need anyone else, just the two of them in the flat all weekend working their way through a carry out and the drugs. Playing records, making love in a sleepy haze, just talking to each other, telling stupid stories. Wasn't most people's idea of a great weekend but it suited them, they were happy then.

She wandered over to the mantelpiece, looked

at the picture of the three of them on the beach at Arran. They'd got a man who was passing to take the picture. McCoy with his swimmers and a T-shirt on, Angela in a bathing suit, two of them sitting on a tartan rug, baby propped up between them. He was looking up at the camera with a big smile on his wee face. Happy Families. She picked it up and ran her finger over the baby's face.

'He looked like you.' She smiled. 'Poor wee bugger.'

McCoy went to go over to her but he couldn't get off the couch. Everything hurt too much. He eased back down onto the cushions, grimaced. 'Tell you what, you can cheer Gibbs up. Let him know I'm black and blue and pissing blood.'

She put the picture down. 'Jimmy? Why would he care?'

'I knew I recognised one of them, just didn't realise it was him.'

She shook her head. 'Whoever did that to you, it wasn't Jimmy. You don't matter that much, Harry. Always did have an inflated idea of yourself.'

'Cheers,' he said, then winced, broken rib was killing him. He reached for the pill bottle on the coffee table.

'What are they anyway?' she asked. He held out the bottle and she looked at them dismissively. 'Amateur hour.' She sat down and opened her handbag, rifled through it and emerged with a couple of yellow pills, looked like they'd fell a horse. 'Take one of these, don't take the other until at least twelve hours after. Okay?'

He nodded and swallowed one over with the last of the Lucozade. 'Jimmy still sorting you out, is he?' She didn't answer, just started putting her coat on. 'That why you left me, then? He got you better stuff?' He was trying to provoke her, but she was having none of it.

She bent over, kissed him. 'Take care of yourself, Harry.'

He held onto her arm, kissed her hand, tried to pull her face to his again, but she slipped out his grasp.

'Not going to work, Harry.'

'Come on, Angela, stay for a drink at least, eh?'

She shook her head. 'Not a good idea, you know that as well as me.' She finished buttoning her coat. 'I'll see you, Harry. You watch out for yourself, eh?'

'What's that supposed to mean?' he asked, but she was gone. Just the smell of perfume and cigarettes left.

He sat there for a while, thinking about Angela and the baby, and Jimmy Gibbs, and who would want to kick fuck out him. He stood up, felt the pill Angela had given him hit and just made it back onto the couch before he was out like a light.

He woke up with a desperate need to pee and the sound of the door hammering. He blinked, tried to rub the sleep out his eyes. Clock on the mantelpiece said five o'clock. Had been asleep for four hours or so. He opened the front door and Wattie was standing there, steaming brown paper parcel in his hands. He held it out. 'Thought you might be hungry.'

They sat at the kitchen table, McCoy wolfing the fish and chips down, suddenly ravenous, realising he hadn't eaten anything for forty-eight hours. Wattie blabbered on as they ate, filling him in about what had been going on at the shop. As expected, still no luck with the gun. The Super was going spare, had authorised as much overtime as Murray wanted. Papers were going mental, reporters trying to follow polis cars, hanging about outside the stations, offering money to anyone with half a story about Bloody January. Whole thing had got worse since the prison service had released the news about Howie Nairn. No luck with the touts yet, none of them knew anything about Tommy Malone or the girl. He'd spent half the day on the phone to the Aberdeen Police trying to find any sort of connection between Lorna Skirving and the Dunlops, anything that would take them forward.

'Any good?' asked McCoy.

'Weren't exactly helpful.'

'What, and you from a wee dump as well?'

Wattie sighed. 'Fucking Glaswegians. Aberdeen is nothing like Greenock, completely different part of the country.'

'All the same to me. They're no Glasgow, the two of them, that's all that matters.'

'Thank fuck, far as I'm concerned.'

'How'd you get on with the records?' McCoy asked.

'Waste of time. Lorna Skirving was never in care or in any sort of reform home. Didn't meet Tommy Malone there.'

'Must've been at Broughton House then,' said McCoy.

'Eh?'

'Girl at Madame Polo's told me she had a boyfriend, lived in the country.'

Wattie looked at him. 'And that means he lives in Broughton House, does it? Countryside's a big place, you know. You don't think you're just so determined this has something to do with Dunlop that you're going to make everything fit that idea?'

'Not Dunlop. Gibbs. We got any other connections between the two, smart arse?'

Wattie shook his head. 'Nope. I went to her flat. Nothing there.'

'What was it like?' asked McCoy.

'Remember Christine Nair's? Like that except scabbier. Some clothes, make-up, magazines, wee radio. Miserable.'

'Waste of time, then.'

Wattie smiled. 'Not quite. Luckily for us the neighbour is a right busybody, must spend all her time glued to the spyhole. I chapped on her door and she invited me in. Gave me chapter and verse. Seems Lorna had quite a few gentlemen callers. Including one regular. She described him as' – he

200

looked at his notebook – 'not smart, sweary.' He only came at night, so she never got a proper look at him, close light's been out for years. Said he tried to kick the door in a few times . . .'

'Tommy Malone?'

'Sounds like it could be.'

'Does that get us anywhere?'

'Maybe we're trying too hard. Maybe Tommy was her boyfriend and she dumped him for this countryside guy. He gets wind of it and shoots her. That Beezy girl said he was out of it. Nutty. Maybe he was just going mental because he'd been dumped?'

McCoy pulled Wattie's half-eaten chips towards him, finished them off.

'Not just an ugly face, are you, Wattie-boy? All these grand theories and turns out it's probably just another bloody domestic,' he said, licking the salt and grease off the chip paper before bundling it up into a ball and lobbing it into the bin.

McCoy shook his head, made his painful way over to the sink and started washing the stink of vinegar off his hands.

'Think it was the Dunlops?' asked Wattie, nodding at his bruises.

'Doubt it. They've enough clout to fuck me over legit. You saw Murray going bananas, all it took was one phone call. Sure I recognised one of them, only saw him for a second but I just can't get it. Thought it might have been Jimmy Gibbs but apparently not. Want to do me a favour?'

201

'What?' asked Wattie.

McCoy held up his taped-up hand. 'Help me get my clothes on?'

Half a slow hour later they stepped out of McCoy's close and onto Gardner Street. They'd managed a pair of jeans, some plimsolls, a jumper, a coat and some scarf he'd got for Christmas from his auntie wrapped round his neck.

'Sure you're going to be okay?'

McCoy nodded. 'Fine. I'm going down to the Victoria for a few, then back to my bed. Just need to get out the house, place is driving me nuts.' Or at least that's what he told Wattie.

'I'd come with you, but I've got a football game tonight. Us against Finnieston . . .'

'Can't miss that. Away ye go.'

'You sure?'

'Aye, beat it. I'll get a cab back up the hill, don't think I'll make it otherwise. I'll see you in the morning.'

A middle-aged woman came out the neighbouring close, pulling a pair of woollen gloves on. 'Thanks for helping me put my clothes back on, Wattie,' said McCoy loudly. She turned and gave them a look, hurried up the hill.

'Half battered and still trying to be the funny prick. I'll pick you up at eight.'

CHAPTER 22

McCoy was still smiling to himself as he walked down Gardner Street. Was beginning to feel normal again, despite the bruises and pains. The bells were going at St Peter's in the next road, six o'clock mass. Sounded quieter than usual, snow muffling the sound. That explained the old couples trying to hurry up the hill. He was taking it easy, walking slowly, keeping to the inside of the pavement in case he needed to lean on the tenement walls for a bit. Didn't want to slip and bash himself off the pavement. He could feel wet coming in through his plimsolls, remembered now why he never wore them. Hole in the sole.

He was halfway down the hill when he noticed the two lads. Both of them were tall. One was skinny, flash looking, all the good gear on, while the other one was just plain massive. He was wearing old jeans and a shirt in the cold, didn't seem to bother him.

They were waiting a few closes down, pulling on fags, looking up the hill at him, pretending they weren't. His heart sank. Looked like they were back to finish what they'd started. He looked up and down the street. No one. Just him and the two of them, last of the stragglers already in St Peter's. Snow was heavy now, wouldn't even be anyone walking their dog or heading to the chippie.

He wasn't up for this, wasn't even supposed to be out of hospital, no way he could defend himself against this pair. They pushed off the tenement wall and wandered up towards him. He swore under his breath. Wasn't any real point in trying to get away, state he was in they'd catch him in two seconds. He stood there waiting for the inevitable, hoping he would pass out quickly.

They approached and stood side by side in front of him, blocking the pavement. The big one smiled at him like he was evil or mental or both. Kept opening and closing his meaty fists. C.O.D.Y. tattooed across the fingers of both in blue ink. The other one was checking up and down the street, making sure no one was around. McCoy thought of crying out, shouting for help, but there was no point, no one was going to hear him.

'McCoy,' the flash one said.

He nodded, didn't seem much point in denying it. The big one leant forward, peered at his black eye. 'That looks sore,' he said. 'What happened?' And then he giggled. Sounded more like a five-year-old than a sixteen-stone brick shithouse.

'Shut it, Jumbo,' said the flash one. 'Behave yourself.'

McCoy wasn't really listening, was just waiting

for Jumbo to throw the first punch, wondering if he could take another doing.

'We didnae mean it.' The flash one was looking at the ground, sheepish. 'Honest. Wouldnae have done it if we'd known it was Stevie Cooper's place. No way.'

And then it dawned. The Ben Duncan. Stevie Cooper's book. Dirty Ally. McCoy felt the tension leave him. Almost felt like crying with relief.

'Got any fags?' he asked.

The flash one nodded, took a packet of Kensitas out the pocket of his leather bomber jacket. He leant in close to light the cigarette and McCoy realised that he was only seventeen, eighteen, lighter shaking in his hands. C.O.D.Y. on his knuckles as well.

'What's your name anyway?' he asked.

'Billy. Billy Leeson,' he said, pushing his wet hair away from his face.

'Jumbo,' said the other one and pointed at his chest. 'Jumbo.'

'Shut it, Jumbo,' said Leeson automatically. Jumbo did as he was told. Shut up and kept smiling. Leeson reached into his pocket again and handed McCoy an envelope. Inside was a wee hardback notebook and what looked like a couple of hundred quid.

'Ten quid's missing,' he said. 'Tell Mr Cooper we're really sorry, we'll get it for him next week. We spent it before we knew; just havenae got it the now. We'll get it, though. Honest.'

Jumbo was listening closely, nodding. 'Honest,' he added.

McCoy put the packet in his coat pocket, shook his head. 'You know how lucky you two are? You found me before Cooper found you. If I was you, I'd get that tenner back to him soon as.' They nodded, stood there looking at him. 'Well, you better fuck off and get it from somewhere then, hadn't you?'

McCoy watched them hurry down the street, big one's sandshoes slapping off the pavement. His whole body was starting to hurt again, ribs and kidneys especially. He took out one of the codeine tablets from the hospital and swallowed it over dry. He needed a drink.

He thought he'd missed her. Knew Murray would go ballistic if he heard he was up and in the shop, so he waited a few closes up the street. Chances were Wattie was right, Lorna Skirving was just a domestic writ large. He'd speak to Murray in the morning, maybe scale things down, didn't seem much point in doing anything else. He was just about to head for home when she came out with Cowie. They talked for a minute then Cowie waved bye and got into his car. She looked up at the sky, put her umbrella up and walked up the street towards him. He stepped out the close and she saw him. Smiled. Then looked horrified.

'My God. Are you all right? I heard you'd been attacked.'

He nodded. The brave soldier. 'I'll live.'

'Christ, I feel terrible now. I spent half last night telling Alasdair and Jackie how rude you were for not turning up. Sure you're okay? You look horrible.'

'Thanks.'

'Shit! Sorry, I didn't mean it like that.'

'That's okay. I do look horrible. Fancy a drink?'

'Yes. Great. And no, you don't.'

He pointed up the road. 'There's a pub up there. The Grove? Supposed to be a bit grotty, though.'

'They took me to the Sarry Heid the first week I moved here. Nothing could be worse than that.'

The Grove was a bit grotty, a proper old man's bar. Susan was the only woman in there but she didn't seem to mind, seemed to quite enjoy the grumbles and dirty looks from the old codgers. They sat down at a table at the back and she took her combat jacket off, shook the snow out her hair. She'd some sort of Victorian-looking blouse on, all lacy and wee buttons up to her neck.

McCoy took a sip of his pint, suddenly didn't know how to start. 'So you're a feminist, then?' he asked and immediately realised that wasn't it.

'Guilty as charged,' she said, smiling.

'What is that exactly?'

She looked at him, dawned on her he wasn't actually joking. 'Simple. Means I believe in equal rights for men and women, equal pay, equal opportunities. We need to redress the balance after centuries of aggressive patriarchy.'

He let the last bit go, he'd got the jist. 'Fair

enough. Doesn't sound too bad. Can't really happen, though. Can it?'

She raised her eyebrows. 'And why's that?'

'Take the polis. In the real world a woman can't do the job properly, just can't. Not strong enough. Not much use breaking up a fight or chasing after someone.'

'Okay, so in your equation all a police officer really needs is brute force and strength, not guile or intelligence, anything like that. That's how the police are selected, is it?'

'Pretty much, aye.'

She laughed. 'At least you're honest. I interviewed a few cops for my dissertation, wasn't a great experience. God save us from the Glasgow Police Force.'

'What? Like me?'

'Maybe you're different. We'll see.'

He jiggled his empty glass at her. 'Another?'

She nodded and he went to the bar. Sneaked a look back at her while he was waiting for the pints. She had a wee mirror out, was flicking at her hair. Maybe he was in with a chance after all.

He put the drinks down, offered her a cigarette. She shook her head, took out her wee tin with the roll-ups.

'I can't make them,' he said. 'Too fiddly.'

She ran the shiny edge of the paper along her lip, started rolling. 'It's not that hard, just takes a bit of practice.'

'And hands that aren't like bunches of bananas. How long you been up here in Glasgow?' he asked.

She thought. 'Since beginning of October.'

'You like it?'

She looked at him, smiled. 'You're not one of these easily offended types, are you?'

'No.'

'Good. In that case, not much. Too dark, too cold, too rainy.'

He feigned a look of total horror. 'You're telling me you don't like Glasgow?'

'You'll get over it . . . Shit!' She slapped her forehead and pulled a folded bit of paper out the front pocket of her jeans. 'Got an address for you. Baby Strange. That woman I was telling you about.'

McCoy took it. 'Kelvin Court. Very swanky. Think Jack Buchanan even lived there.' He looked up. Her expression was blank. 'You don't know who he is, do you?'

'Nope.' She smiled. 'Thought maybe you could help me out a bit. I need to know who actually runs the prostitution business in Glasgow, who the real money goes to. Not the small-time pimps, the real deal. Can you help me get to them, get them to give me an interview?'

'Swapsies? That it?'

She shook her head, looked a bit uncomfortable. 'I wanted to have a drink with you, see you were okay . . .'

'But . . .'

'But I got you Baby Strange's address. That must be worth a favour.' She sat forward, looked serious. 'The more information I can gather, the more accurate my thesis will be. Male exploitation of female sexuality, capitalism at its most truthful and ugly form.'

'Christ, it's no that bad. Some of these lassies make a lot of money.'

'More than the pimps?'

'It's not like that . . .'

'No?'

'I deal with it every day. The pimps and the girls. It's not as split down the middle as you think.'

'Exploitation is exploitation. Seems pretty clear to me.'

'Then maybe you should do a wee bit more research,' he said. 'People's lives are complicated, they—'

'I'm well aware of the reality of these women's lives.'

'That right? Lot of exploitative capitalism up at the university, is there? Pimps and whores wandering round the lectures.'

Regretted it as soon as he said it.

She sat back in her chair. 'No, but what there are, are men like you. Men who can't see past their own inherent sexism. Do you know what it's like to live as a woman, to try and work in a patriarchal world? Know how it feels that the whole time I was trying to explain what a feminist was you were staring at my tits?'

He was going to say he wasn't and then he just couldn't be bothered. 'Well, well, here was me thinking we were having a nice conversation. Turns out all you really want is some names and numbers, and to let me know what a cunt I am.'

'Do you have any idea how offensive that word is?' she asked quietly.

'Come on, it's just a—'

'No, it's not. It's not just a word. That's what people like you always say. Every time you use it you insult me and you insult every other woman.'

'Come on . . .'

'See what I mean? What's next? "Where's your sense of humour?" "Don't take things so seriously?" I've heard it too many times.'

'Christ, I didn't realise I was starting World War Three!'

'It started a long time ago.'

He laughed. She didn't.

She reached for her combat jacket. 'I better go.'

'Look, I'm sorry.'

'Don't worry,' she said, wrapping her long woollen scarf round her neck. 'Believe me, I'll get over it.'

He sighed. 'I don't know what happened. I'm sore all over, stuffed full of painkillers and booze. I'm not usually as much of a cun— . . . of an arse. Honest.'

He tried his best nice-guy smile. Didn't work. She was looking at him like he was the shit under her shoe. Took some change out her pocket, put it down on the table.

'That's for my drinks.'

He watched as she left the pub, amazed he'd managed to fuck it up so quickly and so totally. He downed the last of his pint, then drank the rest of her vodka and Coke. He looked round. Row of old men with bunnets and bad false teeth propping up the bar, talking arse. The place really was a shitehole. His fingers hurt, his sides hurt, all of him hurt, and that was the end of any chance he had of seeing Susan Thomas again. Only one thing for it. He got the barman to call him a cab, ordered a double Bell's and used it to swallow over the last two codeine pills. They started kicking in just as the cab turned up ten minutes later.

CHAPTER 23

'For fuck sake.'

Stevie Cooper was nudging him. He must have fallen asleep.

'Get some of that down you, catch a fucking grip.'

McCoy shook himself awake, took the rolled-up note, stuck it into the wee bag and took a deep sniff. Felt the speed hit him immediately, not so tired all of a sudden. Took a swig of beer, tried to get rid of the metallic taste of it in his throat. He'd gone looking for Stevie after he'd left the Grove, and after a few pubs they'd ended up here. One of Billy Chan's nights, just about the only white faces in there.

Once a month Billy took somewhere over, ran a casino strictly off the books, all bets accepted. Punters came up from Manchester, Liverpool, anywhere there was a Chinatown. Tonight it was being held in a restaurant above Gordon Street. Sign on the door said it was temporarily closed for refurbishment. Only other time McCoy had been at one of Billy's nights it was in an old bakery in Townhead, flour dust coating everyone after a couple of hours. Tonight was busier, had to be fifty or sixty Chinese men seated round the tables, gambling as though their lives depended on it, which knowing Billy they probably did.

They'd been shown to a booth at the back. Six of them sat round a table crowded with drinks, cigars and piles of complimentary poker chips. Stevie, and by extension him, were here as guests of Ronnie Naismith. He'd been running clubs in town for years, since the days of showbands and exhibition dancers. Wasn't the only thing he ran, but he tended to keep his business south of the river so McCoy hadn't had much occasion to run into him.

Now him and Stevie were deep in conversation, empire building. Both of them gabbing at each other as the speed started to take hold. As far as McCoy knew, Naismith paid Stevie a monthly rate to keep his clubs open and free of trouble, and Stevie supplied the doormen and with them his pills and the speed. Worked out for both of them. A girl with a silvery low-cut top whose name he couldn't remember was sitting next to him, holding his hand. He'd some memory of her taking him into the back office, Naismith shouting after them, telling her to make sure he was happy. She'd tried to give him a blowjob, hadn't worked. The codeine, drink and pain were too much to overcome, couldn't rise to the occasion. He stepped away, buttoned up his fly.

She'd looked up at him, terrified, bra and top

on the floor beside her. 'You'll tell Ronnie it was okay? Please.'

He nodded. 'We had a great time.'

She was nothing if not persistent, though. She'd her hand in his trouser pocket now, playing with his cock through the cloth. Seemed to be working this time. He turned to kiss her and Cooper nudged him again.

'By the way, fuck's going on with that cunt Wattie from your shop?'

McCoy turned, girl's hand kept going in his pocket. 'Wattie? My Wattie?'

'Big cunt that looks about eighteen, Ayrshire accent. Been noising up Davey Waters. Came into the Vale telling him he can offer "protection".'

'He's been doing what?' said McCoy. Couldn't believe what he was hearing.

'You heard. Fancies himself, says he'll keep an eye out if Waters passes him a few tips. Fucking clown. He know who he's dealing with?'

McCoy shook his head. 'He's green as they come. Knows fuck all about fuck all.'

'Well, tell the stupid cunt to get a hold of himself. Waters is no daft. Couple of weeks and he would have him in deep. Find himself bought and sold for—' Cooper stopped, peered forward, waved the cigar smoke away from his face. 'Fuck's going on over there?'

McCoy looked up, seemed to be some scuffle going on by the door. He tried to focus, was so out of it was having trouble seeing that far. He could make out a bunch of young guys in dinner suits, five or six of them pushing and shoving, voices raised. Looked like they were trying to get in and it wasn't going to happen. Bouncers were having none of it, had one of them up against the big fish tank, holding him there by his neck.

Isabel, one of Ronnie's girls, was trying to calm everyone down, seemed to know one of the lads in dinner suits. She got the bouncer to let the lad go, was shushing him, pulling him away from the door. Telling the bouncer they were going.

The girl's hand in McCoy's pocket was still working away.

'Want to go back to the office?' she whispered in his ear.

He nodded, stood up, tried to hold his jacket in front of his hard on. Couple of Billy's proper heavies had turned up and were huckling the boys out the door. One was still shouting the odds, Isabel still trying to calm him down. Slicked-back hair, big jaw. He peered again, trying to make sure. Looked like Dunlop Junior. Teddy. The girl pulled at his arm and by the time McCoy looked back he'd gone, Isabel running down the stairs shouting after him. The girl with the silver top tugged at his arm again. The office beckoned.

7TH JANUARY 1973

CHAPTER 24

It wasn't so much that her flimsy dressing gown was open and she didn't seem to be worried about it, it was the fact her nipples were circled in blue glitter that was really distracting. McCoy was trying to be professional, but Wattie had given up, was just standing there staring, mouth open.

'No, I'm her flatmate. She's not here, darling.'

The girl was leaning on the doorway of the flat, smiling engagingly. Seemed distracted, maybe still high on something. Her accent was posh English, all the more surprising given the fact she was black. She yawned widely. 'You'll have to excuse me, I just got in, rather a long night.' She giggled. 'She's at the sound check, I expect.'

'Sound check?' asked McCoy.

'Yes, been a friend of David's for years. Met through Lindsay Kemp.'

'Sorry, eh, miss, you've lost me.'

She giggled again. 'David? Tonight? He's playing in town, at Green's Playhouse I think it is. Should really get some sleep before it starts.'

'What? David Bowie, you mean?' asked Wattie, managing to look up at her face.

219

The girl looked puzzled. 'Who else?'

'Jeez. She knows him? She knows David Bowie?'

'Baby knows everyone, darling, absolutely everyone. It's quite amazing, really. Now if you'll excuse me, the land of nod calls. Ciao!'

She blew them a kiss and shut the apartment door.

'Fucking hell,' said Wattie, shaking his head. 'Did you see those?'

'Couldn't miss them, could have hung a bloody duffle coat on them. Come on, I need to talk to you.'

They walked out the entrance of Kelvin Court and stood under the concrete awning, the rose gardens and lawns in front of them iced with snow. McCoy lit up, coughed. First of the day.

'Davey Waters,' he said.

Wattie was suddenly very interested in the progress of a bin lorry heading up the street towards Anniesland. 'You mean the gun guy? What about him?'

'Stay away from him, that's what. Lucky for you someone's had a word in my ear. Someone like Davey Waters'll chew you up and spit you out before you even know what's going on. Got it?'

'Not sure what you're on about, sir,' said Wattie, eyes still on the lorry.

McCoy sighed. Was going to be like that, was it? 'Don't try and be a fucking smart-arse. Stay the fuck away from him and stop trying to throw your weight about. You think Davey just sits there

220

all day waiting to shite himself off you? Waters has been done for serious assault umpteen times. Would have been done for murder more than once if we had been able to pin it on him. Leave him alone. Stay away. This is Glasgow, not fucking Brigadoon. You hear me?'

'Was only doing what you said,' he sulked.

'What?'

'Connections, how you get ahead.'

'Christ, you're even stupider than I thought.'

'How come we're chasing this Baby Strange up if we think it's a domestic?'

'Because there is a difference between thinking and knowing. Follow things up, complete the picture, do our job. You never listen to anything Murray tells you? Now go and get the fucking car and bring it round. We've got a sound check to go to. Whatever the fuck that is.'

Would have been easier to get into Fort Knox than Green's bloody Playhouse. It took them almost an hour to even get to the entrance. Had to push their way through the crowds of crying and screaming teenage girls. Traffic on Renfield Street was crawling along, periodically brought to a halt by another surge of girls trying to make it across the road to the venue doors. Eventually, after a lot of pushing and shoving, they made it to the door. McCoy held his card up to the glass, a grim-faced bouncer opened the door for them and they were in. Screaming outside abruptly cut off as the big main door closed behind them.

Wattie was all excited, pointing at the posters of past concerts, smiling at every fat bastard carrying a bunch of wires that walked past. Was as cold inside as out, obviously weren't wasting their money heating an empty venue. McCoy wasn't too sure about David Bowie, had seen him on the TV a few times dressed up like some woman alien thing, looked like a freak. He was a big deal, though. Was like getting an audience with the pope. They'd been told by some bloke in a faded commissionaire's uniform to stay put and wait for the manager to turn up. He was going to 'escort them backstage', whatever that meant.

The foyer was echoing with the constant boom of a drum being hit over and over again. Wasn't helping McCoy's hangover one bit. Wattie had stopped one of the technician blokes, was asking him what time the show was. If this went on any longer, he'd be asking him for free tickets. He called him over.

'You're supposed to be a polis, not a bloody teenybopper. Start acting like it.'

'Sorry, just a bit excited. Never been here before. Have you?'

McCoy nodded. 'Last summer. The Faces.'

'Rod Stewart's band?'

McCoy sighed inwardly. 'The band Rod Stewart sings in.'

Wattie looked puzzled. 'Aye, that's them. Was it any good?'

Him and Janey'd smoked two joints before they

went in, half a tab each. Flying. Turned out the security guy used to be a polis, let them right down the front. Drinking from a half bottle, dancing. Band were only feet from them, looked as out of it as they were. Big grin on Rod Stewart's face as he twirled the microphone stand above him. Played 'Stay With Me' twice. Best song ever. Him and Janey shouting it to each other, grins splitting their faces, sweat running off them. Still so high from it all that they shagged each other behind the big bins in the alley across the road when they got out.

'Not bad.'

'Gentlemen?'

A wee bloke in a too-tight dinner suit had appeared, couldn't have got more Brylcreem in his hair if he'd applied it with a trowel. He pointed to the big doors at the top of the stairs. 'If you'd like to follow me.'

They followed him through the doors into the empty auditorium. The 'one two, one two' and the drums were even louder in here, bouncing round the old red and gilt theatre. The place stank of beer, damp and fags, rows of red velvet seats facing towards the stage all as worn as the sticky carpet. They went up a stair to the side of the stage and then through various wee corridors and doors until McCoy wasn't even sure what direction they were facing any more. They stopped halfway down another corridor outside a door with 'Star Dressing Room' written on it in glittery letters. Loud talking and laughing coming from behind it. The wee manager wasn't quite sure what to do. McCoy was getting tired and bored of all this; he reached for the door handle and a voice came from behind him.

'I don't think so, sir.'

He turned and there was a bloke, standing, arms folded, looked like a weightlifter. Cowboy hat, white shirt and a bootlace tie. Unsurpringly, he'd an American accent.

'Can I help you guys with anything?' he asked.

'Naw,' said McCoy, holding out his badge. 'Fuck off.'

He left the manager to explain and pushed the dressing-room door open. The room was crowded. Boys with make-up plastered all over them, a girl strumming a guitar, smell of joss sticks and hair-spray, loud music playing. Some guy in the corner with a sequined jacket and long blond hair was telling a joke, high-pitched laughter as he got to the punchline. McCoy coughed loudly and everyone turned towards him. He supposed the man himself was in here, but he couldn't make out which one he was.

'Looking for someone called Baby Strange,' he said, feeling like a right arse even saying the name.

The room turned again, heads swivelling towards a girl in the corner. She was giving a man sitting in front of her a shoulder massage. His bony white shoulders were bare, was only wearing a kind of woollen swimsuit thing. He looked up. Bright orange spiky hair, funny eyes. That'd be him then. The woman stopped her kneading. She looked as odd as him: tall, stick thin, pure white hair frizzed out, mad make-up like a clown.

'That's me, darling,' she said, inhaling on a pink cigarette. 'Are you the delivery? Thank god, everyone was getting a teeny bit anxious.'

''Fraid not,' said McCoy. 'Polis. I need a word.'

They ended up in the empty discotheque upstairs. Manager showed them to a table beneath an unlit neon sign saying 'Clouds'. A cleaner was tutting, trying to mop up what looked like a combination of dried-up beer and sick from the dance floor. The curved seat round the table was punctured with cigarette burns, yellow foam poking through. Baby Strange looked at it with disgust, then lowered herself down. She started chewing on the edge of a bright blue fingernail. Looked nervous. No surprise.

'What was it you thought we were delivering?' asked McCoy.

She shrugged. 'Some make-up; I forgot to bring it. I promised David I'd give it to him. From Japan.' Her accent was half American and half English. Certain words slipping in and out.

'Shite,' said McCoy. 'Do I look like a fucking make-up delivery boy?'

'I don't know,' she said. 'What do they normally look like?'

McCoy had to hand it to her, she may have

looked like a freak of nature but she was no idiot.

'So what exactly is it you do? Workwise, I mean.'

'Ah, always hard to explain. I arrange things for people. Make sure they go with a bang.' She smiled at them. No takers. Kept going. 'Parties, fashion shows, promotional events . . .'

'How about whores?' said McCoy. 'That's what I heard. Men, women, all sorts. Nothing you can't sort out. That right?'

Atmosphere changed, her face went hard, started drumming her fingers on the table. Wasn't looking for smiles any more.

'What precisely is it I can help you with today, gentlemen?'

'True, is it?' asked McCoy. 'About the whores?'

She stood up. 'I think it's time I ran along. You want to come back and make some more dumb allegations, be my guest. It's your dime. Archie Lomax? Know him, do you? Thought you might. He's my lawyer, on retainer. Be delighted to sit beside me holding my hand. Now, if you please . . .'

McCoy didn't move. 'Archie Lomax. That right? Pretty high-powered lawyer for someone who arranges birthday parties, isn't he? Now, sit back down and start talking. Otherwise we can just wait until your delivery turns up, see exactly what kind of make-up it is, eh?'

She stood there twisting a big red plastic ring round her finger, wondering how to play it. She sighed, sat back down. 'This off the record?' she asked.

'Yes,' said McCoy, lying.

She lit up another pink cigarette. 'Let me try and explain it. There are rich people in this town, rich people who live boring lives. Sometimes they have parties to liven things up a bit. I help spice them up. I have a great Rolodex. I do a great guest list.'

'Including whores?'

'Occasionally, but mostly it's just interesting people. Good-looking kids, artists who want a free meal, bands that are in town. Suddenly these boring rich people aren't boring any more, they're in the *Herald* and the *Scotsman* society pages with Hugh Fraser and Lulu. Suddenly they're hip.'

'And they pay you?'

'Oh yes, honey, they pay. Pay well. Everybody wants to be hip and groovy these days, even boring old bankers. Everybody wants to meet a famous musician, or even a criminal. Maybe you could help me out – starting to get very fashionable, you know.'

'Aye right. So you provide whatever it is people are looking for? That the deal?'

She nodded. 'Within reason.'

McCoy dug in his pocket, brought out the picture of Lorna Skirving, set it down on the table in front of her. 'Provide her?'

She took the picture and looked at it, handed it back. Shook her head. 'I've seen her at a couple of parties, though, usually wrapped round some fat, sweaty businessman. Not really my kind of thing, all a bit low-rent really.'

'Arrange any parties at Broughton House?'

She only took a second to arrange her face again, but McCoy had seen it. Fear. 'No, sadly not, bit out of my league. Practically royalty, I believe.'

'Oh, I think you're being modest. Smart woman like you? I'm sure you could handle them, sort some things out they were looking for. In fact, I think you did.'

She shook her head again. 'Nope. Not me.'

There was no way she was going to give up the Dunlops that easily. Couldn't say he blamed her really. That wasn't going to happen without more of a fight, and more money going into Archie Lomax's account.

She stood up again and looked at her watch. 'David's limo will be here. We're going back to the Albany. Can I go?'

McCoy smiled, shook his head.

'I don't want to miss it.' She was looking anxious, tried another smile. 'First rule of rock and roll, you know, don't get left behind.'

McCoy padded his pockets, found his cigarettes. 'That right? You know what, I think I'll get vice to have a proper look over your wee supply and demand racket. Then I'll get them to have a word in the ear of their pals at the *Daily Record*. Not sure they have a society page, but I'm sure they can work up a nice piece, big picture of you in all your finery. Then you can sit back and watch all your rich clients drop you like a fucking hot brick. That what you want? You're not going to give me the Dunlops, that's fine. I'm a big boy, I can live with it. Give me something.'

She was chewing her lip, bright purple lipstick coating her front teeth. Made up her mind and sat back down.

'Show me the picture again.'

She looked at it, handed it back. 'She did a job for me, one job, year or so ago. A client of mine had a Swedish business associate in town. He was looking for someone who could accommodate his special interests, who didn't mind if he took it a bit further than usual. Her name came up, so I set it up. She did the job all right, no problems, but she stole thirty quid out of his wallet while he was having a shower afterwards. I never worked with her again.'

'She's dead. Someone shot her in broad daylight. Why would someone do that?'

She sat back. 'I've told you everything I know. Finding out who killed her is your job, not mine.'

'We know who killed her. A young guy called Tommy Malone. We want to find out why. She ever meet the Dunlops?'

'I didn't arrange it,' she said evenly.

'That's not what I asked you.'

'I know it wasn't,' she said.

McCoy sat back, sighed. 'Wattie, away and phone Central, get a car here. I'm sick of being taken for a cunt.'

Wattie nodded, stood up. He was halfway across the dancefloor before she said it.

'Okay.'

One little word. Enough. McCoy looked at her. And she began.

'She did a lot of parties for them. I didn't set them up, but I saw her there.'

'Doing what?'

She shrugged. 'Whatever they paid her to. Girl-boy, girl-girl, bondage, S&M, whatever they asked. Seemed to go through their major-domo. Guy with reddish hair . . . John?

'Jimmy?'

She nodded. 'That's him. Stone-cold creep. There was another girl, I think she worked there at the house. Just a stupid girl who wanted people to like her. He loaded her up with acid, let anyone fuck her, filmed it. Some guy called her over in front of everyone, she came running like a lapdog.'

She stopped, lit another coloured cigarette.

'He told her to hold her arm out, she did and he stubbed his cigarette out on it. Smiled when he did it. Told her to go upstairs and wait for him. Called her his toy.' She exhaled, a weak smile through the cigarette smoke. 'Ugly stuff.'

'Why didn't you do anything?' asked McCoy.

'Because I was scared.'

'Of who?'

She shook her head. 'Someone told me she hung herself a few days later. That was the last time I ever went to Broughton House.'

230

'Who was the guy?' asked McCoy.

Nothing. He waited. She wouldn't look at him as she said it, stared down at the floor.

'Teddy. Lord Dunlop's son.'

CHAPTER 25

The force pushed McCoy hard against the car door, Wattie almost on top of him.

'Fuck sake,' he muttered under his breath.

'I cannae bloody help it,' said Wattie as the car pulled out the corner and they managed to straighten up again. Siren was going, light on, the full works. He made out something from the front seat about 'being able to drive a bus through there' as the car accelerated sharply between two Corporation buses and ran a red light.

'I think I'm going to boak,' groaned McCoy as they slammed round another corner doing sixty odd. He wasn't sure why they were going so fast. If she was dead, she was dead, nothing they could do about it now. Brakes went on hard and McCoy groaned as he hit the back of the seats in front of him. Soon saw why they'd stopped: the street ahead was full of men wearing green and white scarves, making their way down London Road towards the car, police on horses trying to herd them away from the other team's burgundy-scarved supporters.

'Did you no fucking realise there was a game on?'
Murray shouted at the driver.

He shook his head. 'Sorry, sir.'

Borders accent. Stupid bugger had to be another
one of Murray's rugby boys. None of them knew
fuck all about football. McCoy was going to say
something about employing Glaswegians in the
Glasgow force, then thought better of it.

'You should have told him, McCoy. It's your lot,'
said Murray.

'So it's my fault now?' he asked.

Murray didn't reply. Just sat there looking
murderous.

The car made a sharp right at the big abattoir
and headed down into Dalmarnock. Glasgow
was a city of villages, of territories marked out
by gangs and old arguments about whether
one road was in or out. He couldn't remember
anyone arguing much about Dalmarnock.
Nobody wanted it.

They pulled up outside a tenement block
marooned in an empty plot of mud pitted with
puddles and broken rubble. The entrances and
ground-floor windows of the flats had been
timbered over by the council, 'STAY OUT –
DANGER' notices just visible under the
spray-painted gang names. Notices hadn't done
much good. Half of the boards had been kicked
in or prised off, splintered ones lying on the ground.

'Kids found her,' said Murray, rubbing at the
condensation on the car window and peering

out. 'In there playing hide and seek. Cannae blame them, not much else to do round here.'

The snow was almost horizontal, wind blowing it hard against the car windows. Nothing else for it, they needed to run. Wind almost took the car door off when McCoy opened it. He ran between a couple of pandas and an ambulance heading for the flats. Thomson came out the close with his raincoat pulled over his head and pointed up.

'Top floor,' he said.

By the look of the place it wasn't only kids who'd been in the building. Doors of the flats had been kicked in, rooms strewn with old blankets, pale ale cans, wallpaper and floorboards scorched black where fires had been lit. Snow was coming through what was left of the glass panels in the stairwell roof; even with that fresh air the place still stank of piss. They trudged up the stairs, shaking snow off their coats, aware of people above them shuffling about, shouting instructions. On the top floor, lights had been rigged up on stands, big battery packs humming. They squeezed past them and into the flat. Wattie pointed to a room lit up like a stage set, harsh white light illuminating everything, including what they were all here for.

A bloodstained sheet wrapped round something lay in the far corner underneath a cracked window. Only clue it contained a woman was the slim ankle and foot poking out the bottom of it. A woman in her late fifties, tweed suit half covered by a white lab coat, was kneeling on the floor beside it. She turned and looked up at them.

'At bloody last,' she said. 'We've all been waiting for the esteemed Mr Murray to cast his eye before we can touch anything.'

'Phyllis,' said Murray. 'Always a pleasure.'

Phyllis Gilroy was a big woman, tall as well as broad, owner of the poshest Glasgow accent McCoy had ever heard. Had been the police pathologist ever since McCoy had joined up. Probably would be after he'd gone. She stood up, straining a bit. 'This weather's not good for my knees, not good at all. I'm going outside for some air and the dim hope of finding some sort of lavatory nearby. All yours, gents.'

She squeezed past them and McCoy started his breathing. Hoped it was going to help. One. Two. Three. One. Two. Three. He moved in, trying to shield his eyes from the lights, knelt down, pulled a corner of the sheet back, saw blood, looked away. One. Two. Three.

He heard Murray swearing, then he moved in beside him, pushed him out the way. 'Fuck sake, we'd be here all day if it was up to you.' He leant forward, grabbed the corner of the sheet and slowly started pulling it away from the body. It came away like a wrapper off a toffee, sticking to the skin as he pulled. McCoy kept his eyes fixed on the ripped wallpaper beyond, trying to breathe slowly. He heard Wattie mutter 'Jesus Christ' under his breath and he looked down.

She was naked, hands tied behind her back with a necktie. She looked young – twenty-odd – and tall. The parts of her body he could see through the sticky blood were bruised. Yellow. Blue. Black. The back of her head was just a crumpled mess of shattered bone, blonde hair thick with blood.

Murray pointed to the back of her head with his shoe. 'Pretty obvious what killed her unless Lady Muck tells us different. Looks like she was knocked about a bit beforehand as well.'

'Do we know who she is?' said McCoy, trying not to look.

'Nope. There's nothing on her,' said Thomson. 'Going to have to try dental records, could take a while. Kids that found her haven't said much, still shell-shocked I think.' He pointed at a carrier bag spilling empty beer cans onto the floor. 'Been the usual alkies up here too, but I can't see any of them having much to do with this.'

McCoy risked another look. 'Doesn't look like all this happened here, there's not enough blood.'

'And where's her clothes?' added Murray. 'You find them?'

Thomson shook his head. 'They've had a look through the building. Nothing.'

'They?' asked Murray. 'Who the fuck's they?'

'Couple of uniforms,' said Thomson warily.

'That right? Fuck's up with you, then? Too bloody important?'

'No, I—'

'Away and have a look yourself, you fucking clown. Now!'

Thomson pushed past them, looking sheepish, and Murray shook his head. 'Is he any use? I'm beginning to bloody wonder.'

'Done?'

Gilroy had reappeared, two dripping wet ambulance men behind her carrying a collapsible stretcher. Murray nodded and Gilroy stepped aside to let the ambulance men through.

'What time is it now?' asked Gilroy, looking at her watch. 'Sixish.' She stared into space, mentally calculating. 'About nine, I'd say. Should have her cleaned up and some idea of what happened. So, until then . . .'

The office was quiet, radio on in the background. They'd been back for a couple of hours, nothing much McCoy could do but wait for Gilroy. Wattie was bent over his typewriter, tongue out, trying to finish his report. McKee filling out his football coupon while absentmindedly dipping his biscuit in his tea.

'Where are we then?' asked McCoy for want of something to say. He'd read through a few reports, made some phone calls, went to see Cowie for a cup of tea. He was bored now.

Wattie sat back from his desk and looked at him.

'Nowhere,' he said. 'No one reported missing in the past couple of days that fits her description. The house to house, if you can call it that, got us nothing. No houses anywhere around really, just a pub. Tried there and nobody saw nothing, no one heard a car. Most of the people that drink there barely know what day it is, mind you.'

'What about the staff?'

'Saw nothing, heard nothing.'

'Great,' said McCoy. 'Know what we have to do now?'

Wattie nodded at the door.

'Perfect timing.' Fat Billy from records was standing there, three overflowing cardboard boxes in his arms. 'Fuck sake, gie us a hand, I'm dying here.'

Wattie took the top one off him and dumped it on his desk, dust going everywhere.

'Got them to pull all the mispers from the past six months.'

'Fuck me, Wattie. You might make a polis yet.'

'You two clowns. *Move.*' They turned. Murray was coming out his office, arm half in the sleeve of his tweed jacket. 'Her ladyship's early for once. Come on.'

McCoy bought the evening paper from the bloke outside the shop, started reading in the car while Murray and Wattie droned on about some rugby match. Lorna Skirving was nowhere to be seen, already yesterday's news. He turned the page. Some bloke shot outside Rolls-Royce in Belfast. Common Market. Train drivers threatening to strike. Bruce and Anthea's secrets of a happy marriage. Usual stuff. He turned the page again and stopped. Big picture of Lord Dunlop and another middle-aged man shaking hands. He skimmed the article. *The Dunlop family and the Mackenzie Trust announce takeover bid of Allied Newspapers. Time for new blood. Looking forward to working together. Share price announced tomorrow.*

'You see this?' He leant forward and passed the paper to Murray. He glanced at it and gave it back.

'Aye, I saw it this morning. Fuck all to do with you, McCoy. Far as you're concerned the Dunlops don't exist.' He looked back over his shoulder at him. 'That clear?'

'Crystal,' he said, sighing.

'Any news on Skirving and that Malone lad? You getting anywhere? Super's been after me to close the file.'

'Not yet. We were pretty sure it was a domestic, seems like Malone had been up at the flat shouting the odds a few times.'

'Were?' asked Murray.

'Are,' said McCoy. 'No real evidence of anything else. She may have had another boyfriend, paid-for private dates, kinky stuff, whips, pain, that sort of thing.'

'Who is he, this boyfriend?'

'Not sure. We're struggling a bit, but I think there's maybe more than just Tommy Malone being jealous and killing her. Doesn't really sound right.'

'Aye well, what it sounds like is the square root

of fuck all to me. Nothing by the morning and I'll have to close it. Domestic it is.'

The mortuary was in Saltmarket down by the Clyde. Funny wee low building facing Glasgow Green. Wattie pulled the car over outside and Murray got out. Wattie watched him go, held his hand up to keep McCoy in the car.

'What?'

'You know who we still haven't spoken to? Bobby.' Wattie pointed to his chest, where the tattoo had been. 'You told Murray you'd do it.'

'Shite,' said McCoy. 'I forgot all about it. Don't let Murray know, for fuck sake. Why'd you no remind me?'

Wattie rolled his eyes. 'Give us a break. Be a waste of time. What's Nairn's boyfriend going to know anyway?'

'Fuck all, no doubt, but we better find out.'

McCoy stood at the back of the room trying to breathe through his mouth, avoiding looking at what was going on in front of him. If bodies at murder scenes were bad, bodies in places like this were somehow worse. It was the white tiles and the enamel buckets and the stink of bleach. The more they tried to cover up what was going on, the worse it was. Gilroy was looking over at him, smirking and shaking her head.

'Leave him,' said Murray. 'He's fine over there. Least he's managed to get in the bloody building this time.'

240

Wattie grinned at him, mouthed 'Wanker'.

The three of them were gathered round the body on the slab. That suited McCoy fine, at least they were blocking his view of what was going on. All he got was the occasional glimpse of a hand or a green sheet through the gaps between them. Gilroy stepped to the side and he saw mottled skin, puff of pubic hair. He looked down quickly, started his breathing, counted the floor tiles. Anything to keep his mind off it. Gilroy's posh voice still managed to cut through.

'Fractured skull, hardly surprising but interesting though. Could have been very light, almost a tap.'

'Eh?' said Murray. 'How come? Half the back of her head's caved in.'

Gilroy took a pen from the breast pocket of her lab coat and pointed at the side of her skull. 'She had a pre-existing hairline fracture. Clear as a bell on the X-ray. She's had it for years, probably had no idea.'

'So anything could have done it? A fall? A punch? Something like that?' asked Wattie.

Gilroy looked amused. 'Well, I doubt it was entirely accidental, going by the rest of her. But a good defence lawyer could certainly argue it.' She moved down the table, pointed with her pen again. 'The bruising is largely centered on her breasts, inner thighs, buttocks. Attack was undoubtedly sexual in nature. The walls of her vagina and anus are bruised and torn.'

'Raped?' asked Murray.

Gilroy shook her head. 'Don't think so. Not in the conventional sense anyway. No trace of semen or rubber. Used something wooden, unfinished, large. Whoever did it was just trying to cause pain, a great deal of pain I would imagine.'

McCoy tried to walk towards them, took one step, felt so dizzy he had to stop, put his hand against the tiled wall to steady himself.

'We've been here before,' he said.

'Lorna Skirving,' said Murray.

Gilroy nodded. 'Took the words out of my mouth, young man.'

McCoy was almost at the slab, was walking slowly, felt like the top of his head was going to come off, like he'd done a huge line of speed too fast. Murray turned, shook his head. 'You sure about this, McCoy? She's no a pretty sight.'

He nodded, tried to swallow the saliva pooling in his mouth. 'Let me have a look.'

Murray nodded and he and Wattie stepped aside. For a moment McCoy thought he was going to go, edges of his vision were blurry, could feel the sweat running down his back. He held onto the edge of the steel table and tried to look. Body was a just a mess of fresh bruises over old ones. There was a handsaw lying by her arm; he tried not to look at that either, blood pulsing in his temples. Murray lifted the gauze cloth off her face and that was that.

*　　*　　*

'Here.' Murray was holding out a plastic cup of water. McCoy took a drink, breathed in the cold January air, felt better. They were sitting on the big sandstone steps of the High Court next door. He didn't have much memory of getting there, was just glad he was out the examination room.

'Sorry about that,' he said.

Murray shrugged. 'Suppose you cannae help it.'

'I thought you were a goner,' chimed in Wattie. 'Lucky you didn't bash your head on the corner of the slab.'

'You ever go to that woman?' said Murray.

'What woman?' asked Wattie.

McCoy shook his head.

'Might no be the worst idea,' said Murray. 'Can't do any harm. Doesn't go on your—' He looked over at Wattie, sitting there all ears, didn't finish his sentence.

'Aye, so they say,' said McCoy. He found his fags in the pocket of his trenchcoat, lit up. Felt better and worse at the same time. Head was spinning but from the nicotine this time, first full drag of an Embassy Regal'll do that to you.

'Isabel,' he said.

'What?' said Murray, looking at him.

'That's her name. Isabel.'

'You know her?' asked Murray. 'How come? Isabel who?'

'Don't know her second name, don't really know her. She's one of Ronnie Naismith's girls, works in his clubs, does a bit of escort work too, I think.'

A bus drew up across the street, scramble to get on, too many people and not enough spaces.

'You're not going to like this,' he said.

'Like what?' said Murray.

'What I'm going to tell you. I saw her last night. I was at one of Billy Chan's casino nights with Stevie Cooper—'

'For fuck sake, McCoy, how many times do I have to tell you to stop seeing that—'

'Dunlop,' he said quietly. 'The son, she was with Teddy. And someone told us last night that he's got previous.'

8TH JANUARY 1973

CHAPTER 26

'What more do you fucking need?'

'More than you've given me, McCoy. A lot more.'

He'd been waiting at his desk when Murray'd got in. Big surprise for everyone. First time he'd been in the shop before 8 a.m. in a long time. Thomson said he'd take a picture for the notice-board, couldn't believe it.

McCoy'd gone through it all last night, went over it again as he was shaving, getting dressed. What he'd say, how he'd convince him. Murrray arrived at half past as usual, didn't look too happy to see him. McCoy gave him five minutes to settle in, then knocked on the office door. He'd started well, all rational and reasonable. Sat in the chair opposite Murray's desk and quietly ran through why he no longer thought they were dealing with a straight domestic. Why they needed to have a look at Dunlop Junior. Hadn't worked. He tried explaining again. Still didn't work. Now he was just shouting. Angry. Knew it wasn't helping but he couldn't stop himself.

'Isabel Garvey was out last night with Dunlop Junior. Dunlop Junior has a history of abusing girls. Now Isabel Garvey's dead. Lorna Skirving was seen at the Dunlops. She died of the same injuries, exact same bloody bruises, and you don't think it's worth talking to them?'

'That's not what I said, so sit down and just listen for two minutes.'

He just stood there, too angry to do what he was told.

'Sit! Now!'

He sat. Pushed his feet out in front of him and crossed his arms.

'If, and I mean if, there is a connection to the Dunlops, we will find it—'

'He was in the bloody casino with her!'

'As were about fifty other people. Including you.' Murray was talking quietly, taking it slow, trying to regain his temper. 'Was she specifically with him, or was she just trying to get the bunch of lads out the place?'

'He was with her.'

'You a hundred per cent on that? She spoke to a group of lads. Maybe he was just one of them.'

'He left with her,' he said stubbornly.

'Sure of that, are you? Half pissed and full of painkillers and you could still tell what was going on? I don't think so.' Murray had his pipe out now, angrily stuffing tobacco down into the bowl. He looked up as if it had just dawned. 'And, by the way, how many fucking times do

I have to tell you to keep away from Stevie bloody Cooper?'

'Come on, Murray, that's got fuck all to do with it. It's the same injuries, that's what matters, the same fucking injuries! I've got a witness who saw him assaulting a girl, stubbing a fucking cigarette out on her arm for kicks.'

'And this witness is going to come forward and give a statement, are they?'

'It's not that easy for—'

'Fucking thought not!' Murray held his hands up. 'I've had about enough of this shite. Young Dunlop will be asked for a statement, same as everyone else in the club that night, that's it. And, believe me, you won't be the one doing it.'

'Come on, Murray—'

'Shut it. It's my decision. Up to me. End of. You're too close, McCoy. Too much history. Think they're going to tell you anything?'

He knew he was probably right. Dunlop's lawyer wouldn't let him within a mile of the two of them. 'Who then?'

'Me. And Wattie.'

'Wattie? What the fuck does he know about anything?'

'Not much, but I do. That okay by you, is it?'

McCoy shrugged. 'Suppose so.'

'Christ, McCoy, I swear it's like dealing with a teenage boy. I've got two of those at home, I don't need another one at my work.'

A knock on the door.

'What!' Murray barked.

It opened and Wattie peered round. 'Sir, can I have a word?'

'Not now.'

'It's important, sir,' he said.

Murray rolled his eyes. 'Jesus Christ, come in then.'

Wattie came in, holding out a sheet of paper. 'The girl,' he said. 'Isabel Garvey. Just had Eastern on the phone. Someone's copped for it.'

McCoy had worked at Eastern for a while. Full of supposed hard men and blokes on the take, crappy shop he'd got out of as soon as he could. Wasn't looking forward to going back. All they had been told was that someone had walked in off the street and told them he'd killed Isabel Garvey. Told them where he'd dumped the body, what kind of sheet it was wrapped in. Wasn't going to be Dunlop Junior, that was for sure.

The front office at the Eastern shop looked the same as it always had. Cream paint yellow with nicotine, worn-through lino and a bench bolted to the wall. The desk sergeant was about as welcoming as an Edinburgh landlady; left them standing there while he took his time phoning through. He put the phone down after a wee chat about Partick Thistle's chances, lifted up the top of the desk and stood aside.

Raeburn was sitting with his feet up on his desk when they went through to the office, hands laced behind his head, big smile on his face.

'McCoy, what you doing here? The sauna's a couple of doors down.' Few of his sidekicks laughed. Murray didn't, didn't even crack a smile, just looked at him.

'Bloke who copped for the Garvey girl. Where is he?' he asked.

Raeburn stood up, realised he better behave himself. 'Still in the cells, sir. He just walked in, said it was an accident. Didn't mean to kill her, he pushed her and she banged her head. He knew all the gen, where she was, where she'd been dumped. Kosher.'

'Who is he?' asked McCoy.

Raeburn looked at his notes. 'One Charles Alexander Gow.'

'Hang on. You mean Chas Gow? Big Chas?' asked McCoy.

'Who's that?' asked Murray.

'Works for Stevie Cooper, heavy at the shebeen in Cumberland Street.'

'Another one of your dodgy pals, is he?' asked Raeburn.

'Aye, he is, and there's no way he did that girl.'

'Fuck off, McCoy, he copped for it.'

'Can I speak to him?'

Raeburn shook his head. 'Can you fuck, it's nothing to do with you.'

'What for?' asked Murray, ignoring him.

'I know Chas, known him for years, just want to hear his side of the story.'

'Well, that doesn't seem too much to ask, does

251

it, Mr Raeburn? Put him in an interview room, will you?' said Murray.

Raeburn didn't move. Murray leant forward. 'I meant now, you cunt,' he said softly. 'Now.'

'He's sweating,' said Murray.

'He always sweats; he's near enough twenty stone.' McCoy held his hands up to the glass, shaded his eyes. Chas was sitting in an orange plastic chair in front of a battered table, tin McEwen's ashtray full of butts in front of him. He was scratching at his neck, looking worried.

'Thanks for that, by the way.'

'Don't thank me,' said Murray. 'That Raeburn thinks he's something. Just another wide boy with a badge.' He stepped back, leant against the wall of the tiny viewing room. 'What are we doing here, McCoy? He's admitted it, knows the details.' He tapped the glass and Chas looked around bewildered. 'That fat bastard in there came in and coughed. Don't look a gift horse in the mouth.'

'That's what worries me. C'mon, let's have a word.'

'All right, Chas?' said McCoy, opening the door.

Chas looked up, surprised and relieved to see him. He was in a bit of a state. He'd a black eye, scrapes down the side of his face, one sleeve of his too-small suit was ripped, yellow nylon shirt showing through. 'McCoy, what are you doing here?'

'Came to see you, Chas.' He looked him up and

down. 'Eastern been their usual hospitable selves, I see. You okay?'

'I'm fine. Sure they knocked me about a bit but I'll live. Irish man in the jail? Happens all the time.'

McCoy pulled out the chair opposite Chas and sat down. 'I heard you'd been telling stories.' He nodded over. 'That man standing over there is Chief Inspector Murray. My boss. He's a good polis, Chas, makes me look like a right amateur, so you better have your story straight, eh?'

Chas took a sideways glance at Murray. 'It's no a story. I already told the other polis. I killed her. Was an accident. We had an argument, I pushed her and she hit her head on the wall. Didn't even hit it hard. Next thing I knew she was dead. I panicked.'

'That right? You and Isabel an item, were you?' He ran his finger round the groove of CUMBIE gouged out the table, looked up. 'I don't want to be rude, Chas, but you're a fat middle-aged bastard who's a bouncer in a brothel. Not really her type. Where'd all this happen, then?'

'Mine. She came back to mine.' He looked up, sweat beading on his shadowed upper lip. He wiped it away. 'She wasnae my girlfriend. I paid her. Told her I'd give her double what she usually got.'

McCoy sat back in his chair. 'Then what?'

'Then she didn't want to go through with it. Said I was stinking, too fat. She couldn't do it. I

253

got angry, tried to force her onto the bed, and that's when she hit her head.'

'That's it? You didn't fuck her. She just bumped her head when you were struggling?'

He nodded.

'Okay, say we buy your wee scenario. What'd you take her clothes off for?'

Nothing.

'Chas? What did you take her clothes off for?'

Nothing. Murray stepped forward. 'Answer the man, Mr Gow.'

Chas looked at them both, ran his fat hand through his greasy hair, coughed. 'I wanted to look at her.'

'You wanted to look at her?'

He nodded, wiped at his eyes. 'She was a lovely wee girl, I just wanted to see her, see what she looked like.' And then his face crumpled. McCoy pulled a hanky out his pocket, handed it over.

'Fuck sake, Chas. How'd all this happen, this isn't you.'

Chas shook his head, blubbering now, hanky held up to his face. 'Don't know.'

'What'd you do with her clothes?'

'In a bin. Stopped the car on the way there, put them in some bin.'

'Where?'

He shook his head again. 'Can't remember.'

'How'd she get the bruises?' asked Murray.

He looked up sharply. 'I didnae do that, I tell you. They were there when I took her clothes off.

Honest.' He looked back and forward between them, trying to make them believe. 'Honest as I'm sitting here in front of you, I didn't batter that girl.'

They were standing outside the station waiting for a panda to be brought round. Line of kids filed passed them, towels under their arms, woman with a whistle at the front. Schools must be back already, holidays over.

'What do you think?' asked Murray.

McCoy shrugged. 'If you'd asked me an hour ago, I wouldn't have believed it. All the forensic stuff, the timings, they check out?'

'Going through them now,' said Murray.

'If they do, it's no really worth arguing about, is it?'

'But . . . there's always a bloody but with you.'

'I've known Chas for years. He's worked in brothels and shebeens for half his life. He's been around the girls, had his fair share of perks and freebies. No sure he'd suddenly flip over one of them. Too much other fruit on the tree.'

'She was a good-looking girl.'

'No more so than most of Ronnie's girls. They're proper escorts. Still doesn't explain the bruising. If he didn't do it, who did?'

The panda drew up and Murray opened the back door. 'Not our problem. Nobody's going to care about that if he murdered her. You coming?'

McCoy shook his head. 'Think I'll walk.'

Murray looked up at the dark sky, heavy with snow. 'Up to you. No more goose chases though.'

Wattie walked into the cafe and looked round. It was warm, steam from the coffee machine and the smell of fried food hanging in the air. Two old ladies nursing cups of tea, a woman with a fat baby on her lap. Took him a minute to see McCoy, sitting up the back in a booth staring into space, absent-mindedly stirring a Pyrex cup of tea. He eased in opposite, waved his hand in front of his face.

'Earth to McCoy.'

He stopped stirring, put the spoon down. 'Got the message then?'

'Aye. Took me a while to find it. What's up with you?'

McCoy shrugged. 'Nothing. Chas. Girls with bruises. The Dunlops. Everything.'

'Thought that Chas bloke had copped for it? They're all happy back at the shop. Open and shut in one day.'

'He did. Sang like a canary. Don't think he did it, though.'

'Christ, you're never satisfied. Why would he cop for something he hasn't done?'

Young girl with a face full of spots and a huge David Cassidy badge on her blouse appeared. She held up a wee notebook and a chewed ballpoint pen. 'What ye wanting?' she asked.

'Cup of tea,' said Wattie. 'And how about a smile?'

'Nae chance,' she said, walking off.

'Charming.' He looked round at the red booths, greasy laminated menus. 'This one of your usual haunts, is it?'

'Pre-existing skull fracture,' McCoy said, tapping his head with his teaspoon.

'What?'

'Isabel Garvey. She had a pre-existing skull fracture and Chas has no proper record. Story's believable enough. He's besotted with a beautiful girl who calls him a sweaty, fat bastard and won't go through with it even after he's paid over the odds. One accidental shove—'

'Followed by a wank after he's pulled the clothes off her dead body—'

'—and it's a tragic accident. He's crippled with remorse and shame. Manslaughter. Good lawyer and he'll get six years, out in four. Looked after inside. That deal could be worth ten grand to someone like Chas.'

'Who's got ten grand?' Wattie sat back as the girl plonked the tea down in front of him. 'Ah, hang on. I get it. The evil Dunlops did it and got Chas to cop to it for them.' He shook his head. 'Come on, McCoy. Tommy Malone shot Lorna Skirving. Chas Gow killed Isabel Garvey.'

'Chas Gow says he killed Isabel Garvey. That's a different thing.'

'Okay, so how'd the Dunlop's find Chas? Not a lot of fat shebeen bouncers hanging out at Broughton House far as I remember.'

'They didn't find him. They've got someone that does that sort of stuff for them. Jimmy Gibbs is ex-polis, he'd know exactly where to find someone like Chas.'

'The Jimmy Gibbs that ran off with your wife? That you don't have any axe to grind with at all?'

'Could have got Tommy Malone the gun as well,' said McCoy.

'Aye, and maybe he was Bible John too. You can't see the wood for the trees on this one. Case is closed; he confessed. It's over.'

McCoy pushed his cup away. 'Not yet; we've got tonight left.'

'Aye? To do what?'

McCoy tapped his heart. 'Bobby. We still haven't talked to Bobby.'

CHAPTER 27

McCoy and Wattie were sitting in traffic in Hawthorn Street. Snow was still coming down fast, windscreen wipers struggling to keep up. The heater was on full, smell of damp coats and cigarette smoke filling the car. McCoy rolled his window down, stuck his head out, trying to see what was going on. Wound it up quick. Freezing.

'Why do we still care about Bobby?' asked Wattie.

'We don't,' said McCoy, yawning. 'But way Murray is at the moment, if we haven't spoken to him and he finds out, then the both of us will be in for it.'

'Still can't believe Howie Nairn was a poof,' said Wattie.

'Aye well, welcome to 1973. Things are changing.'

The car in front started to move and McCoy slipped the car into gear. Pressed on the accelerator, felt the wheels spin on the black ice then catch.

Hawthorn Street ran from Possil to Springburn. People were very concerned with which end they lived at. Nearer Springburn the posher it was.

Distinction didn't mean much to McCoy. Both ends had the same four-in-a-block council flats, wee shops, crappy pubs. People always wanted to look down on someone, he supposed.

They drove under the railway bridge, pulled in by a big sign for the greyhound stadium. McCoy pulled the key out the ignition, radio died. 'Rocket Man' cut off in his prime.

They hurried out the car, coats pulled above their heads, and wrenched the big doors open. Stood in the foyer, shaking the snow off their clothes.

'This it?' asked Wattie, looking round.

McCoy nodded.

'Not exactly Las Vegas, is it?'

'What d'you mean? It's the Ashfield Club. It's better. Billy Connolly's played here, you know. Chic Murray. Glen Daly. Loads of people.'

Wattie looked round the half-deserted club. 'Not the night, though.'

Someone had been keen, gone crazy on the Christmas decorations. Strings of tinsel still hung across the bar. 'Seasons Greetings' signs and plastic santas and snowmen everywhere. A huge silvery Christmas tree blinking in the corner. They walked down the steps, heading for the long bar at the back.

'Shouldn't these be down by now?' asked Wattie. 'Is it no bad luck?'

'Bad luck for the poor cunt who's got to take them down more like. Come on.'

A middle-aged woman with a blonde beehive and cat's-eye glasses was standing behind the bar, framed by the optics and a big pale ale mirror. She walked forward as they approached.

'Boys, what can I get you?'

McCoy nodded at the Tennent's tap. 'Two pints.'

The Ashfield Club was a Glasgow institution. Been there for years, ever since McCoy could remember. Did the lot: dinner dances, bands and comedians, bingo nights. He'd been here a good few times, birthdays, staff nights out. Even came here with Angela once, had a great time. Didn't look like they were going to tonight, though. Half the tables on the floor were empty, only the ones at the front near the stage were busy. Clouds of cigarette smoke sitting over tables filled with pensioners nursing their drinks.

'Quiet the night?' he said.

Barmaid shook her head, pulled the wee silver tap towards her. 'Always are now, son. Telly's killed us, specially on a night like this. Fridays and Saturdays are no bad, though. Still packed then.' She put the two pints down on the bar. 'What brings you two boys here?' McCoy reached in his pocket and she shook her head. 'Polis drink for free in here. Always have done.'

McCoy took a draft. 'That obvious?'

She smiled. 'Been behind this bar for near on thirty years, son, no much gets past me.'

'We're here to see Bobby Thorne. He around?'

She nodded over at the stage. A pianist appeared

out the darkness, lit up in the beam of a red spotlight. 'Just in time. He's coming on. Would have thought you two are a bit young to be seeing Bobby. Old ones love him, though.'

She was right. Clapping and cheers started as soon as he appeared from behind the gold curtain. Bobby Thorne was a wee middle-aged man stuffed into a midnight blue dinner suit and ruffled shirt, big velvet bow tie, pinkie rings on both chubby hands. He smiled, pearly teeth catching the light, and grabbed the microphone.

'How's it going, my good peeps?' he shouted. Pianist running up and down the keys behind him. Rapturous cheers and then he was off, straight into 'Granny's Heilan Hame'.

Wattie looked dismayed. 'Christ, have we got to sit through this?'

'Looks like it. Can't exactly pull him off the stage, can we?'

A group of blue-rinsed women smiled at them as they sat down. They were already clapping along, singing the words before Bobby got there. McCoy supped at his pint and wondered what they were doing here. Nobody cared about Lorna Skirving any more. Wasn't sure he even did. If he was being honest, it was only the Dunlops that were keeping him going. Murray was right. The case was closed the moment Tommy Malone put the bullet in his head. The why and wherefores weren't their problem. He rubbed at his eyes. He was tired, sore, needed his bed. Five more songs and another two pints in, Bobby's act was starting to wear thin. He leant over to one of the women at the next table.

'Is there an interval?'

She nodded, reluctant to turn away from the stage. 'He sings "These Are My Mountains" and "A Scottish Soldier", then he goes off for fifteen minutes. Enjoying the show?'

McCoy nodded. 'Oh aye. Marvellous.'

Bobby wasn't really that bad, just wasn't McCoy's cup of tea. You don't survive thirty years in working men's clubs and variety shows without knowing how to please a crowd. His voice was a surprisingly deep baritone, not bad at all, and he had the patter too. Mother-in-law-jokes, Paddy jokes, stories about wee Glasgow women at the bingo, even got one of the old dears up on stage to serenade her. He'd just launched into 'A Scottish Soldier' when Wattie leant over.

'I didn't realise it was him we'd come to see. My mother's got one of his records. Wonder if she knows he's a poof.'

Bobby did his big ending, took a deep bow and told his 'good peeps' he'd be back after a short interval 'where drink would no doubt be taken'.

Bobby didn't look quite so good up close. He'd undone his trousers, belly poking out, finally free. His wee dressing room stank of his stockinged feet, crossed on top of his bashed patent pumps. His face was orange with make-up, shiny head of hair a fairly obvious toupee. He swallowed back a whisky and looked them up and down. McCoy held up his badge.

'I know who you are. Polis. I've been waiting for you cunts to turn up. Finally find out who did it, did you?'

'Sorry, Mr Thorne. That investigation is still ongoing. We're here on a separate matter.'

Bobby held out his hand. 'Badge.'

McCoy handed it over. Bobby looked at it, and his face crumpled. 'You've got some nerve coming here, McCoy, some bloody nerve. He's dead because of you, dead because of what he told you.' He threw the badge on the floor. 'Get out. Get out my dressing room.'

McCoy picked up his badge, smiled. 'I'll say this for you, Bobby, you've still got it. I remember seeing you at the King's when I was a wee boy. *How Green Was My Valley*. You were good. Let's cut the Oscar-winning stuff and just get on with it, eh?'

Bobby considered for a minute, then poured himself another whisky, looked at the clock on the wall above the mirror. 'Cheeky bastard. You've got ten minutes, then I'm back on.' He knocked it back, grimaced. 'Roar of the pish, smell of the mothballs.'

'You know who killed Howie?'

Bobby shook his head.

'I'm not talking about whoever slit his throat in the showers at Barlinnie, I'm talking about who paid them to do it. I saw the tattoo, Bobby.' He tapped his chest. 'Right above his heart, saw it when he was lying on the tiles, lifeblood draining out of him. Somebody made that happen, Bobby, somebody needs to . . .'

The tears had started. Bobby pulled some paper hankies out of the cardboard box on the dressing table, wiped at his eyes. 'Twenty-two years we were together. Twenty-two bloody years. Longer than most marriages. Nobody bloody cared. Had to find out he was dead by reading it in the paper. Nobody came to tell me, they told his cunt of a sister. Fucking cow wouldn't even let me go to the funeral, got a visit from her and some Church of Scotland minister, both of them looking down their noses at me, telling me if I went I would upset the family. Me! He hated his family, hadn't seen her or them since he was fourteen and his dad chucked him out the house. Wouldn't even let me see the body.'

McCoy sat forward. 'I need you to help me, Bobby. I know you're scared, I know what they did to Howie, but I need you. Without you I can't get them. Howie worked for them, didn't he? Before he went back in?'

Bobby was really crying now, could only manage a nod.

'And those cunts didn't lift a finger to help you, did they? What do you owe them, Bobby? Nothing. Give me something. Tell me.'

Bobby looked at them, was about to speak when the door opened behind them, a girl poked her head around. 'That's your five-minute—'

'Beat it,' said Wattie and pushed the door shut.

'Come on, Bobby. What was it all about? Lorna Skirving. Tell me.'

He took out a cigarette and Wattie was there with the lighter, Bobby's fat hands clasping round his to keep it steady.

He took a deep draw, blew the smoke out the side of his mouth. 'You don't know what they're like. They're evil, the pair of them. Pure. Fucking. Evil. The father and the son. Tag team, that's their thing. One girl between them and they like it rough, very rough. Don't even try. Howie tried, he tried to help that girl and look what happened to him. I mean it, McCoy, it's more than your life's worth.'

Piano music started up and Bobby looked panicked, started to fix his make-up, squeeze his shoes on.

'Come on, Bobby.'

'I cannae, McCoy. I'm no cut out for it. I'm scared. Look at me. I'm a fat, middle-aged poof who's scared of his own shadow. If they did that to Howie, the hard man Howie was, what chance have I got?'

'They both fucked her, that what you're saying, is it? Bobby?' He was leaning into him, voice raised, trying to push him over the edge. 'They fucked her, the two of them. What happened next, Bobby? What happened to Lorna Skirving? To Howie?'

He shook his head. 'I can't,' he said. Started crying again, snot coming down his nose. 'I can't,

McCoy. I can't, I just can't.' He sat there sobbing, shoulders shaking up and down.

McCoy sighed, pulled a hanky out the box, handed it to him. Knew he'd gone too far, too soon.

They stood at the bar and watched Bobby come back on stage, sing another number. Note perfect. Like nothing had ever happened. Like the old pro he was.

'What now?' asked Wattie over the noise of 'You Need Hands'.

'Let's get out of here, can't hear myself think.'

Back outside the snow was still coming down. McCoy looked up at the big flakes whirling through the orange circles of the streetlights. His hand was sore, ribs were sore. No painkillers left. Wattie was standing under the awning watching the people going in and out the brightly lit chippy across the road. He buttoned up his raincoat, pulled his scarf a bit tighter.

'So what happens now?' he asked.

'Nothing,' said McCoy. 'Nothing happens at all.'

'What do you mean? You heard Bobby.'

'Aye, I heard Bobby. The Dunlops like kinky sex. That's all he said. Nothing we can use, nothing that takes us anywhere. Bobby's never going to tell us anything, he's a fucking nervous wreck. Scared for his life. Can't say I blame him. We're in the same place we were before we spoke to him. Time's up.'

'What's up with you?'

McCoy shook his head. 'What's up with me? What d'you think's up with me? I've been kicked to fuck, my hand's killing me, my insides are killing me. I've got a boss who' – he looked at his watch – 'is shutting this case down in less than two hours. Far as he's concerned he's got two murders sewn up. One killer dead, the other one singing like a canary. And I've got some disgruntled old poof who says Dunlop and his son like fucking the same girl at the same time. It's no nice, but it's no a crime last time I looked. In other words, fuck all. What do you want me to do?'

Wattie stepped back from him. 'Christ, okay. Keep your fucking hair on. Just no like you to give up.'

'I tried last time and where did it get me, eh? I almost lost my job. So this time I'm taking the easy road just like I've been told. Everybody's happy. Fuck them. If they don't care, why should I?'

Wattie shrugged. 'That's it then, is it? Case closed, we move on?'

'Looks like it. That okay with you?' he said, knowing he sounded like a petulant teenager, just couldn't stop himself.

'Fuck sake, McCoy. Don't know what you're angry with me for. You're the one that's been dragging me around, wasting time trying to pin something on the Dunlops. Bobby's almost there and you're backing off, and now it's all my fault? Fuck off. It's not my fault you gave up last time—'

'I didn't give up, I went—'

'Aye, went up there pissed is what I heard. Gave the Dunlops the perfect excuse to fuck you over. Shot yourself in the foot. Doesn't come as much of a fucking surprise.'

If he hadn't slipped, his fist would have connected square with Wattie's jaw. As it was, all that happened was he hit him a half-blow on the shoulder and ended up on his arse in the snow. Wattie didn't say anything, just walked away and left him there. Headed off down Hawthorn Street, hand held up for a passing cab.

Didn't even know if she'd be in, didn't have her phone number to call. He parked the car on Hillhead Street, whole body hurting as he stepped down onto the pavement. He looked up; there was a light on at least, had to be a good sign. There was a more than even chance he was going to get the bum's rush but it was worth a try.

He climbed the stairs. Top floor – would be, wouldn't it? – and chapped on the door. A fiddling with the locks and Susan pulled it open. Stood there, looking at him.

'Try again?' he asked. 'I'm sorry I was a dick. Wasn't sure if you'd want to see me again.'

'I don't.'

'Come on, what have you got to lose?'

'What have I got to gain?' she said and closed the door.

He stood there looking at it, at the peeling paint

and the handwritten label with 'Thomas' written on it.

Last try. He bent down, pushed the letterbox open and shouted through. 'You get to examine a member of the Glasgow Police close up. The enemy in all its horrible detail.'

Nothing. Tried again. 'And I'm really horrible, believe me.'

Sound of steps, lock turning, door opened again.

Susan was standing there with half a smile on her face. 'That it? That what you've got to offer? How much of an arse you are?'

'Think yourself lucky. You can make me the star of your thesis. Tell everyone how a Glasgow polis confirmed all your worst fears.'

She considered. 'If you want a drink AND you promise not to be an arse, you can come in for ten minutes.'

He went to step over the threshold. She held her hand up, stopped him. 'Just to be clear. If you think I'm sleeping with you, you're even stupider than I thought.'

'I probably am, but I get the message. Loud and clear.'

She held the door open and he walked in.

She put two glasses down on the kitchen table, opened a bottle of red. Sat down. The flat was warm, candles burning on the table casting a dim light over the old range and a giant Cuban flag pinned to the wall. Record player clicked and a new album fell. *Blonde on Blonde.*

'There. One drink.'

She pushed a half-full tumbler across the table at him.

'What are you really here for, McCoy?' she asked.

'To see you.'

She sat back, didn't look convinced. 'Now why would you want to come and visit me? Must be loads of girls you could go and see, cop groupies, all sorts.'

'There are. They're queuing up. But I wanted to see you.'

'That right? Why's that? You wanted to have another conversation about how patriarchy builds in an expectation that women will do what men want?'

'Wasn't going to be my first choice.'

'Okay, maybe how the female officers at the station spend most of their time being told to make tea for the lads?' She took a sip of her wine. 'And the worst thing is they do it.'

'Or my second.'

'Okay, a long discussion about the failure of society to acknowledge the continuing conditioning of girls to expect less and be happy about it?'

'You finished?' he asked.

'Or maybe you just want to jump my bones?'

'Maybe I do.'

'You're limping, grimacing when you lift your glass up, all battered and bruised. You sure you're up to it?'

He nodded.

'Shame you're never going to find out.'

McCoy's face fell. He looked up and she was grinning at him. 'What's up? Can't take a joke?'

She picked up the two glasses, took his hand, led him out the kitchen. Bob Dylan sang on, asking the sad-eyed lady if he should wait.

When he woke up, she was propped up on one elbow looking at him. He yawned, stretched. She was still looking at him.

'What?'

She smiled. 'You're lying here in my bed and I don't know anything about you.'

'Yes, you do. I'm a polis, you think I'm a male chauvinist pig and contrary to your fears I was more than up to the job.'

She shook her head. 'Add arrogant bastard.' She leant over to the bedside table, got her wee tobacco tin and opened it, started rolling up. 'Tell me something.'

'What? What do you want to know?'

'Cowie said you had a rough childhood, grew up in care?'

'Did he now? Good old Cowie. Yep, wasn't much fun.'

'What happened to your parents?'

He sighed, didn't want to go through this now. Or any other time.

'My dad's an alkie. My mum fucked off when I was about three. My dad tried to cope but he couldn't. Too busy drinking.'

272

'That's rough. Was there no one else around?'
'Yep. My uncle Tommy. Was worse than my dad.'
'So how did . . .'
'You sure you want to hear this?'
She nodded.
'Polis found me wandering about Saracen Street at eleven at night looking for my dad.'
'Jesus.'
'My dad got charged with child cruelty and I got sent to a foster home. That's pretty much how it went until I was sixteen. Too old for care. Bloke that was my foster dad at the time was the only good one I had. Took me along to the station and that was that.'
She lit the cigarette, took a drag, handed it to him.
'I joined the force.'
'So you could help other boys like you maybe?'
'No, because I was used to doing what I was told. You get that way in the homes. Just do what they say right away. Saves you a beating.'
'Where did your mum go?' she asked.
He didn't reply.
'Sorry, if you don't want to talk about it I—'
He held his hand up, stopped her. 'It's okay.' He took a deep drag, blew it out. 'I'd only just started on the beat, was nineteen or so, walking up Saracen Street and I meet this woman who used to live next to us in Vulcan Street. Said she'd met my mum a year or so ago. This woman had been in the hospital for her nerves, as she called it. Met her in there.'

'Her nerves?'

'She was in Woodilee. Big asylum out Lenzie way.'

'And your mum was in there?'

'Had been there for almost ten years.'

Susan sat back against the headboard.

'You asked,' said McCoy. 'Bet you wish you hadn't now.'

'I'm sorry,' she said.

'What for?' he asked. 'It happens. I came out it better than most. There's only one thing about it that's really damaged me, that's had an effect.'

'What?' she asked, sounding concerned. 'What's that?'

'I need to have a cup of tea within five minutes of waking up and I don't know why but I can't make it myself. Can you help a poor damaged soul?'

She stubbed the cigarette out on the tin lid. Pulled the covers back and got out of bed. 'You, McCoy, are one fucking arsehole.'

He grinned. 'One sugar, please.'

9TH JANUARY 1973

CHAPTER 28

'What's all that bloody noise about?'

Wattie's landlady went over to the window and pulled the net curtain aside. Wattie was trying to ignore her, manfully chewing his way through a roll filled with very fatty and very undercooked bacon. She'd a point, though. A car horn had been going on and off for the past couple of minutes.

'Bloody cheek of him. Look.'

Wattie sighed, swallowed half the roll down with a swig of tea, walked over to the window. McCoy was leaning on the side of an unmarked Viva, reading the paper. He dropped his fag, ground it with his shoe, reached into the open car window and pressed the horn again. He was the last person Wattie expected to see that morning. He ignored the landlady's moaning, got his coat and scarf from the stand in the hall, and went out to see what McCoy had to say for himself.

McCoy heard the front door of the house open, folded his paper and put it in his coat pocket. 'You fit? Come on.'

'That it?' asked Wattie, walking down the path.

'Is what it?' he said, and then it dawned. 'Jesus Christ'. He rolled his eyes, then tried to look sincere, didn't work very well. 'I, Harry Vincent McCoy, humbly apologise for trying to punch you yesterday when you were being a cunt. That do you?'

Despite himself Wattie was smiling. 'Suppose it'll have to. What you doing here anyway?'

'We need to be somewhere. Hurry up, I'm freezing.'

McCoy turned the ignition over as Wattie got in, big grin on his face.

'What's up with you?' asked McCoy.

'Vincent?'

'Think yourself lucky you're a prod,' said McCoy. 'I could have been Ignatius.'

The Albany was the best hotel in Glasgow. Didn't stop it being one of the ugliest as well. It was a squat brown skyscraper on the edge of town near the motorway. Flags of every European country jutted out above the entrance, cracking and flapping in the wind. As they pulled up the doormen were busy for once. Attending to men in suits getting out of chauffeur-driven jags, opening doors of taxis full of noisy reporters. They watched as a photographer tried to get himself, two bags and a tripod through the revolving doors.

'What's going on here, then?' asked Wattie.

'Just thought we'd keep our oar in, seeing you were so disappointed in me last night.' He checked his watch. 'Shite, come on, we're going to miss it.'

They hurried through the big brass doors, flashing their badges at a woman with a clipboard and a face like she was chewing a wasp. A sign on an easel in the thickly carpeted foyer directed them up to the Alexander Function Suite. They climbed up the two flights of stairs and made it just as they were closing the wooden doors.

Inside there was a stage set up, rows of gold chairs laid out like pews facing it. Every chair was filled. McCoy recognised some of them, reporters and photographers from *The Herald* and the *Record* mostly. There were even a couple of TV crews, serious-looking men with big heavy cameras and earphones. The air was thick, cigarette smoke sitting above them all like fog. McCoy and Wattie made their way up to the back and stood with the other latecomers lining the wall. Wattie turned to ask McCoy what the fuck they were doing there just as a man in a business suit and glasses appeared on the stage calling for quiet. He waited patiently for the general hubbub of chat to die, leant forward into the microphone and began.

'Good morning, gentlemen. Glad to see so many of you could make it. Let me run through what's going to happen this morning. Mr Forfar and Lord Dunlop will be on stage in a couple of minutes. They will each read a prepared statement, shake hands for the photos and then there will be a short, and I mean short, question and answer period. I'd prefer questions from the financial papers, but if you tabloid boys and girls – and yes that means you, Mary' – the crowd laughed as a woman stood up and took a small bow – 'want to ask questions, make it about the announcement please, nothing else. Got me?' There was a general grumble of disapproval, a few 'Aye, that'll be right.'

'Thought you'd given up on the Dunlops?' asked Wattie.

'Aye, and I thought you'd given up being a smart arse,' said McCoy, grabbing a handout. Two sheets of thick paper stapled together, company logos at the top of each. He started skimming it. *Proud and pleased to announce a dynamic new chapter in the life of the* Glasgow Citizen, *Scotland's oldest running newspaper. James Forfar, long line of newspaper publishers, awarded OBE for his charity work. Lord Dunlop, major force in the Scottish business community.* Usual bollocks. A squeal of feedback and they turned to see the man back on stage at the podium, Dunlop and Forfar standing in the wings.

Flashbulbs popped as they walked forward. Gray Dunlop looked immaculate as ever. Chalk-stripe suit, hair swept back, silver watch chain in his waistcoat. James Forfar didn't. Looked like a bank manager from Arbroath. Dark suit, burgundy tie, toothbrush moustache and a face as long as a wet weekend. From what McCoy could remember he was a Wee Free, strict Baptist, something like that, all blood and thunder. No unions in the workplace, no women at the paper, no working on Sundays. Dunlop smiled and walked towards the podium.

'Good morning,' he said and the room immediately

went quiet. He had presence if nothing else. 'James has graciously asked me to begin.' He turned and acknowledged Forfar, standing off to his left. Didn't look too gracious to McCoy. 'Today is a historic one for James, myself and the companies we represent. So it gives me great pleasure to announce that as of today there will be a merger between the Dunlop Trust and Forfar Publishing.'

As Dunlop rattled on about the new opportunities and a combination of strengths, McCoy's eyes drifted round the room, caught sight of Dunlop Junior. He was sitting in the front row, same chalk-stripe suit, same swept-back hair as his father. Peas in a pod. He thought about what Bobby had told them. Pictured the two of them with Lorna Skirving. Wasn't a pretty picture. What would make a man want to fuck some girl in front of his son? Power? Showing him who's boss? Was beyond McCoy. Not quite sure what was in it for Dunlop Junior. either. Was evidence that he liked stubbing cigarettes out on girls about enough to make him believe Teddy Dunlop had killed Isabel Garvey? He wasn't sure any more. Was that too big a leap to take? Suppose that was up to Wattie and Murray to find out.

Forfar was on now, flat monotone rendering anything he was saying too boring to listen to. The crowd in front of him had already lost interest, had started fidgeting and whispering. McCoy'd lost interest too; something else Bobby said last night was bothering him, about 'Howie trying to

281

save that girl'. As far as McCoy knew, Howie Nairn never did a favour for anyone, especially not a woman. They didn't exist to Howie; unless they were serving him in a pub, he wasn't interested. Why would he be bothered about trying to save Lorna Skirving?

'Fuck.'

He didn't realise he'd said it out loud until the back rows of the audience turned to look at him. He held his hands up in apology and nudged Wattie.

'Come on. We're going.'

They made their way through the crowd to general mutters of disapproval. Wattie managed to stand on the foot of a wee fat bloke with a notepad who tutted loudly and barked, 'Watch where you're bloody going.' More people turned to see what was happening, glad of the diversion.

Forfar droned on regardless, but McCoy saw Dunlop look towards the back of the room, shielding his eyes from the lights, trying to see. His eyes met McCoy's. McCoy tugged his imaginary forelock. Dunlop just looked at him, face blank, blue eyes taking everything in.

CHAPTER 29

Bobby Thorne's house was a trim wee bungalow in King's Park, the very vision of Southside respectability. Neat flowerbeds in the garden, net curtains in the windows, same as all the others in the street. Bobby was standing at the open door with clipboard in hand, tartan slacks and a yellow V-neck jumper, looked like he was en route for the nineteenth hole. He was pointing at various boxes as they were taken out, telling the movers what was going in the van and what wasn't. Wattie and McCoy walked up the driveway, stepping aside to let a boy with a cardboard box marked 'Mementos' get past.

'Where's this stuff going, son?' asked McCoy.

'Into the van,' he said, anxious to get out of the snow that was beginning to fall again.

McCoy wasn't sure if he was being cheeky or just thick. He tried again. 'After that?'

'Goes to the depot, then it's going on the international van. Off to Spain, I think.'

Bobby looked up from his clipboard and saw them. Tried to arrange his face to look happy about it. Didn't really succeed.

'You boys again? Twice in two days? People will talk.'

'You off somewhere, Bobby?' asked McCoy, watching the procession of boxes leaving the house.

'Aye. Spain, Benidorm. Going to stay with my sister for a while.'

McCoy looked up at the darkening sky. 'Don't blame you; weather's getting bad again. You no going to ask us in?'

They sat at the kitchen table while Bobby rummaged in a box full of scrunched-up news-papers, trying to find some mugs. Wasn't having much luck. 'You know what, Bobby, we're no really here for a cup of tea. There was something you said last night; I've been thinking about it.'

'What's that?' he asked suspiciously.

'Howie wanted to help that girl – that's what you said, wasn't it?'

Bobby nodded, looked wary.

'Well, I knew Howie and there is no fucking way he was going to help some lassie he didn't know out the goodness of his heart.'

'You didn't know Howie like I knew—'

McCoy held his hand up. 'Save it, Bobby.' He looked round at the half-packed boxes, the brighter patches left on the orange patterned wallpaper where pictures had been hung. 'That the plan, is it? Ditch this place for a wee retirement on the Costa del Sol? Singing in a few hotels, watching the young lads on the beach in their swimmers?

Miles away from shitey Glasgow and miles away from the Dunlops. Sounds ideal. Don't blame you. Pity, though.'

Bobby sat down on one of the kitchen chairs. 'What's a pity?' he asked nervously.

'That I'm going to stop you going.'

He shook his head. 'No way, you can't do that.'

'Oh, yes I can,' said McCoy. 'And I will. So why don't you make us a cup of tea after all and tell us the story, eh? I don't want you, Bobby – to be honest, I don't give a shite about you – but I want the Dunlops and I'm going to get them. You don't want to talk, that's fine, keep your trap shut, but you'll be stuck here in Glasgow while I make sure they know we've had a wee chat.'

'You wouldnae do that.'

'Oh, yes I would, Bobby. As I said, I couldn't give two fucks about you.' He leant back in his chair, smiled. 'Or you can start talking and the Dunlops won't know a thing about you and me.'

Wattie leant forward, tapped the kettle on the table in front of him. 'Two sugars in mine, thank you, Mr Thorne.'

Bobby disappeared for a while and reappeared with large brown hardback envelope in his hand. 'I never told you this. My name doesn't go near the Dunlops and you let me get the flight tomorrow.'

McCoy nodded.

Bobby sat down, put the envelope on the table in front of him. 'Howie knew Jimmy Gibbs. Knew him from when he was a polis; he lifted him a few times. Called him out the blue a couple of months ago and arranged to meet up. Jimmy knew what Howie was.'

'A criminal, you mean?'

Bobby shook his head. 'Queer. Didnae have any qualms about it. Offered him a deal. The Dunlops were having someone over from America, important business guy, they were having a party for him and they wanted Howie to come. Apparently Howie was his type, would pay him thirty quid to go, and if Howie and this guy got friendly he'd get another thirty.'

'And what did you think about that?'

'Me?' Bobby shrugged. 'Howie was Howie. I learnt long ago not to worry about him having his fun, meant nothing. He always came back to me. That was the important thing.'

McCoy might have believed him more if his speech hadn't sounded so rehearsed. Sounded like he'd got used to having to say it, whether he believed it or not.

'So?' he asked.

'So he went. Was like no kind of party Howie had ever been to, like anyone had ever been to. Drink, drugs, boys, girls, all sorts. He gets talking to Jimmy Gibbs while he's there. He was out of it on something – acid, dope. Kept asking Howie if he wanted anything. Told him he had everything there. Didnae take it, though, the free drink was enough for Howie.'

He took a drink of the tea, lit up a Kensitas and blew the smoke into the air. Wringing the moment dry like the old ham he was.

'So Jimmy tells him to come and see this, takes him into another room with a big two-way mirror in it. That's Jimmy Gibbs' thing, you know, likes to watch and he likes to take photos.'

He tapped the envelope with his finger and pushed it over to McCoy.

McCoy opened it. A dozen or so glossy black and white eight by tens. Some naked girl lying on a bed laughing, wrists tied to the bedposts, another girl bent over her, face in between her legs. Next one was of a big room, looked like an attic. The whole thing was painted white, walls, floor, everything. Even with the mask on he recognised Jimmy Gibbs.

'That's Tommy Malone,' said Wattie, pointing at the picture.

Malone was sitting at Gibbs's feet. He was naked, big smile on his face, arm round a girl with a pentangle painted on her chest. Jimmy Gibbs standing behind them with a hard-on and a severed goat's head in his hand. The blood was dripping from its neck, splashing down onto Malone and the girl.

Next one was of an old man with nothing but a zipped leather hood on. He was bent over a thing that looked a bit like one of the pommel horses you got in a school gym, Howie Nairn fucking him from behind. There were more. More sex, more tied-up people, more beds, more rooms. And there was one that stopped him dead. Felt like the breath had been knocked out of him. He looked up. 'You got anything to drink here?' Bobby nodded, asked Wattie to help him take a couple of boxes off the top of a pile. McCoy slipped the bottom photo into his coat pocket while they were doing it, put the pile back on the table.

'Who are all these people?'

Bobby had found a bottle of whisky, was tipping a slug into each of their mugs. 'Pros, runaways he found at the bus station, rich kids looking for kicks, people that worked on the estate, anyone. Gibbs picked them up everywhere.'

'And Howie had a bright idea, wanted to use the pictures as blackmail.' Was more of a statement than a question.

Bobby nodded. 'He came back full of it. He'd seen someone he knew there, some judge in a pair of frilly knickers getting walked on by a girl in stilettos. Wasn't hard to see how it could work.'

'So what went wrong?'

'The judge didn't play ball like he thought he would. He went straight to Gibbs, told him what was going on. Next thing Howie gets picked up with three shotguns in the boot of his car. You know Howie, he wasn't stupid, he'd never carry anything like that in his car. They planted them.

Got him sent back inside, teach him a lesson, cunts that they are.'

McCoy looked at the photos again. 'What's all this black magic stuff about? That come from Gibbs?'

Bobby nodded. 'He was really serious about it, tried to talk Howie into coming along to one of his ceremonies, as he called it. Howie was having none of it. He'd seen enough of Gibbs and Broughton House. Gibbs had a bunch of kids hanging on him, following him about. All of them off their heads on acid. Thought he was a wizard or some shite. Thought he could do anything. And he wasn't telling them anything different. Was loving it.'

'Like that Charles Manson,' said Wattie.

Bobby nodded. 'That's what Howie said.'

McCoy tapped one of the photos. 'This boy, Tommy Malone. He one of them? One of his followers?' Bobby nodded. 'So let me get this straight. Howie gets me up to Barlinnie, tells me about the girl working in the restaurant. Thought that after Malone had killed the girl I'd get him and he'd lead back to the Dunlops? That was the plan?'

'Think so, except he didn't know the boy would kill himself. He thought you'd get him and he'd spill the whole thing. Gibbs, the parties at Broughton House, everything.'

'Why'd he pick me? Hardly knew me from Adam. How'd he know I had history with them?'

'Gibbs. Gibbs told him.'

'Could Gibbs make Malone kill the girl then kill himself?'

Bobby shrugged. 'Maybe. Howie said they were like disciples, do anything he said. Gibbs told him he'd done it before. Some girl got pregnant, been sleeping with Teddy, the son. Killed herself. Said he made her do it.'

McCoy looked at the photo again. Gibbs grinning, holding up the goat's head, blood dripping from it, dripping onto Tommy Malone's lonely stupid head. No parents, just out of Nazareth House, stuffed full of drugs, girls that would fuck him on Gibbs' say-so. No wonder he fell for it. Fell deep.

'How'd he know about it? How'd Howie know to get me into jail?'

'He was in court the day before. The van that took them through town stopped at a set of lights. He saw Malone, said he looked mad, out of it. Knew something had to be up for him to be away from the estate. Lorna Skirving was his best guess.'

'She wasn't pregnant, though,' said Wattie. 'Why her?'

'She couldn't keep her mouth shut. Dunlop was already worried about it. She'd started blabbing, talking to some prostitute's group or something. Money and a couple of bits of jewellery had gone missing from Broughton House. She was trouble. Could only see it getting worse.'

McCoy picked up another picture. Teddy Dunlop

kneeling on a bed, shoving his dick into a girl's mouth, grasping her hair, forcing her towards him. The girl was Lorna Skirving.

She was trying to look like she was enjoying it. Didn't look like she was. Picture'd been taken through the two-way mirror, must have been taken just as some light seeped in, someone opening the door maybe. You could see a faint reflection of the faces in the room looking through the mirror. One was Gibbs, head thrown back laughing. The other was a man looking intently through the mirror, middle-aged, moustache, dinner suit on.

'Fuck's sake,' Wattie said under his breath. 'Fuck me. Give us that picture.'

Bobby handed it to him, a 'please yourself' expression on his face. Wattie took it, peered at it closely.

'What?' said McCoy, him and Bobby staring. Wattie put the picture down on the table in front of them. Pointed. 'That's Gibbs, yes?' They nodded. 'Do you know who the other bloke is?'

They shook their heads.

'My mum kept scrapbooks, pictures of the royal family. She was mental for them. Me and my sister used to look at them when we were wee. Kept them in the display cupboard. Had about fifty of the bloody—'

'Fuck sake, Wattie!' said McCoy, exasperated.

'Sorry. That' – he tapped the picture again – 'if I'm not mistaken, is Lord Liddesdale.'

The two of them looked blank.

'The Duke of Cromarty.'

Still blank.

'He's the Queen's bloody cousin!'

'What?' said Bobby.

'He's the Queen's cousin, an equerry or whatever you call it.'

They all looked at the picture again. 'I wouldnae know him from Adam,' sniffed Bobby. 'No bad looking, though.'

McCoy put the pictures back in the envelope. Bobby held his hand out.

'Don't think so, Bobby. I need these. You fuck off to sunny Spain and I'll take care of them. Anyone asks, I got them from Howie's cell. Nothing to do with you. Okay?'

'You promise?'

'Cross my heart and hope to die.' He stood up, felt the photo in his coat pocket digging into his side. 'C'mon, Wattie, let's leave Bobby to his packing.'

The movers were outside, leaning against the van, reading the paper, waiting for the nod to start again.

'What do we do with the pictures?' asked Wattie.

'Play it by the book. Show them to Murray, let him deal with it. They're not going to let me anywhere near the Dunlops anyway.' He sat down in the driver's seat, padded his coat looking for his fags, pulled them out and realised he'd pulled out a wee jotter as well. Shite. It was Stevie Cooper's tally book the two lads had given him.

Been so doped up on painkillers the other night he'd forgotten to give him it.

'Need to make a stop on the way back, something I've forgotten to do.'

'What?'

'Drop something off, no take a minute.'

CHAPTER 30

Took them about half an hour to get back across the city. Wattie checked in with the shop on the radio while McCoy looked out the window, watched Glasgow grinding to a halt in the snow, tried not to think about the photo in his back pocket.

'You and Murray got a time to interview Teddy Dunlop?' asked McCoy.

Wattie grunted. 'Joking, aren't you? His lawyer's Archie Lomax. From what I hear we'll be lucky to get near him before next year. Murray's got the high-ups at Central leaning on him, though.'

Snow was coming down harder now, getting misty as well. Wattie switched the headlights on. 'About here, is it?' he asked, rubbing at the windscreen with a dirty chamois cloth. 'Cannae see a bloody thing.'

McCoy pointed at the road running off to the right. 'Drop me here.' He could still feel the rolled-up picture in his pocket. Wasn't quite sure why he'd hid it away, was a base reaction, didn't even think about it. Didn't want to think about it now.

Wattie pulled over and suddenly realised where they were. Memen Road in Springburn. Even he'd heard of that. 'You're no going in there, are you? You'll need a bloody armed guard. They'll smell you a mile off.'

McCoy opened the door, letting a blast of icy air into the car. 'If I'm no back in twenty minutes, you can send in the the Heroes of Telemark.'

Wattie was right to be worried. Memen Road was where angels and polis feared to tread. Was where the council had dumped all the problem tenants. The family gangs of villains, people with feral kids, the alkies, the wife beaters, the borderline insane. Council called it containment. Everyone else called it no-man's-land.

McCoy started walking, ignored the belligerent stares of two ten-year-olds sitting on a wall, anorak hoods up, crisp packet full of glue passing between them. The fences separating the gardens had long been pushed over or torn apart. Pavement and the gardens had become one long line of broken prams, overturned bins and the occasional dumped fridge. The grass, or what was left of it, already covered with a thin layer of the falling snow. McCoy had his head down as he walked, partly to stay out the wind and partly because he was looking out for dog shit or anything worse. Rumour was some copper had stood on an aborted foetus in a carrier bag last year.

He was scanning the ground, didn't see them

until they were right on him. Three big lads. All long leather coats, sideburns and wide flared trousers flapping in the wind. One of them had lost an eye; scar tissue and a weeping slot all that was left. He stood squarely in front of him, put his thumbs in his belt. 'Fuck you want?' he asked. McCoy reached for his badge. 'I know you're fucking polis. I asked what you wanted.'

'Cooper,' he said. 'Tell him McCoy's here.'

Stevie Cooper had gradually colonised all the flats in the last two closes of the street. A kind of fortress guarded by lads looking to get onto his team on one side, old thread works and about half a mile of industrial wasteland on the other. About as far from the long arm of the law as you could get and still be in Glasgow. The Cyclops whistled and a wee girl, seven or eight, appeared out of nowhere. McCoy shook his head. It was January, snow coming down in pelters and all she had on was a wee skirt and a hand-knitted cardigan over a filthy Mickey Mouse T-shirt. Sodden plimsolls completed the misery. Cyclops barked at her, 'Tell Stevie McCoy's here.'

The wee girl nodded seriously and ran off towards the last tenement. The three keepers of the flame stood around trying to look hard. Pinched faces, hands in pockets, stomping their platform boots on the ground to keep warm.

'You no trip over in those things?' McCoy asked amiably. No response. The wee girl came running back.

'He's okay,' she said, panting, breath clouding out in the cold air in front of her. 'Let him through.'

McCoy followed her across the gardens, picking his way between the broken bricks and the icy puddles. She stopped at the last close entrance. 'Fourth floor,' she said, holding out her hand.

McCoy gave her ten pence and she looked at it disgusted.

'Fair enough,' he said, handing over a new fifty pence. 'Away and buy yourself some chips. You must be freezing.'

Was as cold inside the block as out. Most of the flats seemed to be empty, doors either boarded over or kicked in. A pipe had burst somewhere, causing a dripping river of ice on the stairs. McCoy trudged up past a huge 'FLEET COUNTRY' spray-painted on a landing in bright red. Must be Stevie reliving his youth; he'd left those chancers in his wake a long time ago. The fourth-floor flat had a door. A thick wooden one with a brand-new deadlock on it. McCoy knocked, waited as the bolts were drawn and keys were turned. Eventually Billy Weir stuck his head round the door.

'Sorry bout that, some coppers with a big baton thing tried to get in last week. Won't try that again. How's you?' he said, holding out his hand.

McCoy shook it. He liked Billy, he was smart; Cooper thought so too, he'd only come out Barlinnie a year or so ago and he was already being treated as his second-in-command. He held the door open.

297

'He'll no be a minute, come on through.'

McCoy followed him into the warm kitchen, trying to ignore the screams and thumps coming from the room next door. Weir sat down at the Formica table, rolled up the sleeves of his Toulouse-Lautrec print shirt and went back to chopping and dividing the huge mound of speed on the table with a metal ruler. Pushing it back and forward, cutting the powder finer.

'Cup of tea?'

A girl of sixteen or so, skirt barely covering her arse, figure that would stop a clock, was standing by the sink, fag in red-lipsticked mouth. McCoy shook his head, sat down, and that's when he saw him. There was a man handcuffed to the range, kneeling down, trying to make himself as inconspicuous as possible. He'd blood all over his face, nose was at a crazy angle. He tried to smile at McCoy, way a whipped dog would smile if it could. He'd a dark piss stain all down the front of his trousers; smell was coming off him in waves. McCoy nodded down at him.

'What's going on there then?'

Weir looked at the man like he was part of the furniture. 'He's next. Thieving cunt that he is.'

'I'm no, I'm no, it wasnae—'

He only managed to get that much out before Weir leant over and booted him in the stomach. 'Cooper should be done by now,' he said, standing up and booting the man again for luck. 'C'mon through.'

No screams and grunts from behind the door any more, just whimpering. Weir knocked and pushed it open.

'Boss? You okay?'

Cooper was standing in the middle of the empty room. No furniture, just torn floral wallpaper and a stained wooden floor. His usual jeans and short-sleeved shirt were streaked in blood, tidy quiff all over the place. He'd a bottle of Irn-Bru up at his mouth, draining it in long slugs. The whimpering was coming from a man in the corner. He'd blue underpants on and one sock, nothing else. His eyes were swollen shut, scalp cut up, half his hair gone. The foot that didn't have a sock was thick with dark blood, looked like he was missing a couple of toes.

Cooper looked at McCoy over the bottle, eyes glassy and unfocused. McCoy had seen him like this before. Went like this before he ran straight into another gang with razors in each hand, after someone had said the wrong thing, said no when he wanted to hear yes. McCoy hadn't wanted to be around him then, didn't want to be around him now.

'I'm busy,' he said, looking away.

McCoy reached into his coat and pulled out the tally book. 'They owe you a tenner, other than that it's all there.'

Cooper nodded to Weir. He took the book off him and checked the money inside. Nodded. 'Hundred and ninety quid and the tally book.'

Cooper pulled out a couple of pills from his pocket and swallowed them over with the last of the Irn-Bru, then lobbed the bottle at the brick hole where the fireplace had been. It smashed, joined the dozen or so others that had been thrown there before. There was a wee battered coffee table in the corner, a pile of folded shirts and jeans with dry-cleaning tags sitting on it next to four or five different carving knives, a couple of pairs of pliers and a pistol. Cooper walked over, picked up one of the knives, judged the weight of it, picked up another.

'Good wee doggy you are, McCoy, get things done no fuss.'

He was absent-mindedly twisting the tip of the knife into his thigh, oblivious to the hole in his jeans he was making and to the blood running down his leg. He reached into his back pocket and pulled out a roll of fifties. Peeled off five and held them out.

'A tip.'

McCoy shook his head. 'Was a favour, Stevie, don't worry about it.'

'C'mere, you cheeky cunt.'

McCoy knew better than to argue with him in this state. He walked over and Cooper tucked the notes into his top pocket. Was a smell coming off him, something chemical, blood and pennies. Cooper smiled, pulled him close, whispered in his ear.

'You and me, McCoy. You won't let me down.

You and me.' He ran his knuckles across his head, pushed him away laughing. 'Now beat it. I've got stuff to do here.'

McCoy turned to go, anxious to get away.

'By the way,' said Weir. 'Who was it?'

McCoy shrugged. 'Just two daft boys. A thin one and a fat one that wasn't all there. Crapping themselves. Nobodies.'

McCoy just managed to shut the door before the begging started. He stood there listening as it was silenced by what sounded like a kick. He realised the girl in the kitchen was watching him.

'You all right?' she asked. 'Look like you've seen a ghost.'

He nodded. A scream came from behind the door, a thump then another scream.

'How d'you stand it?' he asked her.

'Stand what?' she said.

CHAPTER 31

A fist rapped at the door.

'What you doing in there, you dirty bastard?'

'Fuck off,' said McCoy.

Thomson walked away laughing, shoes echoing on the tiles. Funny thing is, he wasn't that far wrong. McCoy was sitting in a toilet cubicle looking at dirty pictures. Well, one picture, the one that he'd put in his coat. It was a picture of the swimming pool at Broughton House where they'd interviewed Gibbs. It was night-time, pool lit up. There was a rug down on the tiles, two girls on it, both nude, one of them Lorna Skirving.

A crowd of men and a couple of women were looking on. Dunlop was there, silk dressing gown, polite smile on his face, hand in his pocket. Could have been judging the hydrangeas at the county show. Gibbs too, Super 8 camera in hand, even Tommy Malone. It was the figure at the side that was the problem. He'd a towel round his waist, podgy body leaning forward to making sure he could see what was going on. Alasdair Cowie.

He could hear the toilet doors opening again,

two uniforms started pissing in the urinals moaning about how cold it was on the beat. He wanted to give Cowie a chance. Almost ten years they'd been working together, that counted for something. He looked at all the other faces round the rug, scared he would recognise someone else. Just more middle-aged men, cigars in hand, hard-ons tenting their towels.

The uniforms left and McCoy stood up and unlocked the door. He put the picture back in his pocket and went over to the washbasins, wet his hands and rubbed them on the hard, yellow lump of soap on the spindle. He'd just finished when the door swung open, laughter. Wattie walked in, Cowie behind him, both of them smiling.

McCoy put his hand on Wattie's chest as he moved towards the urinals.

'Fuck off for a minute, eh?'

'What? I'm needing a piss.'

McCoy was looking past him, staring at Cowie. 'I need a word with Cowie. Private. Use the other ones.'

Wattie looked at him, looked at Cowie. Both of them silent, just looking at each other. He swore under his breath, turned and left them to it.

'Harry?' said Cowie uncertainly. 'What's up?'

McCoy reached into his pocket and handed him the photo. He took it, took him a couple of seconds to realise he was in it, then looked up at McCoy.

'Quite a line-up, eh, Cowie? Jimmy Gibbs. Tommy Malone. Lord Dunlop. Lorna Skirving and her pal, of course,' said McCoy slowly. 'And you.'

Cowie leant back against the sinks, normal big florid face gone white, looked like he was going to pass out. 'Got any fags?'

McCoy passed him one; he took it, held it up at McCoy's lighter, hands shaking so much he could barely get it lit. He took a deep draw, blew it out, then held his hands up to his face, slumped down onto the sink and started to sob.

McCoy left him a minute or so, couldn't trust himself not to hit him. Cowie stood back up, found a hanky in his pocket, wiped at his face, tried to pull himself together.

'It was one night,' he said. 'You know what my situation is, wife cannae . . . Christ, what a mess.' He splashed some water on his face, turned to face McCoy.

'There's a woman works at the library at the university, Joan. I talked to her a few times when I was in there. One night I went into Curlers for a pint on the way home. She was in there with a couple of friends, all of them dressed up, bit drunk, stoned, I don't know. She called me over and we had a drink, she was laughing at my jokes, kept holding my arm.' He looked over at McCoy, tried a smile. 'I thought I was in there.'

McCoy didn't smile back, just flicked the end of his cigarette into the urinal. Waited.

'They were going to a party out near the Campsies, asked me to go with them. What was I going to say? We got in one of their cars, some posh Edinburgh bloke, a doctor. Soon as we got out of town they started lighting up joints, not my thing but I joined in, car was full of it anyway. Time we got there I was stoned out my box. Didn't realise where I was until later. Huge big modern place—'

'Broughton House,' interrupted McCoy.

Cowie nodded. 'Everyone just trooped into this big swimming pool bit, clothes were already lying everywhere. Towels being handed out. So I joined in.' He tried another smile. 'Proving to myself I was as free and liberated as all the rest of them.'

McCoy waited for him to carry on.

'There were women everywhere . . . People having sex in the pool, could hardly believe what was going on. Joan was all over me, smoked another joint, there was some kind of whistling, people shouting the show was about to begin. Two girls lying on a rug playing with each other, everyone standing round trying to pretend it was a usual Friday night, me included. Joan starting kissing my ear, telling me it was turning her on; we went for a wander, found some wee room with a couch in it . . .' He faded off. Tears in his eyes again.

'I swear, Harry, I didn't do anything. Didn't even speak to Lorna Skirving, never saw her again after that night.'

'Just waltzed into the Shish Mahal with the big news about her fucking autopsy. Never mentioned anything. It's not fucking on.'

'I wasn't sure it was her. I was so fucking out of it. I couldnae be sure, didn't seem worth telling you.'

'That right? Decide that, did you?'

'My wife—'

'Fuck you and fuck your wife, Cowie. Didn't care much about her that night, did ye?'

Cowie was shaking his head, tears running down his face, snot coming out his nose. 'I swear, Harry, swear on my life, that was it. One night when I didn't have to sit on the couch waiting to change her, carry her up to bed, lay out her medicine, listen to the clock fucking ticking and ticking.'

'If I find out you're lying to me, Cowie, I swear I'll crucify you. I mean it. I'll kick your fucking head in, then I'll take this picture to Murray and you'll be out on your arse, no pension, no nothing.'

Cowie was nodding, head still down. 'I'm not lying, Harry. I swear it. On my life.'

McCoy didn't want to look at him any more, was reminded of the man in Cooper's room, same terrified look, same pleading in his eyes. He folded up the photo, stuffed it into his pocket and left, Cowie shouting after him all the way down the corridor.

The two of them had been sitting at their desks for going on four hours. Shifts had changed; night guys had come in, half of them back out on calls already. McCoy looked at his watch. Half eight. He'd handed the photos over to Murray after he'd left Cowie, told him the story, told him who the man in the reflection was.

Murray had looked at them, scratching his stubble every so often, cursing quietly, then spent the rest of the afternoon in his office, door shut, phone glued to his ear. Chief Constable had been in and out a couple of times. Looked angrier than he usually did. Murray had told him and Wattie to sit tight, say nothing to nobody and wait. Which is what they'd done. Now McCoy had run out of fags and his empty stomach was gurgling, making itself heard. Chief Constable had appeared again twenty minutes ago, tall man in a business suit with him. Wattie was reading yesterday's *Record* for the third time when the door opened and Murray's head appeared.

'You two. In.'

The man in the suit was called Mr Cavendish, no further explanation. Whoever he was, he was in charge, Murray and the Chief fussing round him like waiters. He was sitting behind Murray's desk, short hair going grey at the sides, pinstripe suit, kind of face you wouldn't remember.

'Sit down,' he said without looking up. Wattie and McCoy sat down on the two orange plastic chairs, looked up at their bosses but their faces were set; they weren't giving anything away. This was Cavendish's deal all right. He finished flicking through the file on his desk, closed it and looked up at them.

'These are difficult times,' he said. 'A time for

difficult decisions. There are strikes in the ship-yards and in the mines, IRA bombs in London, power cuts. Our country is under siege. The last thing we need is another problem, another erosion of our values, another assault on our beliefs. It's up to us to protect it.'

McCoy was half listening, half trying to work out exactly who this guy was. Wattie was listening hard, looking terrified. Cavendish's suit was too expensive for him to be Special Branch, so was his accent, public school with a hint of Edinburgh. MI5 maybe? Home Office? Whoever he was, he was in full flow.

'It is our duty to make sure of the safe running of this country. That we keep order, irrespective of who threatens it. That we stay true to what is best for this country and its people, that—'

'Sorry to interrupt, Mr Cavendish, but what's that got to do with us?'

Cavendish didn't look happy about being inter-rupted. He sat back, narrowed his eyes. Murray and the Chief Constable looked like someone had thrown a bucket of cold water on them. McCoy knew he should've kept his mouth shut but he was tired, hungry and he needed a smoke. He'd done his bit and handed the pictures over, didn't much care about Cavendish, whoever he was, and his speech about the world teetering on the brink. He sat forward. In for a penny.

'You got us in here because I gave Chief Inspector Murray there a picture of Lord Liddesdale and

Jimmy Gibbs watching Lorna Skirving getting a cock shoved into her mouth. Teddy Dunlop's cock, to be exact. The same Lorna Skirving who was later murdered by a bloke who worked for Lord Dunlop. I've handed the pictures over, played by the book. I've been a good boy. So if you don't mind me asking, who the fuck are you?'

Wattie was looking between the two, looked terrified, eased over in his seat as far from McCoy as he could get.

Cavendish turned to Murray. 'As far as I understand, that particular case is now closed? The murderer shot himself at the scene.'

Murray nodded. Correct. 'It is closed,' he said tightly. 'And you, McCoy, you fucking behave yourself.'

'What point are you struggling to make, Mr McCoy?' asked Cavendish.

'You know fine well what I'm saying. Dunlop's up to his neck in this. I know it, Murray knows it and now you—'

'So what exactly is it we know, Mr McCoy?' he said icily. 'Do we have any proof of Lord Dunlop's involvement in the murder of this girl?'

McCoy looked at Wattie. His eyes were fixed firmly on the floor in front of him. No help there.

'No reason to look at him, Mr McCoy, it's a simple yes or no question. Do we have any proof?'

McCoy shook his head. 'Not yet, but if we had a bit more time—'

Cavendish held up his hand. 'I'm not sure we

need any more time. According to your superiors here and the procurator fiscal, the case was closed today. So as far as I can see there is nothing to be gained by anyone knowing about this picture.'

'What, you're telling me to just forget it exists?'

'Precisely so,' said Cavendish. 'And it's not just me who's telling you. You recently became a detective, which means you signed the Official Secrets Act. As of four o'clock this afternoon this photograph is covered by said act. Any discussion by you of its contents or indeed its very existence would mean your immediate arrest, the loss of your job and a lengthy jail penalty. All covered by a D-notice. No one would even know it had happened.' He pulled a sheet out the file in front of him and put it in front of Wattie, then took a silver fountain pen out his jacket.

'Mr Watson, could you sign it too, please?'

Wattie looked at Murray and the Chief. The Chief nodded. 'Go on, son. Sign it.'

McCoy watched him sign. 'You can't do this.'

Cavendish took the form back and tucked it into his file. 'I just did.'

'Aye, well, it won't finish there, I'm—'

'No, you're not. Whatever you think you are going to do, you're not. You're playing with the big boys now, Mr McCoy, and we don't play fair and we don't play nice.' He opened the manila file and McCoy caught a glimpse of his photo stapled to the corner of the top page.

'On the surface it looks like you've done rather

well. Detective at age thirty. A fast promotion for anyone, never mind a Catholic in the Glasgow force. Especially a Catholic with your kind of background. Children's homes and the like. Your superiors speak highly of you, say you're bright, clever, destined to go far.' He sat back, smiled. As welcoming as a shark. 'I, however, take a different view. A very different view.'

He picked up a page from the file, scanned it. 'It seems you have made rather a habit of harassing the Dunlops. Wild accusations of murder. Drunk on duty.' He tutted. 'Not very clever.' He looked over at him, at the black eye and scrapes on his face, the two fingers bandaged together. 'Looks like your reckless behaviour goes on unabated. Professionally and personally you are a mess.'

He replaced the page and picked up another. 'May as well go through it all while we're here, eh? Steven Paul Cooper. Runs most of the crime in the north of the city. Good friend of yours apparently; cosy little chats in his saunas and the like. Seems you're rather fond of trying out his merchandise.'

He put back the paper and closed the file. 'You know what's ironic, Mr McCoy? You sit here in front of me full of moral indignation and self-righteousness and yet it seems to me you're just another bent copper. A bent copper I would happily have got rid of were it not for the appeals from your superior officer here.'

McCoy looked at him, thought about the two

hundred and fifty quid in his top pocket and the nights with Janey and the drugs and the favours he'd done Cooper. Didn't know how Cavendish knew it all but he did.

Cavendish shut the file. 'Do we understand one another, Mr McCoy? Mr Watson? Understand what is at stake here?'

Wattie nodded. 'Yes, sir.'

McCoy stood up. 'Can we go now?' he asked Murray.

Murray looked at the Chief, who nodded. Cavendish stood up, held out his hand to shake. Wattie shook it. McCoy didn't. Cavendish shrugged, looked amused.

'I mean what I say, Mr McCoy. We play dirty, so forget all about that photograph. As far as you two are concerned it doesn't exist. If I ever hear different I'll destroy you, grind you into the dirt like the piece of worthless shit you are.' He smiled. 'Now fuck off out my sight. You're turning my stomach.'

CHAPTER 32

Wattie and McCoy walked out the back door of the station, anxious to get out and as far from Cavendish and what had happened as possible. A bottle-green MG turned into the backcourt, wheels kicking up slush. It stopped and Phyllis Gilroy manoeuvred herself out, all wrapped up in a sheepskin car coat, fur hat and leather gloves.

'Ah, Mr McCoy. Hoped I might run into you.' She ducked back into the wee sports car and got her briefcase off the back seat. 'Have something rather interesting for you.'

'What's that, then?' asked McCoy, mind elsewhere.

'Girl we found in the abandoned house, remember her?'

He nodded. 'Isabel Garvey.'

'That's the one.' She stopped, looked at them. 'What's up with you two anyway? Look like you've lost a fiver and found a shilling.'

McCoy shook his head. 'Nothing. Long day. The girl?'

'The girl indeed. We found a good few carpet fibres under her fingernails, she may have gripped onto it at some point during the evening. We couldn't identify the bloody stuff anywhere. Didn't match any of our standard domestic samples, right pain in the bahookey. Collins in the lab, smart boy, made it his mission to find out where they came from. Sent them off to some friend of his who works for the Met.'

'And?'

'And they came from the carpet in a car, it seems,' she said, taking off her hat and attempting to rescue her hairdo.

'Chas's car?'

She finished pushing and patting it into shape, checked it in the wing mirror, turned to them and smiled. 'Wouldn't think so. Not unless he's won the pools lately. Bloody stuff came from a Rolls-Royce Silver Cloud.'

Neither of them spoke as they drank their first pints, both too absorbed in what had just happened. They were sitting up the back of The Kiwi, as far as they could get from the crowd of cops coming off their shift gathered round the front door. McCoy hated The Kiwi, too near to the shop, too many coppers, but he wanted a drink soon as. Wattie was sitting there looking like he'd been hit by a truck, face ashen as he brought the last of his pint up to his lips.

'Another?' asked McCoy.

Wattie nodded, swallowed the dregs back, looked at him.

'What?'

'Think all that means I'm fucked, never going to get promoted?'

McCoy shook his head. 'Naw. Not you.' He smiled, tried to lighten the mood. 'Me on the other hand, I'm a dead man walking. Tennent's?'

He still looked terrible when McCoy brought the drinks back. He sighed, put the pints on the table, thought he'd be as well to just get it out the way. 'Okay, spit it out. What do you want to know?'

'That guy Cavendish. Who was he?'

McCoy shrugged. 'Don't know. Special Branch, Home Office, fuck knows. Whoever he was he's a cunt.'

Wattie wasn't looking at him, was rubbing his finger through the film of beer on the table, making lines. 'The things he said about you. They true?'

'Some of it. I know Stevie Cooper, we go back a long way, since we were wee boys. He tells me a couple of things, I tell him a couple of things. Like I told you, you need contacts in this game. I've got Cooper. Murray plays golf every so often with Naismith. Doesn't mean he's bent or I'm bent, it's just the way it is.'

'You ever take money from him?'

'Fuck off. Any more of that and I'm going to get offended. Of course I havenae. You ever seen me do anything bent?' Wattie shook his head. The necessary white lie believed. 'Cooper runs some girls and, bless me, Holy Father, for I have sinned,

I've slept with a few of them. Not all of us are as straight down the line as you.'

'What about you and the Dunlops?'

'Christ, Wattie, I've been interrogated enough today. Give us a break.' He sighed, may as well get it all out. 'Jimmy Gibbs was a good polis and then he wasn't, got caught up with all sorts and then he got done by Discipline. I got dragged through the shite with him because I worked with him and he didn't lift a finger to put them right. Thought me involved would take the heat off him. Then he gives the fucking Masons' handshake and gets invalided out, no questions asked, while I get parked on my arse in Kilmarnock for four months. I got pulled in every few days until they finally realised I was clean. Meanwhile Gibbs had got a job at the Dunlops', big car, good money. Him and Angela out on the town every weekend while I tried to stick my life back together.'

'So you went after him?'

McCoy shook his head. 'Naw, not that exciting. That girl killed herself on the Dunlop estate. I got sent out to have a look. Gibbs acted like the cunt he'd become. I went back that night after four hours in the pub, was going to tell him what I really thought, maybe give him a kicking, who knows. Trouble was Lord fucking Dunlop was back from London, so I started in on him instead. Not my finest hour.' He sat back, lit up. 'That okay with you?'

Wattie nodded.

'Thank fuck for that. Thought I was back up before the Discipline.' He waggled his empty glass. 'Now go and get us a pint.'

Three pints later they weren't feeling so bad. McCoy had told some of his old war stories, the funny ones. Man arrested for fucking his dog, time some jakey threw up all over Murray, the old chestnuts. Wattie put his glass down, was about to get them another when he remembered.

'Miss Gilroy. I forgot all about her, what she said.'

'Shouldn't have bothered remembering, no going to do you any good,' said McCoy.

'Dunlop has a Rolls-Royce, places him with the girl on the night she died.'

'I'm sure he does and I'm sure it does. Makes no fucking odds though, not after this afternoon. Do you want to go in tomorrow and start shouting about the Dunlops to Murray again?'

Wattie shook his head.

'No. Me neither. Thing about people like Dunlop is they don't forget. Behind all that money and accent he's just like any other thug. Holds a grudge until he's ready to do something about it. I'm barely hanging on by the skin of my teeth as it is. He gets angry again, losing my job will be the least of it. You'll learn, Wattie, some of them get away, nothing you can do. Just have to learn to fight another day. Get us a short as well.'

Wattie spent the next half-hour telling McCoy what a great team they were, how they were going to be pals forever. McCoy nodded, tried to look like he was listening hard, then put him in a taxi. He looked at his watch. Half eight. Better get a move on.

The cab dropped McCoy off at the Cartwheel at the bottom of Byres Road. Susan was already there, sitting at the table. Both of them ordered steak, bottle of red wine. Any awkwardness went with the first glass. He ended up telling her about his early days on the beat, his funny stories, party pieces. She laughed, made him tell the one about the burglar's false teeth twice. She'd interviewed Baby Strange the day before, found her 'amazing', wanted to maybe shift her thesis around, make it more about her. McCoy nodded, looked interested, didn't mention what she'd said about Broughton House, didn't want to spoil the atmosphere.

After their steaks, she made him have a tiramisu so she could have a spoonful then ate the whole thing. McCoy ordered another bottle of red wine and when it came they got the waiter to open it and took it with them, walked arm in arm up Byres Road, heading for her flat.

And now she was asleep, softly snoring beside McCoy. He'd tried to sleep but it was no use. He got out bed, pulled his trousers on and went into the kitchen where the gas fire was still on. He sat at the table, smoked a cigarette. Didn't mean to do it but the notepad was right in front of him.

He skimmed through it; lots of talk of female empowerment and the economic misogyny of conventional prostitution. He was about to give up when it caught his eye.

INT. *How have your relations with the police been?*

B.S. *What do you mean? (laughter)*

INT. *Have you ever been arrested?*

B.S. *Once, a long time ago. Nothing to do with prostitution. Shoplifting!*

INT. *The police . . .*

B.S. *Circles I work in now? They seem to have been taken care of, not really a problem. You meet some at parties, smoking dope, whatever, wouldn't know they were police unless they told you.*

INT. *And they get involved in the sexual side of things?*

B.S. *Sometimes.*

INT. *How?*

B.S. *The usual way! Sometimes it's a freebie to oil the wheels, as it were, and sometimes they come back as punters. Join in like everyone else.*

INT. *And they don't cause trouble?*

B.S. *No. Well, one did. Turned out to be a real creep.*

> INT. *How?*
>
> B.S. *Came to one of the parties and saw a girl there, she was a performer really.*
>
> INT. *Performer?*
>
> B.S. *Sex show, you know. Her and another girl. Anyway, found out where she lived, where she worked. Started turning up, harassing her. Told her he'd have her arrested unless she did what he wanted. Really creepy.*
>
> INT. *And this was when you had the house in Chelsea?*
>
> B.S. *No, it was here. Poor girl came to me for help. What could I do?*
>
> INT. *What happened?*
>
> B.S. *She said she'd tell his wife and he beat her black and blue . . .*

'You been up long?' Susan was standing in the kitchen doorway, dressing gown on.

He turned. 'Half an hour.'

'Come back to bed, I'm freezing.' She came over, embraced him. 'What time is—'

He felt her stiffen as she saw what he was reading. 'Susan, I . . .'

She let him go, walked over to the sink, turned the tap on and let it run, filled up a glass.

'I'm sorry, it was just on the table.'

'That really what you're here for, is it? A little snoop around? A little read of a confidential interview, see if there's anything you need to know?'

'Come on, it's not like that.'

'Really? That's exactly what it looks like.'

'Susan . . .' McCoy started.

'I should have known. Once a policeman, always a policeman. And here was me thinking that despite it all, all the macho tough guy stuff, that you were good underneath. You know something? I even thought you might actually like me.'

'I do.'

'No, you don't, Harry. You just think you do. This is what you really like.' She waved at the notebook on the table. 'Checking up on people, spying, finding things out you're not supposed to know.'

'That's not true.'

'Yes, it is. I don't really blame you for it. It's your job, it's you, it's what you are.' She drained the glass, set it upside down on the drainer. 'Do me a favour. Just don't use me to do it.' She walked away, went into the bathroom, slammed the door.

McCoy sat back. Wished desperately he'd never started reading it, but he had. He got his clothes out the bedroom, put them on quickly, left Susan a note. *Call you tomorrow.* Eased the door shut behind him and walked down the stairs onto Byres Road. He needed a drink after that.

The lights were off, place was dark for the first time he could remember. He chapped the door, expected Big Chas for a minute then remembered. No answer. Chapped again.

'Fuck off. We're closed.'

He leant into the door. 'C'mon, Iris. It's McCoy.'

'I don't give a fuck who it is, we're closed. Now fuck off.'

He rapped the door harder. 'I've got money. Come on, Iris, be a pal, I need a drink. Come on.'

The lock was pulled back and Iris stood there in the gloom. Took him a second or two to realise it was her. No make-up, faded dressing gown pulled round her, hair in a net.

'Well? Come in before you let all the bloody heat out.'

The flat was dark, all the doors closed. He followed her towards the light coming from the half-opened door at the end of the corridor. Iris's room was tiny, wee couch with antimacassars, armchair, telly, framed pictures of doe-eyed Victorian kids on the walls, Jim Reeves softly singing from the radiogram. It was warm, smelt of perfume and the remains of mince and tatties sitting on a plate by the chair. He eased himself down onto the couch and looked around. 'I've never been in here before.'

'Aye, and you won't be again. What's up with you anyway? Thought you polis were the ones who dealt out the beatings?'

'Doesn't always work out that way.'

'Gin's all I've got,' she said, pouring him half a tumbler.

'What happened? Where is everyone? This cause of Chas?'

She snorted. 'As if. Cooper no tell ye? We're shutting down. Supposed to be moving to some fucking sauna in Duke Street. His instructions.

Fucking liberty it is. Twelve years I've run this place and now I'm supposed to sit behind a desk handing towels to punters.' She swallowed a good half of her gin over. 'Good mind to tell him to shove it up his arse.'

'What about the girls?'

'Couple of days' holiday until they do the new place up. Except your wee pal that is, she's fucked off.'

'Janey?'

'She no tell you she was going?' She sat back in her armchair, looked amused. 'And here was me thinking you two were peas in a pod.'

'Where'd she go?'

'Nae idea. Got up one morning and the wee cow had gone. Told Cooper but he didnae give a shit, served her purpose as far as he was concerned.'

'What does that mean?'

She shrugged.

'Come on, Iris. Stop being a narky cow for once in your fucking life. Tell me.'

'Needle marks on her arms, passing out while the punters were riding her. No that good for business, is it?' She mimed sticking a syringe in her arm. 'I tried to tell her to stay away from that shite. Laughed in my face, asked me what the fuck I knew about it.'

McCoy swallowed the gin over, grimaced and held out his glass for another. 'I didnae think she was intae that, didn't think she was that bad.'

'She wasn't, just couldnae say no, not to him.'

'Who?'

She shook her head. 'Cannae see what's in front of your fucking face, can you, led by your dick like all the rest, same old fucking story.' She poured another half tumbler. 'This is your last; after this you're out.'

He padded his jacket, found a squashed packet of Regal and lit up. 'You think Chas did it?'

She laughed. 'You taking the piss?'

'Who put him up to it?'

'How the fuck should I know? Somebody did. You're the polis, you find out who.'

'He ever mention a Jimmy Gibbs?'

She shook her head. 'That who told him to do it?

McCoy shrugged. 'Think so.'

'He was a shite doorman, only ended up here when they couldnae use him anywhere else. Only chance he'll ever get to make a bit of money. Cannae blame him, I suppose.' She swirled the oily gin round in her tumbler, looked into the fire.

Way she looked when she talked about him made McCoy think the rumours about her and Chas might be true. 'You gonnae miss this place, Iris?'

She shook her head again, tried to smile. 'No this place. The life maybe. Mind you, hasnae been the same for years. Used to be the shebeens were the places, after the war. Used to love working them, busy they were, six, seven nights a week.'

He smiled. 'Heard you used to be a pro, eh, Iris?'

'Aye I was, nothing wrong with that. I was a good-looking girl back then, just wasnae any good at it. To make real money you have to convince the punters you're having a good time. I couldnae manage that so they started me looking after the booze, then the girls. Much more my style.'

'Maybe the sauna'll be okay?'

'Aye, and maybe it won't. Come on, you, move it. I need my bed.' She pulled a drawer of the dresser open and took out a half bottle of whisky, handed it to him. 'Take this with you, save me pouring it down the sink.'

CHAPTER 33

He looked up and down the street; no chance of getting a taxi in this weather. Only one thing for it: walk. At least he'd the half bottle to keep him warm. Snow must have been on the whole time he was in Iris's. The streets and the buildings were covered, quiet, sound all muffled. He opened the whisky, took a swig and grimaced. Watered down. Good old Iris, cheap until the very end.

The Dunlops had a Rolls, he'd seen it at the press conference, seen it up at Broughton House. No doubt that was where Isabel had ended up, fingers clawing at the carpet. What could he do with that, though? Maybe needed to take some of his own advice and let things go. Maybe Chas had been right: he needed to move on, stop seeing Cooper with the easy birds and the easy drugs. Murray and the Chief were going to be watching him, maybe it was time to keep his head down, stick to the straight and narrow for a while. Couldn't do any harm. He took another swig. Only a couple of days late with his New Year's resolutions. He'd holidays he had to take as well.

Next week off maybe. No more Dunlops or Cooper. Maybe go up north for a few days. Clear his head.

He'd just turned off Hyndland Road into Havelock Street when he saw the lights. Three pandas were parked round the edge of the wee swing park, lights spinning, flashing blue on a huddle of plainers over by the iron roundabout. He recognised Gilroy's wee MG parked over at the fence. Must be something big to get her out her bed on a night like this. A uniform with a big overcoat was guarding the park gate; he showed him his badge and he lifted the rope, let him duck under.

As he got closer he saw the familiar outline. Trilby, tweed coat, pipe in hand. Murray. He was talking to Wattie, pointing back at the road. Wattie saw him and called him over. He walked over, wishing he hadn't come in. Last person he needed to see tonight was Murray, especially when he was pissed.

'McCoy, what you doing here?' asked Wattie.

He took his hands out his pockets, rubbed them together. 'Nothing. Was on the way home and I saw the lights. Sir,' he nodded at Murray, who nodded back. Both of them awkward. 'What's the story anyway?'

Wattie nodded over to a young couple with blankets round their shoulders, looking scared. 'Winching couple climbed over the fence, drunk, fancied a wee burl on the roundabout and found him. Young guy, late teens, twenty, not long dead. Been given a right going over as well.'

'Do we know who he is?'

Wattie shook his head. 'Doesn't seem to have any ID or anything, pockets are empty. Got a tattoo, though.' He pointed at his knuckles. '*Come On Die Young*. Looks like he did. Should be called in as missing soon. You all right?'

McCoy nodded, hoped he was wrong. 'Can I see him?'

'No like you, McCoy. Thought you hated blood. He's over there.' He swept his arm towards the swings. 'Be my guest.'

He walked over just as they managed to get the lights hooked up, area ahead suddenly flooded with white light and the huge spindly shadows of the swings. He eased through the plainers, following Murray. Said a prayer under his breath.

The boy was lying face down, blood-stained jeans and underpants halfway down his legs. His shirt was torn and bloody; back a mess of stab wounds. He'd one arm folded beneath him, the other stretched out towards the lights, blue ink letters just below the knuckle of each finger. *C.O.D.Y.*

Gilroy was buzzing about, instructing the two ambulance men spreading a tarpaulin out on the ground beside the body. One knelt by the boy's shoulders, the other by his feet.

'Careful now,' she said. 'At the count of three. One, two, three!'

They rolled the body over and McCoy found himself looking, just like he knew he would be, into the face of one of the boys who'd taken Cooper's tally book. Billy Leeson.

'Fuck,' he said, looking away.

'What's up?' asked Murray. 'You know him?'

McCoy shook his head. 'No, sorry, just the usual. You know me.'

Murray looked down at the boy. 'All the gear on as well. Some poor bugger who wished he'd never gone out the night.'

The boy's print shirt was dark red and soaking. Right eye swollen and black, looked like his front teeth had been knocked out. Gilroy carefully eased the sides of the tarpaulin over him and the ambulance men started fastening belts around his shrouded body. Job done, she eased off her gloves and stuffed them in her jacket pocket.

'Mr McCoy, we meet again. What are you doing here? I thought Murray and Wattie were taking care of this one?'

'They are. I was just passing.'

'So, what's the story?' asked Murray.

'Provisionally?'

Murray sighed. 'Provisionally.'

Gilroy nodded. 'Male, late teens, five foot ten or thereabouts. General wear and tear, scratches, minor cuts and abrasions. Seems to have lost three of his teeth or, to be completely accurate, two and a half, the other half's still in there. Two major centres of interest. Two deep wounds in his chest, one piercing his lung, the other going straight into his heart. Carving knife or something similar, serrated. Ninety-nine per cent the cause of death.' She grimaced. 'I can only hope those wounds were inflicted before the other one.'

'The other one?' asked McCoy.

'Mmm. Seems someone has shoved the same carving knife up his back passage and given it a good twisting round.'

'Fucking hell,' said McCoy.

'I'm not given to bad language, but "fucking hell" indeed,' said Gilroy.

'Must have got on the wrong side of someone pretty important,' said Murray. 'Let's see if we can find out who he is pronto. Fingerprints are bound to be on file.' He dug his gloves out his pocket, put them on. 'Not much point in me standing here all night. Wattie, get a fingertip search going, keep the park closed and get that bloody tent up before the press get here.' He turned to McCoy. 'You want a lift?'

McCoy shook his head. 'I'm only a couple of streets away. I'll walk. Don't think you'd get a car up Gardner Street in this snow anyway.'

Murray looked up at the clumped flakes falling from the sky. 'Could be right. Seems to me you might be better on this mess. Keep you occupied. Let Wattie think he's running it, keep an eye out.'

'Babysit, you mean?'

Murray nodded. 'Keep your head down for a

330

week or so, until we're sure Cavendish isn't coming back. Okay?'

'Fine by me,' said McCoy. Least he could do.

Murray walked out the circle of light, down the slushy path towards the pandas. McCoy watched him go. Looked like they were back on an even keel. He turned back to the red churned-up snow, the outline of where the boy had been. Poor fucker had got on the wrong side of someone, right enough. And all because of him.

Wattie approached, blowing into his hands. 'What you doing lurking about this time of night?'

'Couldn't sleep.'

'Nightmares about Cavendish?' asked Wattie, smiling.

'Something like that. What you doing here?'

'Couldn't sleep either, better off here, see how they do things like this, see what I can learn.'

'Thought I was supposed to be teaching you?'

'You are. Just that sometimes you don't explain things very much.'

Was a fair point. 'You trying to make me feel guilty?' asked McCoy.

'Don't think I could do that if I tried.'

'Too right you couldn't. Stick by Murray, he's the only one who knows what he's doing. Don't let any of the uniforms take the piss. This is your scene, they do what you want.'

Wattie saluted. 'Yes, sir.'

'Murray say anything else about Cavendish?'

'Not much. Just told me to keep my head down, that it would blow over.'

'And the rest?'

Wattie looked sheepish. 'Told me not to pick up any of your bad habits. Don't fraternise with the enemy, don't drink on duty, don't get stuck on one path, keep the options open.'

'Not bad advice, might try following it myself.' He stuck his hands in his pockets, walked off, heading for the gate.

He sat by the fire when he got in, didn't put the lights on, just let the orange bars light up the room. He kept sipping at the half bottle; tasted rotten but it was working. He found his wee red jotter on the mantelpiece, the one he'd bought when all this started. Seemed a long time ago now. He opened it up. Picture of Lorna Skirving from the paper with a big question mark beside it. List underneath: *Worker? Punter? Boyfriend? Hired?* Next page, *Howie Nairn: How connected to the girl?*

He sat down, leant against the wall. Looked at her picture again. 'Howie Nairn. How connected to the girl.' He sat there for a while, sipping the whisky, watching the passing headlights stretch the shadows of the furniture across the wall. By the time the sun had started to turn the sky a bluish pink he'd worked out what he had to do. He got up, ran his head under the kitchen tap, suffered the cold to wake him up. He put his coat on, shut the front door behind him and walked down to Dumbarton Road to find a taxi.

10TH JANUARY 1973

CHAPTER 34

McCoy stepped off the train and joined the crowd shuffling towards the inspectors. He gave his ticket over and turned his coat collar up. Dundee was so cold it made Glasgow seem tropical. Icy sleet was coming down sideways, heavy grey sky sitting just above the roofs of the town. The station was opposite the Tay; river was as grey as the sky, moving slowly, branches and twigs floating past. He'd only been here once before, hoped he'd never have to come again. He'd interviewed a bloke the Dundee boys had in custody for sexual assault, Murray sure he was responsible for two rapes in Glasgow. Turned out the bloke was friendlier than the Dundee polis were. Not too keen on Glaswegians up here as a rule.

There was a wee cafe just across the road, steamed-up windows and a *Fisher and Donaldson Served Here* sign. He waited for a couple of buses to pass, crossed the street and went in. Place was warm and crowded, customers and staff joking with each other. He ordered a tea and a bacon roll, found a quiet corner. He'd stopped at the

R. S. McColl's in the station and bought a paper and a brown hardback envelope. He slipped the picture out his pocket, tried to look at it without anyone seeing it. Cowie still there in his towel, Lord Dunlop in a loosely belted dressing gown, Dunlop Junior beside him, hand rubbing his dick through the towel round his waist, all of them staring at Lorna Skirving pushing a dildo up the other girl's arse. Father and son, pillars of the community. Should be enough. He put it in the envelope and sealed it, wrote *Mr James Forfar* in big letters across it and *to be opened by the addressee only* across the back. He downed the last of his tea and made his way over to a group of painters in splattered white overalls sitting near the counter.

'Any of you boys know where Forfar Publishing is?'

Had to get the bloke to tell him a few times before he got it, thick Dundee accent more than he could decipher. Turned out it wasn't too far.

Dundee on a sleety January morning. Had to be more miserable places, he just couldn't think of any. Forfar Publishing turned out to be a large Victorian building, red sandstone, looked like a town hall or a library. A uniformed concierge pulled the door open for him and he walked into a marble-lined hall. There was a wreath of poppies lying on the floor beneath a memorial for the Forfar workers killed in the two world wars. He scanned the names; not a single Irish or Catholic one amongst them. Wasn't only

336

unions Forfar didn't like. The woman behind the desk peered at him over half-moon glasses as he approached.

'Can I help you?'

He smiled his best smile. 'I hope so,' he said, holding up the envelope. 'Just come from Glasgow on the train. Urgent delivery for Mr Forfar, has to be opened by him personally.'

The woman took it. 'I'll see he gets it.'

'Thanks very much. Apparently he has to see it as soon as possible.' He tried to look as gormless as possible. 'Something to do with a merger?'

'Ah, you should have said.' She reached for the phone and McCoy mouthed 'Thank you' and left her to it.

Couple of hours later his train rumbled into Queen Street Station. He rubbed his eyes; he'd been in and out of sleep the whole journey, making up for last night. People were standing up, getting their luggage off the racks, putting on coats and scarves. It was done now, no going back. Picture should be enough to make the Wee Free stick choke on his morning tea. Have another think about his merger with the upstanding Dunlops. He yawned, stood up, started shuffling along the train corridor. Hitting the Dunlops financially was all he could do now, getting them on Lorna Skirving or Tommy Malone or Isabel Garvey was never going to happen. Even if the photo managed to torpedo the merger, it wasn't going to bring them down. What it would do was cause them a fair bit of trouble and a good bit of money and that was enough. For now.

He got off the train, glad to be back in sooty, grimy Glasgow, and made his way through the station to the rank at Queen Street. Didn't have to wait long. He opened the back door.

'Where you off to, pal?'

'Memen Street,' he said. One down. One to go.

CHAPTER 35

Same three lads with the leather coats, same wee girl taking the message to Stevie, same trudge over what was left of the gardens in Memen Street. Same climb up the frozen close. McCoy rapped on the door, glad he couldn't hear anyone getting battered this time. Maybe he was in time to stop it.

Billy Weir only opened the door a crack this time, looked worried. 'Bad time, McCoy. Come back later, eh?'

'I need to speak to him, Billy. Now.'

'Aye well, he's busy.'

Standing there arguing wasn't going to get him anywhere so he booted the door as hard as he could. Billy went flying, the door bashed off the inside wall and he was in. Billy was up quick, shouting the odds, exactly what he'd hoped for. The door to the room opposite was wrenched open and Cooper was standing there. Shirt off, greasy quiff hanging over his eyes, hammer in his hand.

'Fuck's going on here?' he asked, glowering at Billy.

'Cunt bashed his way in, couldnae stop him,' said Billy, looking furious. 'Sorry, boss.'

Cooper was breathing heavy like he'd been running, fine spray of blood across his nose and mouth. 'If you're so fucking desperate to see me, McCoy, come on in.'

He held the door wide. McCoy could hear crying, could see blood on the wooden floor, footprints walked through it. That room was the last place he wanted to go. Didn't have a choice. He stepped past Billy, went in and Cooper shut the door behind him.

He was too late. One of Jumbo's sandshoes was off; foot a pulpy mess of broken toes and blood. He was lying facing the wall curled up, crying, crying like a child who'd lost his mum. He turned his head round, broken nose splattered over his face, slash down his left cheek, wound gaping. McCoy's stomach turned and he looked away quickly.

Cooper stuck a rolled-up note deep into the pile of speed on the mantelpiece and took a huge snort, grimaced, wiped at his nose and took a swig from one of the screwtops lined up beside the mound of powder. 'You want one?' he asked, holding out a bottle. McCoy nodded, took it.

Cooper watched him, mimed McCoy's shaky hands. 'What's up wi' you?'

McCoy shook his head. 'Nothing. You know me, bit squeamish.' He nodded over at Jumbo. 'You finished?'

Cooper snorted. 'Not by a long shot. Why? What's it to you?'

'Come on, Stevie, leave him, eh? He's just a daft boy, didnae know what he was doing, hasnae the sense. He's had enough of a doing, eh?'

'That's for me to decide. My business.'

McCoy held his hands up. 'Fair point, fair point. I'm no telling you what to do, Stevie, just asking a favour.'

Cooper put the bottle down, looked at him, eyes narrowing. 'What is all this anyway?'

McCoy tried a smile. 'Let's just call it a guilty conscience, eh? I didn't think you'd be so heavy on the two lads.'

Cooper didn't smile back. He walked over to Jumbo, grabbed the neck of his shirt and pulled him round. He was whimpering, trying to roll up in a ball, trying to get away. Cooper kicked him square in the stomach and he lurched forward and threw up a dribble of watery sick. McCoy looked away again.

'McCoy,' Cooper shouted. 'I'm over here. Get your eyes off the fucking floor and look at me!'

He tried to breathe slowly and looked up. Cooper was standing over Jumbo now, hammer in hand. 'You no too keen on the rough stuff, eh? No want to get your hands dirty.' He sat down hard on Jumbo, who let out another whimper. 'Two cunts take the piss out of me and they get what's coming, that way everyone knows who's the boss. Simple stuff, McCoy.' He was twirling the hammer round in his fingers. Stopped it with the handle pointing at McCoy.

'Want a go?'

McCoy shook his head.

'Tough.'

Cooper put the hammer down and grabbed Jumbo's wrist, forced his hand flat onto the floor, fat fingers spread out. C.O.D.Y. He was whimpering and crying, squirming under him, trying to get his arm free.

'Do it and I'll think about letting him go.'

'Fuck sake, Stevie, you must be joking.'

He looked at him, at the look in his eyes, knew he wasn't. Didn't know what kind of game he was playing but he didn't see what else he could do. If he walked out, Jumbo would be dead in a couple of hours anyway. He walked over and picked up the hammer.

'No fucking about,' said Cooper. 'Do it like you mean it.'

He knelt down beside them, lifted the hammer up, tried not to think about what he was about to do, and hit Jumbo's hand with as much force as he could. The noise was horrible, a scream of real agony. He felt his stomach turn, knew he couldn't be sick. Not now.

Cooper grinned at him. 'Good man.'

McCoy dropped the hammer and walked over to the window, pushed it open and breathed in the sharp cold air. Ignored the screams as long as he could. Turned round just as Cooper got off

Jumbo. McCoy's stomach lurched as Jumbo raised his hand and half his forefinger was left behind, flattened into the wooden floor.

He took his beer off the mantelpiece, drank half of it in one go. Cooper came over, familiar rolling stride, slapped him on the back.

'Didnae think you had it in you.'

'You going to let him go now?'

He smiled. 'No.'

'You cunt, Cooper, you said—'

'What I said was that I'd think about it, and that's what I'm doing. C'mon.'

He walked out the room and McCoy followed, didn't want to look back at Jumbo, at what he'd done. The noises coming from him were bad enough.

'Out,' said Cooper, as they walked into the kitchen. Billy and the girl looked up. They were sitting at the table working on a huge mound of yellowish speed, folded paper wraps lined up, ready to be filled. Was so much of it McCoy could taste it in the air, metallic, chalky. They shuffled past them, Billy still not looking happy.

Cooper pointed to the speed on the table. 'See this? Waste of fucking time. Cannae sell it for more than a couple of quid a gram. Fucking kids at the dancing, that's it. No repeat business. But this . . .' He dug into his jeans pocket, pulled out a tiny wee plastic bag half full of gummy brown powder. 'This is different. Things are changing, McCoy, changing very fast, and I'm going to be

343

riding the wave. New connections, new ways of doing things, making money. Smack's only a part of it, I've been expanding my contacts.'

'You been giving it to Janey?'

'Janey? Aye, she cannae get enough of it, sort of a guinea pig, see how much we need to cut it. Why?'

'She gone, disappeared. Iris doesn't know where she is.'

'Hang on, you're no still fucking her, are ye?' He shook his head. 'I telt you before, McCoy, she's just another whoor. Smacked-out whoor now, good for nothing. No getting your fucking hole, that it?' He walked over to the door. Shouted. 'Helen! C'mere, hen.'

The girl came back through and Cooper grabbed her by the hair, forced her down onto her knees. 'Want her to suck you off? She'll do it now, do anything I tell her.' He twisted her round to face him. 'That right, hen? You'll do anything I say,' he said.

She nodded, was sobbing, make-up starting to run. Cooper laughed and let her go. She crawled over, grabbed onto McCoy's belt, tried to undo it. He stepped back, shook his head.

'No fancy it, eh, McCoy?'

He shook his head again, was pressed back against the kitchen wall trying to get away from the crying girl. Cooper grabbed her, told her to fuck off. She started to say something and he slapped her across the face. 'Move it, I said!'

She scrambled out the room and Cooper sat down at the kitchen table. McCoy wasn't sure if it was just the speed, but he looked half mad. Paranoid. He spoke quietly, slowly.

'Need to know you're with me, McCoy. If you're not, you've got one chance. Walk away.'

'C'mon, Cooper, it's been a long time. I just wondered what happened to . . .'

Cooper looked at him. Face splattered with Jumbo's blood, eyes black and dilated, fist opening and closing. 'Yes or no?' he said.

What was he going to say? So he said it. 'Aye, I'm with you.'

Cooper leant back in the chair, face slack with relief, and McCoy suddenly realised Cooper was as lost as everyone else. No family, always on the lookout for the polis or whichever villain was next to have a go, no proper girlfriend. No one round him except people whose wages he was paying. Only person he really had, the only person he had any connection with, was him. He sat down at the table.

'I'm here, Cooper. Have been since we were wee boys, eh?'

Cooper nodded.

'But you know what, pal, you're taking too much of that stuff.' He nodded at the pile of speed. 'It's no helping you, eh? Making you mental. Well, more mental.'

Cooper smiled. 'Cheeky cunt. Like I need your fucking advice. Wasnae for me you'd still be eating that fucking dinner in the home.' He took the wee bag of smack out again. 'You gonnae listen this time?'

McCoy nodded. 'Where'd you get it anyway? Thought it only turned up once in a while, tiny wee amounts.'

Cooper brightened, sat up. 'Not any more. Billy Chan was back in Hong Kong a couple of months ago, set up a regular supply. Started coming in last month. He's offering it to me and Ronnie Naismith. And there's the problem.'

'What?'

'Only make real money if you control the whole supply and that's what I'm going to do. Going to end up ugly, though, and that's where you and your fat pal next door come in.'

'I don't get it.'

'Murray. Been in Naismith's pocket for years. He goes easy on him. That needs to stop.'

McCoy looked at him like he was mad. 'Murray? You're taking the piss, aren't you? He's as straight as they come.'

'That right, is it? Big house in Bearsden, three boys at posh school. How do you think he pays for that on his salary?'

'He comes from money, from down in the Borders, Hawick.'

Cooper shook his head. 'Fucking polis, thick as shit, the lot of you. All that rugby shite's pulled the wool over your eyes. Think his dad was some fucking doctor in Hawick or something? His dad was a fucking farm labourer, he got a sports scholarship. Give me a fucking break. He's had his nose in the trough for years, same as all the rest of them.'

McCoy shook his head. 'No fucking way, someone's been telling you porkies. I've worked for him for years, he's as straight as they come.'

'Cannae fucking tell you anything. Okay, suit yourself. I still need Naismith out the picture, need his protection shut down, need him put away for a few months until I get it all sorted out. You fix that and I'll let that fat cunt next door go.'

'How can I sort something out that doesnae exist?'

Cooper just held his hand out. 'Deal?'

McCoy shook. At least it'd get Jumbo out of there. He'd worry about the rest later.

McCoy was leaning into the back of the car, door open. 'Listen to me, Jumbo. Right? Billy here's going to take you to the Royal, to A&E. You go in there, tell them you got attacked in the street, didn't see who did it. Right?'

Jumbo nodded, was looking at him intently. Ready to do anything his saviour asked.

'You got anywhere you can go after that? Aunties? Uncles? You need to get out of here for a while.'

He nodded again. 'Auntie Peggy. She lives by the seaside in . . .' He strained, trying to think. 'Girvan.'

'Fine. You get out the hospital – say nothing,

347

remember – then you go to Central Station and you get a ticket for Girvan. Here . . .' He dug in his top pocket, took out the money Cooper had given him the other day. 'You give your auntie half of this, tell her you need to stay for a few months.'

'A few months,' he repeated.

McCoy nodded. 'You do that and then you come back and I'll get you a job with Mr Cooper. Right?'

He shook his head violently, started crying again.

'It'll be okay, he's a friend now, everything's changed. Honest.' He leant over the front seat. 'He's ready, Billy. You take him to the Royal, then put him on the train.' Billy nodded, didn't look very happy about it.

McCoy turned back to Jumbo. 'I'll see you when you get back, eh?'

Jumbo nodded. McCoy kept his eyes on his face, trying to avoid the smashed and broken hand. 'I'll see you.' He went to get out the car and Jumbo grabbed him, embraced him, started crying again. McCoy looked at Billy, embarrassed, patted Jumbo's back. 'You're all right, son. It's all right now.'

11TH JANUARY 1973

CHAPTER 36

'Hold your fucking horses!'

The hammering had woken him up. He'd tried to ignore it at first but it wasn't going away. He'd got home, fallen asleep on the couch. He looked at his watch: eight o'clock, he'd only been asleep for a few hours. No wonder he felt terrible. He slid the bolt in the door and pulled it open.

'You stupid fucking cunt,' Jimmy Gibbs said. 'You stupid, stupid cunt.' He barged past him and walked into the flat.

'Come in,' said McCoy, shutting the door behind him.

Gibbs was all suited and booted, reddish hair combed into a neat side shed. Must have come straight from Dunlop. He walked into the living room, lighting up as he went. He supposed he'd expected him, just wished he'd been in a better state to deal with it. Gibbs chucked his match into the fireplace and turned to face him.

'You got any idea the trouble you've caused?'

McCoy sat down at the table, yawned and scratched his chest. 'What do you want anyway,

351

Gibbs? I was in my bed. And by the way, how much did you have to pay Chas Gow to get him to take the rap for Isabel Garvey?'

'I haven't a fucking clue what you're on about, McCoy. The rest of them. Where are they?'

McCoy was reading the back of yesterday's *Record*. Well, pretending to. 'I give up. The rest of what?'

'The photos, you fucking clown.'

'What photos is that? I've no got any photos.' He looked up, smiled. Couldn't resist it. 'How's the merger going, by the way?'

Gibbs shook his head. 'Still acting the smart prick, aren't you, McCoy? You're nothing but a fucking amateur.'

He sat at the table, was about to put his elbows down then noticed the toast crumbs and spilt milk, snatched the *Record* over and leant on that instead. His sleeves hitched up and McCoy saw it. The bottom half on a pentangle tattooed on the inside of his wrist.

'That work, does it?' he asked, pointing at it. 'All that devil worshipping shite. Help you get to fuck teenagers, does it? Much acid did you have to give Tommy Malone to fry his brain, get him to do what you want?'

'Tommy did what he wanted to do. I didn't have to make him do anything.'

McCoy looked at him. Realised. 'You actually believe all this shit, don't you, Gibbs? Really fucking believe it.'

Gibbs pulled up his sleeve. Blue pentangle was there and there was something above it too. An inscription in blue copperplate writing. McCoy leant forward and read it. *'Do as thou wilt is the whole of the law.'*

'What's that supposed to mean?' he asked.

'It means you don't understand what you're dealing with. What we are capable of.'

'We? What, you and the Dunlops? You're getting ideas above your station. You're just another servant, as far as they're concerned. There's no "we". You're just another one of their houseboys.'

'I didn't think someone like you would understand. It's all a bit above you, McCoy. Bit too much for your brain to take in.'

'Maybe you're right, Gibbs, maybe I'm just too thick to understand how drawing pentangles on stoned teenagers gives you an excuse to treat them like pieces of shit.'

'As I said, it's beyond you, McCoy. You just don't get it, never will.' Gibbs smiled at him. 'Lord Dunlop and I had a cosy wee dinner with Forfar, talked him through the art of faking photographs. Told him all about unscrupulous business rivals who would do anything to stop this merger going through. Dunlop told him exactly how disgusted he was by that faked photograph, that it was an obscene abomination, the product of a sick and godless mind.'

And then Gibbs was up and out his chair before McCoy knew what was happening. He grabbed the empty milk bottle from the table as he jumped up and smashed it down on McCoy's head. It shattered and McCoy fell backwards. Gibbs was on top of him instantly, knees pinning down his shoulders, jagged neck of the bottle pushing into his cheek. Gibbs' face was in his, smell of cigarettes on his breath.

'Listen, you cunt, because I'm only going to say this once. I want the photos. All of them. You've got until the end of the day tomorrow.'

'Get the fuck off me,' said McCoy, struggling to get out from under him.

Gibbs looked him in the eye. 'End of the fucking day,' he said, and pushed down on the bottle. McCoy felt the pressure on his cheek, then it gave way and he screamed as Gibbs pushed the glass deep into his skin.

CHAPTER 37

The cars were circling. Cortinas, Vivas, Hillman Imps. Family cars full of family men just looking, plucking up the courage or making a choice. A car pulled over every so often, girl leant in the window, did the deal, then got in. Glasgow Green was a good step down the ladder from the leafy square of Blythswood. And where he was going was even worse.

McCoy walked past the girls leaning on the Green railings, smoking, trying to stay warm in their miniskirts and wee tops, and headed down towards the dark lane running by the back of the old box factory. The road hadn't been used for years, was littered with broken wine bottles, cigarette packets, used condoms. A huddle of figures was gathered round a fire in an oil drum down at the end. They were either very young or had reached the ends of their working lives. Nothing in between.

The old girls were falling down the slippery slope, no use in the saunas or the shebeens, or even for the circling cars two streets away. The younger girls all looked the same. Thin, too thin, black circles under their eyes, runny noses, desperation written all over their faces. Couple of them approached, tried to smile.

'All right, fella, what you after?'

McCoy held up his badge and any hope they had on their faces died.

'Looking for someone. Girl called Janey.' Nothing. He dug in his pocket, pulled out two quid. The girls looked at the notes, couldn't take their eyes off them.

'She's no here,' the taller one said. 'She was here earlier on, got a couple of jobs. Some old guy gied her two quid just to suck him off. Lucky cow.'

'Where'd she go?' he asked.

They didn't look at him, didn't take their eyes off the money in McCoy's hand. 'Where d'you think? To score.'

'Where would that be?' asked McCoy.

'Anywhere. There's loads around just now. Good stuff tae.'

McCoy held out the money, their eyes followed it like a dog following a stick. 'You see her, you tell her McCoy's looking for her. She knows where she can find me.'

He couldn't look at the hunger in their eyes any more, held out the notes. They snatched them, were straight off up the road. McCoy knew he was probably wasting his time but he had to try, try and find her before she got in so deep she couldn't get back out. He'd tried a couple of the shelters, roads at the back of the Tennent's brewery and then the Green. Knew that's where she was probably going to be working, was kidding himself with the other places. Heroin doesn't take any prisoners. Couldn't find her. Wherever she'd gone with her score, she'd disappeared.

By the time he got into the office it was after three. Radiators had gone on the blink; some pipe had burst with the cold. Everyone was sitting at their desks with their coats on, hats and scarves. Wattie was on the phone, had some sort of mittens on, looked like a big kid. He hung up and came over, handed him a note. *Call Jean Baird.* Took him a minute to remember who Jean Baird was. Madame Polo. What was she phoning him for? Was just about to pick up the phone when Murray appeared round his office door and shouted on him and Wattie.

'You two okay?' he asked as they walked into his office. Then he noticed McCoy's cheek. 'What happened to you?'

'Shaving,' said McCoy.

Murray raised his eyebrows, shook his head. 'Shaving, my arse.'

'No, thanks.'

'Aye, very funny, McCoy. That body the other night, the one in the swing park? Have we identified him yet?'

Wattie shook his head. 'He'd nothing on him, nobody knows who he is. No fingerprints on file either.' He looked glum. 'Think we'll have to try the mispers books.'

Murray thought. 'He looked like he was a small-time boy. One of the troops. Sort of person McCoy knows.'

McCoy nodded. 'Might do. Think I should try it?'

Wattie nodded, looked relieved. 'Good idea.'

'Well, get up to Saracen, Milton, Springburn, ask around, you've got contacts up there. Find out if anyone knows who he is.'

They nodded, stood up.

'He was serious, that Cavendish,' said Murray. 'Talking about the Official Secrets and that. You never saw those photos, never heard of them. I'll say it again. Just keep your head down, get back to some proper polis work. Don't give him an excuse to come looking for either of you. Clear?'

'You still going to interview Teddy Dunlop?' asked McCoy.

'Am I fuck,' said Murray. 'As you well know. Now beat it.'

McCoy and Wattie made their way to the back of the shop to see if there were any pool cars around.

'You go ahead, see if you can find one. I'll no be a minute,' said McCoy.

Wattie nodded, kept walking down the corridor. McCoy waited until he'd gone and pushed the door to Cowie's office open.

Cowie was sitting behind his desk typing something, didn't look up as he came in. 'Mr McCoy! Sit yourself down. If I don't finish this paragraph now, I'll lose track of the whole bloody—'

'Lorna Skirving.'

The typing stopped. Cowie looked up. 'What about her?'

'That's why you were waiting about outside Murray's office, wasn't it? Waiting to see if you could get a heads-up on the coroner's report. See if the bruises you'd given her were still there. Lucky for you someone else had had a go at her since, managed to give her a whole new set. No wonder you were so cheery when you turned up at the Indian.'

Cowie looked at him. Blinked. Sat back in his chair.

'The neighbour. Wattie had a chat with her. She told him all about her boyfriend turning up at her door. Thought it was Malone at first. Why wouldn't I? But then I thought about what she said. Said he was "untidy, messy". Now who does that sound like?'

'That's a load of shite,' said Cowie.

'All that crying and pleading. It was only the once, poor me with my crippled wife, I'm so sorry, I don't know anything. But you did. You knew Lorna Skirving and you made her life hell. Harassed her, blackmailed her into sleeping with you. Beat her black and blue when she threatened to tell your wife.'

'Harry, come on, we can talk about this, it doesn't—'

'You're fucked, Cowie. It's over. No pension, no Pass Go. Out on your fucking arse.'

'You don't have any proof.'

'Don't I? You want to bet on that? What do you think Murray's going to do when I tell him you were fucking a murder suspect and you didn't tell anyone? Give you a pay rise?'

Cowie stared at him. Swallowed. 'What can I do?'

'Nothing. Resign. Get the fuck out this office.'

'I'm nineteen years in, Harry. I need that pension. Without that me and the wife, we won't survive. She'll have to go into a home. Please, Harry, be a pal. I need—'

'You know what, Cowie? I don't give a shit.'

Cowie was white, all the colour gone from his face. Looked desperate, broken, like he was about to cry.

'What if I had something to trade, something I could tell you?' he said.

Taken longer than McCoy thought it would, but he'd finally got him there.

'Like what?'

'Something about the Dunlops.'

'What the fuck do you know about them? Far as I could see you were just standing there with your dick in your hand.'

Tears started. Cowie wiped them away with the back of his hand. 'Teddy,' he said.

'The son?' McCoy asked. 'What about him?'

'All I know is the women I was with wouldn't go near him.'

'Why not?'

Cowie shrugged. 'That's all I heard. Maybe I can try and . . .'

McCoy turned, walked away. Was almost at the door when Cowie shouted after him.

'Harry! Please!'

The noise cut off as he shut the door behind him.

'You going up to ask around?' said Wattie, nodding towards the north of the city.

'Me? That not supposed to be *we*? You not supposed to be showing me what you can do?'

'Sure, sure, no problem,' said Wattie, pulling a pair of woolly gloves out his coat pocket. 'Just thought you might get on better on your own, people more likely to talk.'

'And . . .?'

'And it's the football club Christmas dance the night,' he said, grinning.

'Christmas was two weeks ago.'

'I know, they have it in January. Supposed to cheer everyone up.'

McCoy shook his head. 'Off you go.'

'Cheers, McCoy,' he said, pulling a woolly hat on. 'I owe you.'

'Aye, you fucking do.'

McCoy watched him hurry past the big hospital gates and down the hill into town. Wattie didn't know it but he'd saved him a problem; he'd been trying to work out how to get rid of him. Didn't need Wattie standing there in some pub in

Springburn while a bloke told them his pal Cooper had done the boy in, everyone knew that.

If the real story came out, he was fucked, up to his arse in it. Murray couldn't save him this time. He'd delivered the boys wrapped up like a parcel so Cooper could make dog meat out of them. Needed to find him quick. A taxi passed, yellow light shining weakly in the fog. A miracle in this weather. He hailed it and got in, told the driver to take him up to Springburn.

The driver gave up around the fire station, didn't want to go up the hill, too scared he'd get stuck. McCoy got out, didn't give him a tip, ignored his moaning and started trudging up the hill. He could see his problem, though. If anything, the snow was getting worse, was almost horizontal now. Both sides of the road were lined with abandoned cars, most of them already half buried. The streetlights weren't doing much good against the snow and the fog, barely lighting up the way ahead. He walked up past the fire station and crossed the bridge; railway tracks below were covered as well, no trains running tonight.

He was almost at the Bells when he saw it. A car was making its way down Balgrayhill towards him. It was a dirty big black Rolls-Royce. Didn't see many of them in Glasgow, never mind in Springburn. He stood outside Bells and waited, wasn't surprised when it drew up beside him and a driver in a cap and greatcoat got out.

'Mr McCoy? I've been looking for you. Lord Dunlop would like a word.'

'That right? Well, tell Lord Dunlop I'm busy.'

'He has a suite at the Albany.' He gestured to the car. 'Will only take us ten minutes to get there. You'll be back here within the hour.'

'Tell you what . . .'

'Mason,' said the driver.

'Tell you what, Mason. Why don't you get in your big car and go and get Dunlop? If he wants to talk to me, I'll be in this pub here for the next hour. Tell the mountain to come to Muhammad.'

Mason nodded, got in the car and started it up, clouds of exhaust fumes in the icy night air. McCoy pushed the door of the Bells open, watched it drive off down the hill.

Sitting in the pub brooding and waiting wasn't doing him any good, Isabel Garvey, Tommy Malone, Lorna Skirving going round in his head. Who knew how many others the Dunlops had chewed up and spat out? How many of the runaways they found floating in canals, the pregnant girls who hung themselves out of desperation, the ones already living rough on the Grates had run into people like the Dunlops? Jimmy Gibbs leading them like some pied piper towards Broughton House and the cameras in the walls and the pentagrams and the handcuffs on the bedside table?

He ordered another pint, drank a whisky at the bar while he was waiting for it to be poured. Sat back down and tried to get his mind onto something else. Couldn't.

He'd just finished his second pint, pretty sure Dunlop wasn't coming in, when the door opened. Just like a cowboy film everyone stopped talking and turned to look at the stranger in the doorway. An old boy let out a low whistle, taking in the bespoke suit, the dark blue cashmere coat and the kid-leather gloves Dunlop was peeling off his elegant hands. He looked around, spotted McCoy in the gloom of the dingy pub and came over.

'Happy now, are we?' he asked. 'Made your point?'

They sat at a wee table at the back, hammered copper table top sticky with spilt beer, ash and soggy beer mats. Punters in the pub weren't shy; they were taking a good look at Dunlop, trying to work out what he was doing there. Too rich-looking to be a polis, not flash enough to be a landlord. Dunlop lifted up the gin and tonic McCoy had got him, peered at it, didn't look happy. No ice, no lemon, just a warm oily liquid in a smeared glass.

'What do you want?' asked McCoy. All he wanted was rid of him. He was sick of it. Sick of Dunlop, sick of Gibbs, sick of them getting away with it.

Dunlop took a sip of his drink, tried not to grimace. 'Was that Gibbs?' he asked.

McCoy's hand went up to the plasters on his face. 'Yep.'

'My apologies. He has a tendency to step over

the mark. Can be useful sometimes, as you can imagine. No real harm done, I hope.' He smiled.

McCoy wasn't playing. No chitchat, no exchanged smiles. He took a long swig of his lager, wiped his mouth of the foam. 'That Rolls outside, that the one Junior took Isabel home in the other night?'

'Sorry?'

'C'mon, Dunlop, you can do better than that. That night slipped your memory, has it? Let me see if I can help you out. It was the night your son raped her, stubbed cigarettes out on her, kicked fuck out her, then punched her so hard her skull fractured. Isabel Garvey was her name. Lovely lassie, lying in the morgue now. Ringing any bells?'

McCoy should have known better. Should have known he was wasting his time. Dunlop didn't say anything, was like water off a duck's back, didn't even flinch. Just wasn't interested.

'I need those photographs back, McCoy. That's what I came here for. I hoped you could be reasonable. It's not in either of our interests to have to bring the big guns in.'

'Who's that, then? The Chief? The mysterious Mr Cavendish? Not sure the old school tie will survive pictures of you and Junior fucking either end of a dead eighteen-year-old girl. You know what? Despite you sitting there looking like butter wouldn't melt you must be worried. Deep down inside you're shitting yourself. Otherwise there's no way you would be sitting here in the Bells trying not to breathe in in case you catch something.' He shook his empty glass at him. 'Now away up and get me another pint. I'm thirsty.'

Contempt flashed across Dunlop's face. He was about to say something, thought again and didn't.

'Right decision,' said McCoy, holding his gaze. He held out his glass. 'Tennent's.'

Dunlop took it, made his way to the bar, drinkers parting to let him in, barman at him straight away. Privileges of wealth even extended to a shitehole like the Bells. Dunlop still thought he had the rest of the pictures. Thought he'd only handed over the one with the two of them and Lorna Skirving in it. Didn't know Cavendish had them all. For some reason Cavendish was keeping that news to himself. Supposed that's what men like Cavendish did. Kept things in case they needed them one day. Well, he wasn't going to tell Dunlop any different.

Dunlop came back, put the pint of Tennent's down in front of him. 'There you are. Now, what I need is for—'

McCoy laughed. 'You still think you can call the shots, don't you? Don't you get it? You're fucked, Dunlop, completely fucked. So why don't you shut it and I'll tell you what's going to happen.'

Dunlop looked like he'd been slapped in the face, wasn't used to being talked to like that. He was keeping his temper; just how difficult that was for him was written all over his face.

'I'll give you the photos back but I want something in return. You're not going to give me, Teddy . . .' McCoy shrugged. 'I can see that. I'm a reasonable man, but I want him gone. Your wee tag team needs to split up. No more shared girls scared out their wits, fucked all ways then battered black and blue or worse. Send the wee fucker off to the colonies, one of your rubber plantations, diamond mines, I don't care. Just somewhere away from here.'

Dunlop thought, nodded. 'We have interests in Canadian forestry. Saskatchewan. That far enough?'

McCoy nodded. 'Doesn't sound like you'll be that sad to see him go.'

'Have you any children, McCoy?'

McCoy shook his head. No way he was talking about Bobby to someone like Dunlop.

Dunlop shrugged. 'They can be a burden as well as a joy. Teddy has always been a, how shall we say, troubled boy. That trouble is going to come home to roost at some point. I'd rather that happened in Canada than here.'

'Is that a confession?'

For once Dunlop looked like an ordinary man, a man who, despite all his wealth, couldn't do anything about his own flesh and blood. 'It may take a couple of days. He's not been at home.'

'No? Where is he?' asked McCoy.

'As I said, Teddy is a complicated boy. He goes AWOL every so often. Sometimes it's a drugs and alcohol binge, sometimes he checks into a clinic for a rest and sometimes he just disappears. Is that it?' he asked, going to stand up.

McCoy shook his head. 'Nope. I want Gibbs.'

Dunlop raised his eyebrows. 'Gibbs? That could be problematic. He's taken care of family business for the past five years or so, knows where—'

'The bodies are buried?'

A humourless smile. 'Not quite. Despite your paranoid fantasies. Rather more prosaic I'm afraid; we'll need a handover, confidentiality agreement, etc. He may not know where the bodies are buried but he knows enough, more than enough. He won't be happy. I'll need a couple of days, a deal will have to be struck. Recompense made. Will be tricky.' He sipped his drink, grimaced again. 'What are you actually going to charge him with, if you don't mind me asking?'

McCoy ticked off on his fingers. 'Conspiracy to supply illegal drugs, sexual assault of a minor, trading in and manufacture of pornography. All sorts. Don't you worry, I'll find enough to put the cunt away for a good few years.'

'So it will be in the papers?'

'Bet your life. They'll have a fucking field day. But at least they won't have the photos, and without the photos they won't have that much. I'm sure one of your expensive lawyers will be able to minimise the damage.'

'I can't imagine you're stupid enough not to have made copies.'

'Nope. I've seen enough detective films. They're

in a sealed envelope in a lawyer's office; anything happens to me, he opens it and sends it straight to the press. Believe that's the usual procedure.'

Dunlop swallowed over the last of his drink and stood up. 'As I said, I'll need a couple of days.'

'Junior gone. Gibbs handed over, no protection.'

'And if I don't?'

'And if you don't I give the pictures to the papers and to the police. Will make the Headless Man trial look like a fucking tea party.'

Dunlop pulled his gloves back on. 'Anything goes wrong I'll ensure your police career is over.'

McCoy laughed, hadn't taken Dunlop long to get back to his old imperious self. The Dunlop that always wins, that looks after number one no matter what, that fucks over anyone to do it. The Dunlop McCoy hated more than anyone he'd ever met. The Dunlop he couldn't even look at any more. 'Fuck off before I change my mind.'

That was more than Dunlop could take. He'd kept his powder dry but now he leant into McCoy's face. 'Now you listen to me, you ignorant little fucker. I've tried to be civil—'

McCoy punched him in the face. Hard. Dunlop's nose exploded, blood splattering all over his face, his tie, his good silk shirt. McCoy pulled his fist back and punched him again and Dunlop went down, flat out on the sticky, beer-stained carpet. McCoy stepped back, knew if he didn't stop now he never would, that he'd kick Dunlop unconscious and keep going.

Dunlop was up on his elbows; he looked half surprised and half terrified. He held his hand to his nose, tried to stop the bleeding.

'I told you to fuck off,' said McCoy. 'I'm not going to tell you twice.'

Dunlop scrambled up, headed for the door, head down, banged it open and was gone. McCoy knew it was pointless, would no doubt come back on him, but he didn't regret it. It was a little victory in a situation where he was never going to get the big one. He walked up to the bar, ordered a pint and wiped the blood off his knuckles with a bar towel.

'On me,' said the barman, as he put it down. 'Fucking snobby cunt never left a tip.'

CHAPTER 38

Wattie grabbed him as soon as he walked into the shop. 'Murray's looking everywhere for you. He's up at the hospital.'

'Shite. What's he doing there? And what you doing here? Thought you were going to some dance?'

'I was, until Murray got wind. Got a right doing.'

'What's at the hospital?'

Wattie shrugged. 'Didn't tell me, just told me to get you over there. Soon as. I was just coming to look for you.'

Wattie drove. Traffic was down to a bare minimum, nobody wanting to go out in the weather unless they really had to. Half the roads were blocked, cars abandoned in the snowdrifts. Radio was reporting power had gone down in the Southside, car accidents everywhere, bridges closed. McCoy swore and switched it off. Ignored Wattie's protests. Wattie was hunched over the wheel, rubbing at the windscreen, trying to make out where they were through the condensation and the snow.

'Can you no go any faster?' McCoy asked.

'Aye, no problem. Just as long as you want to end up under a fucking bus. What's up with you anyway?'

Didn't reply. Didn't shut him up, though.

'That bloke from the play park?' Wattie asked. 'Any luck?'

Took McCoy a minute to realise what he was talking about. Had forgotten that's what he was supposed to be doing up in Springburn. 'No, no really. This weather's shut everything down, nobody out and about. Place was deserted. We can try again tomorrow.' Wattie seemed to buy it, went back to rubbing the end of his coat sleeve on the windscreen.

A bus had conked out in the snow in Argyle Street. A crowd of cold and angry passengers were standing outside it, conductor trying to explain what was going on.

Murray had his pipe going when they pulled up, was pacing up and down the pavement outside the big A&E entrance trying to keep warm. Held it up as they approached.

'No let me smoke this in there, so I'm out here in bloody Antarctica.' They moved towards the door and Murray put his arm across Wattie's chest. 'Not you, son,' he said. 'Give us a wee while, eh?'

Wattie started to protest, could tell by Murray's face it wasn't a good idea, walked back to the car muttering at the injustice.

'That bad, is it?' asked McCoy. 'Do I have to

go in? I fucking hate these places, Murray, can we no—'

But he was talking to the back of Murray's coat. He sighed and followed him in.

'I thought you'd want to know.'

They were standing by a bed looking down at Janey. McCoy stepped forward, held her hand through the sheet. He clasped it, held it into his body. His vision was getting blurry; tear rolled down and made a dark spot on the green sheet. He sniffed, wiped the back of his hand across his face.

'What happened?' he said.

'Kids found her in an empty flat in Partick. Syringe still sticking out her arm. Did you know?'

He nodded. 'Sort of. Tried to find her yesterday, didn't realise how bad it had got.'

'They think she'll pull through, but they can't say for certain. She was lucky, three others this week found dead. It's like a fucking plague. Young kids, all of them. She got any family?'

'I don't know. Iris'll know. Try Iris.' He was still staring at her. Remembered waking up on those mornings at the shebeen, frost on the windows, her wrapped around him, both of them too cold to get out of bed. He always gave in first, jumped up, put the electric fire on, then jumped back in. Two of them talking and laughing, waiting for the room to heat up. Realised now how happy he'd been then, how much he'd missed her.

'You all right, son? You want some time?'

McCoy shook his head. Didn't want this to be what he thought about when he thought of her. The stink of floor cleaner, the IV going into her bruised arm, the rows of beds. He stepped back and Murray put his arm round him, patted his back.

'I'm sorry, son. Shouldn't happen to someone this young. She'll make it, I know she will.'

McCoy took out his cigarettes and lit one with a shaky hand. He inhaled, felt dizzy, wanted to feel dizzy, wanted to feel anything but how he was feeling now.

'There's gonnae be more of this, McCoy. Got a feeling this is only the beginning. Never used to get this stuff up here and now it's turning up everywhere. Your pal Cooper know anything about it? This is serious, need to get him put away before any more girls are lying in beds like this—' Murray stopped, realised McCoy was staring at him. 'What's up with you?' he asked. 'You okay?'

McCoy wasn't listening to him. What Cooper had said about Murray and Naismith – was that why he was really here? Was Murray showing him Janey, thinking he'd give him Cooper? Was all Murray's sympathy just about leaving the field wide open for Naismith?

'You all right?' asked Murray. 'You've gone a funny colour.'

He didn't want to look at him, didn't want to think it could be true. 'Just need some air,' he said, pushing past him. 'Some fresh air.'

He sat in the A&E reception for a while, trying to take on board all that had happened. Trying to work out what he believed and what he didn't. Murray had been like a father to him, more of a father than his own had ever been. Was he really dirty? Cooper didn't tend to make things like that up, wasn't his style. Whatever he was, Stevie Cooper was straight down the line. And whatever he was, he was the reason Janey was lying in the hospital. And who was he, sitting there judging them? Hadn't been doing so well himself. Janey, Susan back to thinking he was a cunt, Billy Leeson dead, Jumbo beaten to within an inch of his life.

'You can fuck off too!' He looked up and a uniform was trying to huckle a girl out of A&E. She was drunk, skirt too short, street girl.

'I'm waiting for my pal!' she screeched. Took a swipe at the uniform. People waiting giggled. A cry of 'Batter him, hen.' McCoy smiled too and then he remembered. Jean Baird. He hadn't called her back.

CHAPTER 39

'Thought I'd come in person,' said McCoy. Madame Polo, or Jean Baird, whatever her name was, had opened the door herself, bit of a surprise, he'd expected a maid. Uniform the girl was wearing last time must have been for something else entirely. Madame Polo held the door open, led him into a sort of reception room. She poured them both a whisky from a crystal decanter and came straight to the point.

'Elsa, the girl you met last time, is missing. She didn't turn up for work, wasn't at home, nobody knows where she is.'

'Maybe she just took off? They must come and go in this business.'

She looked at him. 'They?'

'Sorry, the girls.' McCoy felt suitably chastised. Susan was right, she really was like some kind of headmistress.

'Not Elsa. She's as reliable as they come. No way would this happen unless something was wrong.'

'What could be wrong?'

Madame Polo looked down at her drink. 'I may

not have been as forthcoming as I might have been the last time we spoke.'

McCoy didn't say anything. Waited.

'Elsa told me she did a job with Lorna Skirving and her boyfriend. He wanted two girls.'

McCoy nodded.

'She was blindfolded the whole time, part of the scenario. He didn't want her to know what was coming.'

'Which was?' asked McCoy.

'She didn't say, didn't want to talk about it. But whatever happened she wouldn't go with them again. Lorna asked her and asked her, offered her double money, seems the boyfriend had taken a shine to her. Didn't work. She point-blank refused.'

'And you're worried she's gone off with the boyfriend?'

Madame Polo nodded. 'And not come back.'

'Who's the boyfriend?'

'As I said, Mr McCoy, discretion is the key to my business. I am not going to identify any of our clients.'

'Teddy Dunlop – was it him?'

She nodded, just a slight tilt of her head. Enough.

McCoy sat back, watched Madame Polo get up, make her way back towards the drinks cabinet. No way he could go back to Murray with this. The fact it was the Dunlops wasn't enough to get fired straight away, but he could hear him now: 'Where's the evidence?' There wasn't any, just a very bad feeling in the pit of his stomach.

And the only person he could think of to help him try and get rid of it was the last person in the world he wanted to see. Still, blood, of whatever kind it may be, was thicker than water.

Madame Polo handed him a half-full tumbler.

'Will you help?' she asked.

He nodded. 'Can I use your phone?'

McCoy was waiting outside the Bon Accord for twenty minutes or so, getting colder and colder, before the Silver Zephyr drew up. Cooper stepped out, hit the roof a couple of times, shut the door and the driver drove off into the foggy night. Cooper turned his collar up, blew into his hands and walked over.

'So, what's the big problem?' he asked.

'Need a bit of help with someone. Off the books.'

'That it?' said Cooper.

McCoy pointed behind him to the townhouse next to the hotel. 'In there. We should go round the back.'

'That's the big emergency? You need me to batter someone for you? Fuck sake! I could have sent Billy.'

'You going to help me or not?' asked McCoy.

Cooper turned, headed towards the townhouse. 'Let's get it over with.'

They made their way past the lit-up windows of the Bon Accord, sounds of a party going on inside, towards the lane that would take them behind the row of buildings. They turned into the lane, feet sinking into the soft, undisturbed snow. A fox jumped down from an open bin, disappeared through a gap in the fence. Their breath was blowing out in front of them, clouds in the freezing air.

There was never going to be a good time to say it, but he had to do it before they got in the house.

'Janey's in the hospital,' he said. 'Overdose.'

'That right?' said Cooper, chewing at his thumbnail. 'No real surprise.'

'No, not considering you put her there.'

Cooper turned to him, laughed. 'I did what?'

'Smack. Got her hooked while she tried out your fucking strengths for you. Then you chucked her out the shebeen when you didn't need her any more.'

Cooper shook his head, looked amused. 'Christ, if I'd known she was that good a gobble I'd have kept her on. I told you before, McCoy. She was a whore. End of. A druggy wee whore. Throw a fucking stick at the Green and you'll hit twenty of them. Life goes on. I run a business, no a fucking rest home for junkie whores.'

McCoy knew he should let it go, but he couldn't. Couldn't stop himself. Kept picturing her at the hospital, the two of them in her room, laughing, dancing to the Rolling Stones like stupid teenagers. 'Didn't fucking care, did you? Knew me and her had something, you didn't give a shit about her. About me.'

'Fuck this,' muttered Cooper.

'You could have—'

McCoy didn't get to finish his sentence. Cooper was all over him, hands round his neck, pushing his head hard against the wall of the lane. He was in his face, spitting through clenched teeth.

'Three fucking years of you crying and pishing the bed, everyone lining up to give the scaredy wee cunt a kicking. And me, I took care of them all. Kept you away from the nuns and Father fucking Brendan's tickle time. I was the one the brothers beat to fuck; I was the one that got put in that fucking lock box for days at a time. No you. Was that no enough? And just for the fucking record, Janey only went with you for the drugs you brought.'

'That's no—'

'Aye, it fucking is. Iris told me. So next month when the proper smack comes in it's going to be run by me and Billy Chan because he'll have Murray in his pocket and Naismith will be in Barlinnie and you're going to make that happen.' Cooper grabbed McCoy's head, hit it off the wall behind him. 'Right?'

McCoy nodded, put his hand to the back of his head, felt blood. Cooper looked like he had in that room, taking a hammer to Jumbo on the floor. Gone somewhere else.

'What?' he shouted, knocking McCoy's head off the wall again. 'I didnae hear you! What?'

'Yes. Yes,' he managed. Cooper pushed him back against the wall again, then let him go. McCoy slid down, ended up sitting in the snow.

'I fucking saved you from getting your arse fucked and your head kicked in for years, McCoy. Don't you ever fucking ask me what I've done for you!'

Cooper stepped back, wiped at his mouth with his sleeve, turned and walked up the lane, stopped, punched the wall with his fist. Did it again. McCoy winced: he was hitting the wall as hard as he could. He pulled his fist back to do it a third time.

'Stevie! Stop it!'

Cooper turned, blinked at him, seemed to come to. He walked back, held out his hand and McCoy took it, like he always did. Cooper pulled him up. Storm seemed to have passed; he looked like his normal self again.

Cooper spat in the snow, took out his fags. Looked up at the back of the townhouses.

'Now, are you going to tell me what the fuck we're doing here?'

CHAPTER 40

McCoy pushed the wooden gate open and he and Cooper walked up the garden path. Light was spilling out from the kitchen windows, illuminating the snow-covered lawn. McCoy wiped some of the frost from the window with his sleeve and they looked in. He tried the door handle. Unlocked. Lucky for once.

They stepped into the kitchen and closed the door behind them. Stood for a minute, just listening, trying to get their bearings. The house was almost as cold as it was outside. Seemed empty, unlived in. Cooper pointed to the light coming from the half-open door to the hallway. The hall floor was flooded, a good couple of inches of water. Easy to see where it had come from. Water was running down the stairs, spilling over the sides, dripping onto the floor below.

They splashed through into the big front room, feet leaving watery footprints on the dusty floorboards. A grand piano covered in a thick stoor of dust and some furniture covered in white dust-sheets. The walls were covered in animal heads. Elk, a zebra, even a lion. Glass eyes staring at them. Complicated arrangements of regimental shields and swords beside them, shining in the gloom.

They stepped back into the hall and McCoy shouted as loud as he could. 'Dunlop? You here?'

His voice echoed in the empty house. Nothing. He tried again. 'Dunlop? Elsa?' More echoes.

There was nothing on the first floor but a couple of empty rooms. Nothing on the second either but a mouse that skittered across the floorboards of the back bedroom, disappeared under the skirting.

'Might be barking up the wrong tree here, McCoy,' said Cooper.

'Probably, but we should check the whole place. Come on.'

They climbed the next set of stairs. The water was running down from the third-floor landing, through the railings and falling onto the stairs below. They splashed through it, kept heading up.

'What the fuck is all this?' said Cooper, waggling his foot to get some of the water off.

'Probably a burst pipe, no heating in this bloody place,' replied McCoy.

One of the doors on the third-floor landing was closed. McCoy nodded at it, Cooper pushed it open and they went in.

'Shite,' said McCoy.

The room was furnished properly this time, was even warm. Beyond piles of clothes, a four-poster bed dominated the middle of the room, white sheets on it stained with blood.

Cooper moved in, looked at the bed and stepped back. 'Sheets are still wet with it.'

There was a pile of scud mags on the bedside table, *Jezebel* lying on the top, open at the picture of Lorna Skirving. McCoy picked it up. Knew then he was in the right place.

'Dunlop!' he shouted. 'Glasgow Police. You here?'

There was a half bottle of Haig on the sideboard. Cooper twisted the top off and took a swig. Handed it over. McCoy took a swig, put the bottle down.

'What the fuck happened in here?' asked Cooper, looking at the blood dripping from the bed onto the floor.

'I don't know,' said McCoy. 'Nothing good.'

'You got anything on you?' Cooper asked.

McCoy shook his head. Cooper pulled a knife out from his back pocket, handed it to him. 'Take this.'

'What about you?' McCoy asked.

'I can take care of myself.'

'One more floor to go,' McCoy said.

'May as well get on with it.' Cooper nodded at the door. 'Let's go.'

They got to the top of the last set of stairs. Three doors on the landing.

Cooper pointed at one. 'I'll take this one. You check the other.'

McCoy nodded, headed for it as Cooper walked the other way down the corridor. He pushed the door open and stepped in. Felt the whoosh of something heavy coming towards him and pain exploded in his face. Noise of someone running as he fell to the floor, another wave of hot pain and then everything was dark.

'McCoy! McCoy!'

He could hear him, but he couldn't see him. Just a fuzzy shape blocking the light. He blinked a few times and Cooper's face came into focus.

'You okay?'

McCoy nodded, put his hand up to his face, felt the blood. 'Fuck!' He held onto a set of drawers, managed to hoist himself up. His nose felt wobbly, definitely broken, could feel a big gash across his right cheek as well.

'Am I okay?' he asked, looking at Cooper.

'You'll live.' Cooper pulled his T-shirt over his head, bundled it up and held it to McCoy's forehead. Pressed hard. Ignored McCoy's yelps of pain.

'You see him?' he asked.

McCoy shook his head, wincing as he did. 'Heard him running away.'

Cooper took one of McCoy's hands and held it against the T-shirt. 'Keep that held tight on the cut.'

'How come you know first aid all of a sudden?' asked McCoy.

'You kidding me?'

McCoy looked at Cooper. At his bare torso

marked with the scars from slashes and knife wounds.

'Sorry,' he said.

'Keep the pressure up, press it hard,' said Cooper. 'I'll check next door.'

He knew he shouldn't, but as soon as Cooper disappeared he pulled the T-shirt away and had a look at it. It was red now, soaked in blood. He felt a rush of dizziness, quickly held it back against the wound. He didn't even know if it was Teddy Dunlop who had hit him, just knew whoever it was had hit him hard. Really hard.

McCoy tried to fish his cigarettes out his pocket with his free hand. Wasn't doing very well. He pulled the T-shirt away and groaned when it stuck to his hair, blood already congealing into a syrupy mess. He'd just managed to light up when he thought he heard something. He froze. Listened.

'Cooper?' he said, realised he was whispering. Said it again, louder this time. 'Cooper?'

Nothing.

'Cooper?'

Nothing.

Then he heard it. More of a whisper than anything else. 'McCoy?'

'Cooper? You there?'

A thick splash of blood arced up the floral wallpaper. It was still wet, glistening and dripping. McCoy pressed himself against the doorframe, heart going.

'Cooper?' he whispered. 'Cooper?'

No reply.

He tried again. 'Stevie? You there?'

He edged himself along the wall and into the room. Made himself look down. Cooper was lying in a growing pool of blood, dark red seeping across the pale bedroom carpet.

McCoy knelt down beside him.

'Stevie, it's me. What happened? You okay?'

He wasn't. He'd a huge wound running from his shoulder all the way down his back. The sides of it were gaping open, glimpses of bone, yellow fatty tissue.

Cooper opened his eyes. Grimaced. 'Cunt had a sword.'

'It's okay, don't move. You'll be okay,' said McCoy.

'Was hiding behind the door, got me soon as I stepped in.'

'Christ! Just be quiet, keep your strength. Okay?'

Cooper nodded. Grimaced again. 'It's fucking sore.'

McCoy pulled the sheets off the bed, tried to wrap them round Cooper's body, stop the blood pouring out the wound. Wasn't doing much good, was like trying to stop the tide. He tried to keep talking, wasn't sure Cooper could even hear him. He was barely conscious, eyes flickering every so often. The blood was getting everywhere, warm and sticky, covering Cooper, covering McCoy. He was doing okay, dizzy but still functioning, just needed not to pass out, not now. He'd done the best he could with the sheets, stuffed them into the wound, blood seemed to be stopping a bit. Wasn't enough, though. Cooper needed a hospital and fast.

He stood up. 'I'll no be long, just need to go downstairs and phone an ambulance, you'll be fine for five minutes, eh?' Wasn't much response, was talking more to himself than anyone else. He turned to go and Cooper's arm shot out, grabbed at his ankle. McCoy jumped.

'Don't let that cunt get away,' Cooper managed to get out between shallow breaths.

The grip on his ankle loosened and McCoy bolted downstairs, heading for the ground floor. He found the phone in the kitchen and called the shop. He thought it was going to ring out, then Wattie finally answered.

'Central. Watson speaking.'

'Wattie! Listen to me. Get to Park Circus as quick as you can, bring anyone in the station. Number 12!'

'What? That you, McCoy? What's up?

'Just fucking do it. Call an ambulance as well!'

'Okay. Murray's here and Thomson, I think. I'll bring them. You okay? What's going on?'

'Just get here, Wattie. Now! The ambulance!'

He'd just put the phone back in the cradle, cutting off another 'What's happening?' from Wattie, when he heard a whir, the sound of a turntable spinning, arm going down onto a scratchy record, and suddenly there was music. He stepped back, wasn't sure why, as it boomed down the stairs. He was so surprised he just stood there and listened. The Animals' 'House of the Rising Sun'. The last plaintive 'And God, I know I'm one' finished and the needle skidded across the empty grooves, lifted and dropped again at the beginning of the disc. The song started up again.

'There is a house in New Orleans, they call the Rising Sun.'

McCoy did something he never thought he'd do again. He crossed himself. And then he started to climb the stairs.

CHAPTER 41

McCoy was spooked, scared of the creaking of the house, the wind rattling the windows, the squeaks of the floorboards under his feet. He tried to tell himself to stay calm as he climbed, but he could feel his heart thumping in his chest. The record finished, whirred and the song started up again. It was definitely coming from the top floor, getting louder as he climbed.

'Oh Mother tell your children, not to do what I have done.'

McCoy stood on the top-floor landing. He'd come this far. Had to keep going. The open door at the end of the landing was the only place Teddy Dunlop could have gone. Connecting doors between the three rooms meant they had missed him, let him get away. He moved forward, music getting louder the nearer he got to the room. He stood outside, got himself ready, then pushed the door wide open.

'Dunlop, you in here?' he shouted.

Nothing. He stepped in, wary of him jumping out again, but the room was empty. He breathed a sigh of relief and looked round. The record player was on the sideboard by the window, record spinning round. Music was totally distorted now, the volume turned up too high for the wee speaker. He walked over, broken glass crunching under his feet, and pulled the needle off. The music stopped instantly, a sudden feeling of a pressing silence, an absence of sound.

The room was sparsely furnished – a sideboard, a rumpled single bed. No Dunlop. Part of him was relieved. He could go back downstairs now, sit with Cooper and wait for Wattie and the ambulance to arrive. He'd tried. Dunlop must have got past them somehow, made it out the house.

He stepped out the room, knelt down to wash the blood off his hands in the water on the floor and that's when he saw it. A slit of dim light in the panelling at the far end of the landing. He could pretend he hadn't seen it. Walk away. No one would know. But he would. He stood up.

It was a door, made to look like another piece of panelling. He pushed and it opened into a huge bathroom, white tiles everywhere. Two overhead fluorescents fizzed and flashed, barely penetrating the fog of steam. Water was pouring over the sides of an old freestanding bath, both taps going full pelt. He leant over to turn them off and jumped back in fright.

Elsa was in the bath. Nude. Face serene under the pinkish water, dead blue eyes staring up at him. He turned the taps off, noise sank from a gushing to a steady drip into the water. He breathed deeply, made himself take another look. Blood was clouding up from her mouth and from between her legs. Steady red flow coming from the two gaping slash marks across her neck.

He looked down at her, found himself saying a prayer for her under his breath. No atheists in a foxhole, they say.

As soon as he stepped out of the bathroom he felt a cold breeze across his wet skin. Took him a second to work out it was coming from a door in the back of the landing. He walked over, breeze getting stronger, and opened it.

The door opened onto a box room empty but for a pile of old sheets and a box of plates. The slanted roof had a window held up by an iron pole. Wind must have been blowing in all night, snow was lying in a semi-circular pile on the wooden floor beneath it. McCoy pushed the window open, hauled himself up through the gap and looked out.

The townhouse roof sloped down to the gutter, then the long drop to the street below. McCoy swayed. Behind him the roof ran up a good twenty feet towards a group of sooty terracotta chimneys silhouetted against the night sky. There were footprints in the snow leading up to them. He got himself up onto the roof and started making his way gingerly up the slope. Fucked if he was going to stop now. He started upright then went down on his hands and knees, afraid of slipping and falling the hundred feet to the street below. He made it to the chimneystacks and looked around.

He edged his way round, keeping his back to the chimneys, arms splayed out, gripping on. Teddy Dunlop was sitting on the other side, back against the brick base, bloody sword resting across his knees. He nodded at him as if he'd just seen him in his local.

'McCoy, wasn't it?'

McCoy looked at him warily, then sat down, didn't seem to be anything else he could do. He was freezing, soaked clothes making it even colder than it was. At least the chimneys were warm – next door must have all the fires going. He pressed his back against them, tried to stop shivering.

'Nice here,' Dunlop said, looking out over the view of the city below. 'Peaceful.' Turned to McCoy. 'How's the nose?'

'I'll live.'

'Sorry about that. I thought it was one of my father's goons come to tidy up then take me away for a little rest cure. Electroshock therapy. Heard of it?'

McCoy shook his head.

'Nasty business.' Dunlop held out a pack of cigarettes; there was blood on them, but McCoy didn't care. He took one, he needed it. He took a sideways look at Dunlop as he held out a Zippo to light it. He didn't look good. He'd lost weight; collar of his shirt was too big for his neck. The suit he'd on was as wet as McCoy's, half with water, half with blood.

Dunlop tapped the sword with his finger. 'My

great-grandfather's apparently. Was on the wall downstairs. Took it with him to Africa to kill some Boers. I don't doubt he succeeded.'

'What's been going on here?' McCoy asked evenly. 'You want to tell me about Elsa downstairs?'

He sighed, looked out over the view, flicked his cigarette end out into the darkness. 'Elsa? What is there to tell?'

'Well she's lying dead in a bathtub for a start.'

He sighed. 'Does it matter? It's done now.'

'Yes, it fucking matters! She was a nineteen-year-old girl with all her life ahead of her and because of you she's lying dead, bleeding from fucking everywhere.'

Dunlop looked at him, smiled. 'So you're my confessor, are you? Not quite what I expected, I have to say. Elsa is dead because Elsa stopped being fun,' he said.

'Fun? Jesus. What's that supposed to mean?'

He turned, smiled. 'You know something? You can see it in their faces, see the exact moment they give up. It's like a kind of hope goes, a light goes out in their eyes.'

'Give up what?' asked McCoy.

'Give up thinking the pain's worth it. Elsa finally realised she wasn't going to be Mrs Dunlop and that it wasn't ever going to stop and I saw it in her face. So she . . .'

'She what?'

'So she wasn't any fun any more.'

'Jesus Christ.'

The wind was getting stronger, gusting hard, blowing the snow against the chimneys and against them. Dunlop turned his collar up, stuck his hands deep into the pockets of his jacket. 'Don't be so disgusted. The pursuit of fun is a big thing in our family.'

'What does that mean?' McCoy asked.

He took out his cigarettes again but the wind was too strong now, even for his Zippo. He tried a few times, then gave up and threw it over the edge.

'I was sixteen. That was the first time my father brought a girl, a prostitute, into the equation. Fun for all. And do you know what happens after a while, when you and your father have sex with a prostitute?'

Dunlop turned, looked at him. McCoy shook his head.

'You get bored. Inured. Jaded. What my father thought was some sort of holy transgression you see as just another night. So you start to look further abroad, for that thing, that experience that's something more. That really is fun.'

He slipped his hand round the handle of the sword, lifted it up, pointed the tip out into the dark, to the city below.

'I grew up in that world down there, but there's nothing left for me here now. Only one more person to be delivered and then I'm done.' He turned to McCoy and grinned. 'Looks like fate has given me exactly what I need.'

McCoy started backing away. Knew it was

useless. He didn't have a chance up here against Dunlop; he was younger, at least as strong. If he could get downstairs again then maybe, but not up here, up here he didn't have a hope. A slate slid out from under his foot and they watched it tumble down the roof, over the side and into the darkness.

Dunlop stood up, brushed himself off and smiled. 'Come on, McCoy, that's not going to work, is it? Back over here, if you please.' He raised the sword. 'Now.'

McCoy swore under his breath. 'You don't have to do that, Dunlop.'

'On the contrary, I do. I very much do.'

'Why? You'll not get away. Patrol cars are on the way, I called them from downstairs.' Realised how desperate he sounded, how useless.

Dunlop looked off over the side. 'As if I care about that.' He raised the sword, pushed the tip against McCoy's shirt. The skin broke, a bloom of red blood appeared on the white cotton. McCoy breathed, waited. Wasn't sure why but his mind drifted back to Arran. To that day with Angela and Bobby, the day they got the man to take the picture of them on the rug. To being happy.

'You're going to help me, Mr McCoy. I'm off to pastures new.'

McCoy started backing away, knew he had no chance. Knew he had to try. He took another step back, was trying not to slip when Dunlop suddenly flipped the sword in the air and caught the tip of it in his hand. He smiled, held the handle end out to McCoy.

'Take it.'

McCoy shook his head.

'Take it.'

Dunlop was holding the sword at arm's length, blood seeping through his fingers as gripped the blade, the handle only six inches or so from McCoy's face.

He took it in his shaking hand and Dunlop leant forward, pushed his chest onto the tip of the sword.

'Now,' he said. 'Now, Mr McCoy, do it now.'

McCoy adjusted his grip, got the sword firm in his hand, held it for a few seconds.

Dunlop whispered. 'Do it.'

He thought of Elsa dead in the bath, Cooper's life draining away downstairs. Tommy Malone. Lorna Skirving. All the damage Dunlop and his father had done. Dunlop was pushing himself forward; McCoy felt the pressure give and an inch or so of the blade disappeared into Dunlop's chest.

'Do it.'

He could end it all.

'Now, McCoy.'

But without Teddy he didn't have Dunlop Senior. And he was as guilty as Teddy was. He wanted them both. Both alive. Both on the stand. Both guilty. He dropped the sword.

Dunlop shook his head. 'Don't have it in you. I should have known.'

Before McCoy knew what was happening Dunlop

397

was running down the roof at full tilt, slipping and sliding on the snowy tiles until he reached the edge and disappeared into the darkness.

He heard it before he could make it to the edge of the roof. The whump as his body hit. He scrambled and slid down to the edge, grabbed onto a big TV aerial and peered over. Dunlop had landed on the road just outside the front entrance of the Bon Accord Hotel. His body was splayed on the ground, arms and legs at impossible angles, blood already starting to spread out beneath him into the snow. Two men were running towards the body, looking up, trying to work out what had happened. More people appeared, a ring formed round the body. A man came out the hotel with a blanket. He heard the distant sound of sirens, looked up, could see the flashing lights of the ambulance and the pandas coming down Woodlands Road. A patrol car stopped beside the body and Wattie and Murray got out. Ambulance men rushed into the house with a stretcher.

McCoy looked up at the heavy sky and watched the flakes spiralling down. Wind was up too, clouds scudding across the sky. He started shivering, not sure if it was the wet clothes clinging to him or what had just happened. Either way it was time to get back inside, to get in out of the cold.

20TH JANUARY 1973

CHAPTER 42

The Royal was Glasgow's biggest and oldest hospital, huge black building on the High Street, original red sandstone obliterated by years of soot and dirt. Ward 12 was at the back, took McCoy a while to find it. Knew he was there when he saw Billy Weir standing at the doors smoking. He nodded as he approached.

'How's the patient then?'

Billy shook his head. 'Doc says he'll be fine. Just needs to be in here for a couple of weeks, keep as still as he can.'

'Bet he's enjoying that?'

'Oh aye, effing and blinding non-stop. Most of the nurses have already refused to go near him.'

McCoy held up a copy of the *Daily Record* and a brown paper bag of grapes. 'Wish me luck.'

He heard him as soon as he pushed the door open. Couldn't really work out what he was on about but heard the words 'cunt' and 'fuck' enough to know he wasn't happy. A nurse pushed past him, heading for the door, hands up to her face, tears in her eyes.

He pulled up a chair and sat down beside the

bed. Cooper was lying face down, encased in heavy bandages from his shoulders to his waist, face turned to the side, squashed into the pillow.

'Fuck you laughing at?' he asked.

McCoy held his hands up. 'Me? Nothing. How you doing?'

'Me? Fucking great. How d'you think? Stuck here for another two weeks, cannae bloody move, nurses having to wipe my arse for me. It's fucking great.'

'Come on, at least you're going to be okay. Was touch and go for a while, you lost a lot of blood.'

'Aye, so I hear. That cunt really dead?'

McCoy nodded. 'Splattered all over the pavement.'

'And you're getting a medal for it?'

'Yep. Thought he was going to kill me. Amazing the strength you get when you're that scared. Just went for him, knocked the sword out his hand and managed to get him over the side before he got me. Back in the good books. Murray's golden boy again.'

'Glad to hear it; be easier for you to sort that cunt Naismith out. I need that doing, hear me?' He winced, wasn't supposed to even be talking, never mind threatening.

'I hear you.' McCoy put the grapes down on the wee bedside cabinet and opened the paper. 'Football?'

Cooper nodded, sweat on his forehead. Sixty-seven stitches, major muscle damage in his back.

He wasn't going to be the man he'd been, but McCoy wasn't going to tell him that. He started reading the football reports, was only five minutes or so in when he realised Cooper was asleep. Not surprising given the bottles of painkillers lined up on the cabinet. He shoved a couple of grapes in his mouth and opened the paper, looking for the TV page. He stopped chewing when he saw the headline. Wasn't big, halfway down a page. *LORD DUNLOP – NEW TRAGEDY.*

He scanned it. *Drowning accident . . . victim Jimmy Gibbs, 34 . . . found by housekeeper.*

He shut the paper. They really didn't fuck about, the rich. Just did what they had to do to protect themselves, no matter what it was.

Cooper was snoring now, scarred hands lying on the blue blanket. Whatever Cooper was, he was amateur hour compared to Lord Dunlop. Son not even buried yet and he'd still made sure Jimmy Gibbs wasn't going to be talking to the polis or the press. Or anyone.

People like Dunlop Senior didn't end up with scars all over their hands, sword wounds on their back, lying in a dingy ward of a public hospital. Not them. They moved through the world untouched, no matter what they'd done. For people like Gray Dunlop, deciding to get rid of Jimmy Gibbs was like deciding to wear the red tie today instead of the blue. A decision easily taken and as easily forgotten.

Outside, the snow was gently falling, covering

Glasgow in a fresh white layer, hiding the dirt beneath. McCoy started walking down towards town. He passed the cathedral, group of wee kids standing in a line outside, waiting for the tour.

He'd been signed off for three weeks on the condition he went to see the shrink. Compulsory. Mood he was in maybe he'd tell her why he really hated the sight of blood so much. He stopped, lit a cigarette and watched them file in, one by one. Looked about seven or eight, same age as he'd been when it happened. He looked up at the falling snow, felt it fall on his face. Then again, maybe some things were better off staying secret.